VINE HILL ROAD PRESS

Also by
M. L. Doyle

Fiction
Master Sergeant Lauren Harper Mysteries:
The Peacekeeper's Photograph
Canceled Plans (companion short)
The Sapper's Plot
The Ranger's Revenge (Spring 2014)

Nonfiction
I'm Still Standing;
From Captured Soldier to free citizen, my journey home
With Shoshana Johnson
(Touchstone, 2010)

A Promise Fulfilled,
My life as a Wife and Mother, Soldier and General Officer
With BG (Ret.) Julia Cleckley

Romance
The Limited Partnerships series
Part I - Charlie
Part II - Luke
Part III - Wolf
Part IV – Derek
Limited Partnerships Omnibus

The Sapper's Plot

By

M. L. Doyle

VHR
PRESS
VINE HILL ROAD PRESS

While the author has attempted to present as realistic a view of
military life as possible, liberties were taken for literary purposes.
This is a work of fiction and should be treated as such.
Any similarities to persons living or dead, real or imagined,
is purely coincidental.
That's my story and I'm sticking to it.

Edited by Gale Deitch
Cover design by EarthlyCharms.com
Author photo by Chad T. Jones

DEDICATION

For the men and women of
the 364th Mobile Public Affairs Detachment,
Fort Snelling, MN
and all others who answer the call to serve.

Sap-per, n. U.S. Army engineer specialized in digging and building fortifications, constructing combat expedient bridges, roads and air fields and handles the disposal of bombs, mines etc.

Chapter 1

Someone retched loudly behind me and, in sympathy, my own stomach clenched in a painful heave. Sweat trickled down the middle of my back and pooled around the clasp of my bra before it continued its downward trail, the slow progress made my skin feel like a thousand bugs crawled on it. The high-pitched warble of insects sent a constant undulating note into the air and contributed to that crawly feeling on my skin. Aside from the jungle thrum and the horrible human noises that went on and on, no one made a sound. Everyone around me stood frozen in place.

Like everyone else, I kept staring at the cement slab, hoping something would begin to make sense. The more I stared, the more a creeping sense of pressure built on my lungs. Breathing was already difficult in the thick jungle humidity. Looking at the thing buried in cement intensified my near panicked desire for fresh air.

We stood in the frame of what was intended to be the foundation of a simple, two-room school building. The engineers had completed the wooden frame a couple of days before, and today, were scheduled to pour the cement slab.

Someone had already been busy with the cement and left a horror in their wake.

A section of concrete had been poured and smoothed in the center of the frame. In the middle of the smooth surface, rose a sudden swelling, a mound that sloped to the outline of a shoulder. Dark green camouflage fabric poked through the cement and the unit patch, usually sewn onto the right shoulder of the uniform, sat clearly visible on the sleeve. At just above the elbow, the arm disappeared again until it resurfaced a little further away. Four fingers stood frozen, sticking out of the hardened floor. More flat concrete led the eye to a protruding knee, the green camouflage pattern decorated with flecks of dried cement.

Whoever had poured the cement, had taken the time to smooth around the mounds, even smoothing between the shoulder and hand, between the hand and the knee, making the floor appear exactly the way it should have, save for the gruesome corpse frozen in the center.

The expert trowel work gave me the willies. The killer had left a message with the smoothing of the cement, clearly an ugly message, the meaning unknown. I didn't think I wanted to understand what it meant.

"Sick son of a bitch," I mumbled to myself.

Soldiers and people from the local village stood around staring at the body. The news team I had escorted to the site, Tony Cordovan and his videographer, Juka Dropic, stood close behind me. One of them breathed loudly, his breath whistling through his nose.

Cordovan and Dropic were the reason I'd been ordered on this mission. An investigative news team from Minneapolis, they claimed they wanted hometown coverage of the humanitarian mission and the National Guard soldiers from Minnesota, but the news team had a reputation for finding scandal where it didn't exist. Their request to come along had alerted Army leadership to the potential for bad press in the middle of the jungle. My orders were to keep an eye on them and try to figure out what they were after.

The orders had come at the last minute and I'd been furious to get them. Everyone knew I'd just returned from a deployment, a mission that had almost cost me my life. They all knew I needed rest, but I'd been ordered here anyway. The thing that really pissed me off was that I'd been forced to cancel the vacation plans I'd had with Sergeant Major Harry Fogg of the British Royal Army, plans I'd looked forward to for months and a period of relaxation I needed. Badly.

And now, evidently I'd brought the news crew to a murder scene. The suck factor of this last minute mission continued to increase exponentially.

Aside from the musky smell of the jungle, a decidedly pungent odor hung in the air, like someone had doused a dung heap in cheap perfume. I took shallow breaths and when that didn't work, pulled up the collar of my uniform to cover my nose and mouth. That didn't work either.

The man who had been loudly retching finally gained control of his stomach, but now his sobbing filled the air.

"Bobby! Oh god, Bobby!" he cried.

He crouched on the ground inches from the body. With his arms wrapped around his knees, he rocked back and forth, eyes wide and mouth open in a silent wail.

I wondered how he knew who it was under the concrete, until the glint of a gold ring caught my attention. A large stone surrounded by a signet-type setting identified the hand now frozen in death.

Looking at that ring, the hand and the placement of the knee, another bit of information became clear. Bobby had been fighting. He had been alive when someone poured the concrete on him.

The impressions of small paw prints and the thin pronged prints of birds were scattered around the corpse, evidence the jungle's scavengers had already been at it. On closer inspection, white bone sticking out of the ravaged flesh of his hand proved almost too much for my already upset belly.

I spun away from the repulsiveness and walked smack into Dropic. Mumbling an apology, I made my way to our vehicle, past several soldiers, most of them looking as green as I felt. Leaning on the hood of our truck I took deep shaking breaths. The memory of the smell lingered in my nose. Breathing through my mouth didn't help, only intensified my regret that I'd eaten breakfast hours earlier. After a few moments, I was able to stand, walk to the passenger side and sit down in the vehicle, my legs hanging outside the door. I grabbed my water bottle from the floor of the truck and took deep gulps of lukewarm liquid, then poured more into my palm and splashed my face a few times.

When my breathing slowed down, I caught a glimpse of myself in the truck's side-view mirror. My caramel-colored skin looked dusty brown and unhealthy. My hair had started the day in the usual way, as a long, wildly curling mane, French-braided while it was still soaking wet. The tail was shoved up under the braid so that it was off my collar and secured with a fat barrette. Despite my efforts, fuzzy wisps of dark hair stuck up around my head, making my face look narrow and drawn. The lines of red in my brown eyes and puffy bags underneath didn't help. I looked like crap.

I'd started the day in a freshly starched and laundered uniform. The pants had almost stood by themselves and made a sound like separating Velcro when I forced my legs into them. Now, my summer-weight jacket was already soaked through with sweat and the only thing holding the pants up was the black web belt I wore. Even my boots, which I had, out of habit, spit-shined the night before, were already covered in a thick coating of dust.

The news team along with our driver, Sergeant Alfred Mora, and I had packed sleeping bags, food and equipment to keep us for a week into the back of our Humvee and left Soto Cano Air Base along with the engineers just as the morning birds began to chirp.

Taking the advice of the combat engineering unit's First Sergeant, Donald Dodd, we tagged along with their convoy following the long line of vehicles for almost two hours to make it to Los Flores, a tiny mountain village in a remote region of Honduras.

"It doesn't matter if you've got an eight-digit grid coordinate," Dodd had said with a mouth full of tobacco chew and his boonie cap, the floppy brimmed hat made for jungle use, pushed back on his head. He pointed at the dot on the map that indicated our intended destination. "See, all along here, Sergeant Harper? There aren't any roads going in or out of there, ya see? You could be bouncing around that jungle for days and never find the place." He spit a long stream of tobacco juice on the ground to emphasize his point, avoiding my eyes and looking apologetic at his need to spit.

At first, Dodd had tried to talk me out of going along, using every excuse, including the remoteness of the location and even that I would be the only woman at the engineering site. Eventually, he'd understood that I wouldn't be deterred and that I would be bringing the news crew along whether he liked it or not. He hid his displeasure well, but every time he looked at me or the reporters, I could see irritation lurking behind his gaze.

Once we left Soto Cano, our convoy traveled on asphalt roads for only forty-five minutes before the roads turned to dirt. Fifteen minutes later, even the dirt road petered out. The rest of the slow and bumpy route had followed dried creek beds, mule trails and no trail at all save for tire marks, evidence that vehicles had traveled this way in previous trips. Pickup trucks, a wrecker, a five-ton truck and a hodgepodge of other vehicles made the slow journey through the jungle to this remote village. Two deuce n' half's, aptly named for their two-and-a-half-ton capacity, carried most of the engineering unit soldiers, the combat Sappers who would be building a school house instead of their usual mission of blowing things up, digging defensive positions and the like.

Driving behind one of the Deuces, I watched the soldiers bouncing around in the back, grateful for my seat in our Humvee. We were seat-belted in, but I still had one hand braced on the dashboard, one hand holding onto an overhead pole, and my ears closed to the comments and complaints from our passengers.

We began the ride from the base camp with the windows open and the steamy Honduran air whipping around inside the vehicle. Once we hit the off-road portion of the trip, we zipped up the plastic flaps that served as windows for protection from tree branches that slapped and scratched us along the way. Cordovan had trouble getting his window closed. He fiddled with it for several minutes but couldn't get the zipper to budge. Eventually he was whacked by a snapping branch and his face now carried a scratch across his cheek.

As we loaded the vehicle in the morning, I'd noticed, that while Dropic's gear was smart, well-used, outdoorsman gear, Cordovan's was sparkling new department store stuff, purchased more for the label than its durability. Even the hiking boots he wore, while high-priced Gortex footwear, would probably barely last the one trip. It was further confirmation that the reporter was out of his element, had left his comfortable city reporting behind to gain access to the story he was after.

His bio and the tapes of his reports I had studied told me that Tony Cordovan had a reputation for investigating white collar crime, government misdeeds and city scandals confined to more civilized surroundings. Now here he was, in the heat of the jungle. Whatever brought him out here had to be something significant, something controversial, or Cordovan wouldn't have made the trip. It was worrisome.

Not to mention that I'd just delivered them to a murder scene.

A young sergeant in the vehicle next to mine talked over the radio to the headquarters' Tactical Operations Center in Soto Cano. Several solders stood around listening to the exchange. The officer in charge of the TOC had practically been asleep when I signed out with them that morning; only one other person had been on duty at the time. I imagined they were scrambling to figure out what to do about this sudden turn of events.

"Secure the area and wait for instructions," was the response on the radio.

"How we supposed to secure the god damn area when we don't have any weapons? What a load of crap…" the young sergeant said in exasperation to the men standing around him. Into the radio he said, "Roger, that. Out."

The state of alert on a nation-building exercise usually remained low. We hadn't come here with defense in mind. Weapons were not authorized. We only wore helmets while traveling in vehicles, no flack vests, and only military police, the few sent to Honduras, were issued weapons. As far as I knew, there weren't any MPs at this remote construction site so there was little chance a single American weapon was available. There weren't any fences around the site, no defensive positions, no guards, and it appeared the only communication link we had with the main base was through the radios in the vehicles. Secure the area? With what?

The young sergeant climbed out of the Humvee, slammed the door behind him and cursed all the way back to the murder scene.

The sound of footsteps on the gravel behind where I sat in the vehicle caught my attention. Dropic walked to the back of the truck and I cursed under my breath, knowing what he was about to do. In confirmation, I heard the rip of the zipper as he opened the rear storage compartment. Further shuffling confirmed he was pulling his video gear out of the truck.

Unlike most Bosnians I'd met, Dropic, was a large man in size and voice, who wore his hair below his shirt collar, his beard short and untrimmed, his cargo pants loose and wrinkled, his photographer's vest pockets filled with spare batteries, clamps and cables, and a wide infectious grin that masked his impatience with his TV personality partner. Dropic's video camera and tripod looked small and lightweight in his beefy paws.

Why did he have to be Bosnian?

I was afraid of him. It was irrational, I knew. He hadn't threatened me. In fact, he'd tried to be funny, charming even. Still, his voice, his accent drenched me in memories that left my insides feeling liquid. Dropic was just a guy trying to do his job and had nothing to do with the brutal nightmares I carried with me after my time in his war-torn country. He didn't resemble the men who had attacked me, the men who had brutalized me, held me prisoner and almost enslaved me.

He didn't resemble the man I had killed.

My rational mind knew all these things, but it didn't matter. Upon meeting him, his voice, his accent had stirred up memories still too vivid, too raw to ignore. It didn't help that he smoked the same damn cigarettes they had smoked. The smell of the unfiltered Camels, the sight of the red package in his hands was enough to make me tremble. God, I hated the smell of those things.

The exhaustion I felt now, the exhaustion that seemed to have settled in my bones so deep I sometimes felt like I could curl up and sleep for weeks, stemmed mostly from the fact that, almost nightly, I'd jerk awake at three a.m. with the smell of horse, hay and those damn cigarettes in my nostrils, the nightmares so vivid I relived the experience over and over again.

None of that was Dropic's fault, but every time I heard his accent, every time I smelled the cigarette smoke that seemed to cling to him like a second skin, I couldn't help but blame him for it. Why the hell did he have to be Bosnian?

I moved to the back of the truck where Dropic hiked his battery utility belt around his waist and snapped the fastener in place. I steeled myself for the confrontation, freezing my liquid insides to hard ice.

"That is an American soldier. You will not shoot video of his body." I said.

The steady and commanding sound of my voice surprised me and stoked my confidence. When he ignored me, some of that confidence leaked out. He continued to gather his bulky equipment. He attached a small light to the top of the camera and plugged the attaching wires in place. His glance flicked to me for a moment, then he reached into his bag and grabbed a handheld microphone. I crossed my arms over my chest, trying to still my shakes. He wasn't going to make this easy. At a murder scene like this, I thought it unlikely that any solder would be willing to talk to him, but evidently he intended to try to get them to talk. A dark smirk played at the corner of his mouth as he hefted the gear from the truck. I stopped him with a hand on his arm and felt his considerable muscles tense. His smirk became a glare. He looked eager and ready to argue his point.

"You can't stop me," he said.

"Yes, I can."

"What happened to freedom of the press?"

"This isn't America."

He opened his mouth to say something, then stopped, realizing what I said was true. After a moment, he shook his head as if to brush an insect away and tried to step around me. I stepped in front of him, putting my hand in the middle of his chest.

"Shooting video of dead American soldiers is not permitted. Ever."

"You can't cover this up," Dropic said in frustration. "This is news."

"It won't be in a week."

He towered over me, his jaw clenched in frustration. If he had bothered to look closer, he would have seen my knees tremble. I tried to push the brutal visions out of my head, the ones from Bosnia. He sounded so much like them. His intimidating presence felt like them and the way he towered over me, made me feel trapped, as trapped as I had been under their brutal care. If he moved at all, I feared I would flinch. I widened my stance and managed to stand my ground.

Dropic slowly absorbed the truth of what I said. He had come here in my vehicle. He didn't have remote satellite uplink equipment with him and there was little chance he would find the technology needed in this isolated place. He would have to physically drive the video somewhere to feed it to the vast news machine. There was no way for him to get his video out without my help, and I wasn't going to help him.

He pressed his lips together and leaned over me as if he wanted to get physical but restrained himself. His nostrils flared in frustration, his nose hairs whistled and I got a strong whiff of his tobacco breath. It took every ounce of my will to stare back at him. He finally called to Cordovan over my shoulder.

"I should feel homesick. She's acting like we're in Tito's Yugoslavia or something. She's won't let me get the footage."

Cordovan strolled over, his safari jacket looking crisp despite the damp jungle heat. Somehow he had rearranged his black hair to its perfectly coifed state. I felt rumpled and dirty next to his faultless appearance. Up close, I noticed his black eyes were slightly bloodshot, the skin around them puffy and sagging. Those slight imperfections made me feel a little better.

Cordovan surprised me by shaking his head.

"Don't overreact, Juka. We don't need shots of the body. That's an American soldier buried under there. Have some respect."

"Have some respect?" Dropic repeated incredulously. "Who are you trying to kid?"

I felt a bit incredulous myself. The false note of sincerity in Cordovan's voice, the solemn look on his face, the way he strolled over with his hands buried in the pockets of his crisply ironed jeans, it seemed all too casual.

"I'm sure Sergeant Harper is concerned about the family. Seeing that video would be horrible for them," Cordovan said. He shuddered to demonstrate his empathy.

I narrowed my eyes at him not believing a word of it but if he intended to stop Dropic from shooting the video, I wasn't going to complain. The body wasn't going anywhere for a while. Maybe he figured they could get the footage later.

"You can't control the news," Dropic barked at me. "You people never seem to learn. Government's crumble over such things. And don't forget, Mai Lai, Watergate, Lewinski…"

"That's enough, Juka," Cordovan interrupted, angrily. "She's not covering up a murder. Just preventing you from shooting video we probably wouldn't show on the air anyway."

Dropic stopped, his mouth open in shock. He looked at the gear in his hands, and I got the impression he wanted to throw everything down. Finally, he stormed away in the opposite direction of the crime scene hauling his gear with him. I was grateful for his departure and used the excuse of brushing hair out of my face to see if my hands were still shaking. They were. I cursed under my breath. Falling apart every time I talked to the Bosnian was not an option.

"Thank you," I said to Cordovan, surprised my voice was steady.

He shrugged. "I didn't do it for you. I simply don't approve of that kind of sensational video."

I had researched Cordovan's action news reports. The times he had chased people from place to place, the glare of the camera lights making the subject look guilty no matter what they may have done. The doors slammed in his face, the hands in front of the lens. I wondered what he was up to.

They had agreed to follow my ground rules, signing the formal agreement before they left Minneapolis. Break the rules and they would be denied access to the military controlled construction site. Perhaps Cordovan was simply following the rules. Perhaps, whatever had originally brought them to this place was bigger than a body buried in cement. I didn't like it.

He turned back to the scene at the foundation.

"Do you think he was alive when they poured the cement on him?"

"I think so, yes."

"Looking at that," he shook his head. "Makes it hard for me to breath."

"Yes."

"How could someone do such a thing?"

There was no way to explain it.

"So much for this band of brothers idea," Cordovan said. "Soldiers killing each other like that."

I thought he had taken a leap to assume a soldier did it, but I kept my mouth shut. Cordovan peered at me waiting for a response. When he didn't get one, he scanned the crowd of villagers. "They have probably never seen anything like this." Twenty or so villagers had gathered along the forest line to watch the events at the clearing where their new schoolhouse was to be built.

The adults seemed of uniform height, just over five feet. The men wore checked or stripped button-down cotton shirts over dusty dungarees, floppy straw hats pulled down on their heads. Their faces were a mass of brown, weathered wrinkles.

The women, their hair pulled up or plaited down their backs, wore cotton dresses with aprons and knee socks, their feet in worn sneakers. Barefoot children stared wide-eyed, some hugging the legs of their mothers.

"Doesn't leave much of a good impression, does it?" he asked.

Honduras had seen its share of civil war, war with neighboring El Salvador, rebel groups and guerilla warfare. I didn't think violence was such a stranger here.

I gazed around the crowd. One boy of about six wore a t-shirt with a grinning Bart Simpson on the front. A teenager, maybe fifteen, wore a Lakers jersey, his hands shoved into the back pockets of the jeans he wore low slung around his hips. I hadn't seen any satellite dishes, but the village had generators so it was possible they had internet access somewhere. There could even be videogame consoles in some of the homes. Movies, music and video games meant they had been exposed to plenty of barbarity.

"It's not as remote as you might think," I said. "I bet some of these kids could quote you lines from your favorite action movies,"

Cordovan shrugged. "That may be true. But do you think any of them have met Americans in person before? It's a shame to think that we're simply reinforcing the violent Hollywood stereotype."

As uncomfortable as it made me, his assessment was probably right. These missions were meant to leave positive impressions, provide humanitarian relief, make friends. We weren't making any friends today.

Someone behind us cleared his throat. Cordovan and I turned to find three men standing with hats in hand, obviously waiting to speak with us. The man in front stood out in the crowd. While most of the villagers were dark brown and weathered from sun or their hard work, or both, this man's skin was much lighter, almost white and smooth, as if his life had been easier, certainly with far less time in the sun than anyone else around us. He wasn't noticeably taller, but he stood erect, as if he weren't afraid to look life in the face.

He introduced himself and the other two men to us in Spanish. I could understand the names at least. Senor Bonilla was the one doing all the talking and introductions. When we shook hands, I noticed his were soft and clean. Senor Bonilla was not a laborer.

Senors Rioja and Egberto barely looked me in the eye. Their clothes were well worn but seemed to be their Sunday best as if they had dressed for the occasion. They had taken extra effort to comb their hair and clean up their cowboy boots, but dirt remained under their fingernails and unlike Bonilla, their hands were hard, cracked and calloused. Working men.

I wasn't sure what made Rioja and Egberto more nervous, meeting Cordovan and me, or being around the confident Senor Bonilla. Bonilla did a lot of talking, gesturing at them at the village, doing a little bowing to Cordovan. I figured someone would clue me in if it were necessary. Bonilla directed a question at me.

"I'm sorry, I don't speak Spanish."

The three men looked surprised. Cordovan made apologies for my lack of the language. I was accustomed to people assuming I was Hispanic, my brown skin and dark, curly hair, led many to make the wrong assumption. I felt no inclination to outline my heritage for the men.

"Mr. Bonilla is a sort of mayor of the village," Cordovan finally explained. "He is welcoming us and offering his assistance. He expresses his regret at this unfortunate death." Cordovan looked at me, as if waiting for me to respond.

"Tell him thanks for the condolences. I'm sure his assistance will be appreciated when the investigators arrive," I said.

Cordovan translated, then seemed to wait for more from me.

"I'm sorry that this tragedy has interrupted the important work we're doing for your village," I said.

Again, once he completed the translation, Cordovan turned to me as if there should be more for me to say. I had to be careful. My authority extended to escorting the media team, not representing the humanitarian mission to the village leadership. It wasn't my place, and I didn't like Cordovan shoving me into the position.

I glanced at the men who waited patiently. Rioja and Egberto looked down or away from me as soon as our eyes met. Bonilla, however, made his own appraisal. He checked out my boots, my body and stared at the name tapes on my uniform. When his eyes met mine again, he smiled darkly. I decided I didn't like the soft-handed man.

"Please tell Mr. Bonilla that I'm just a visitor to his lovely village, with no authority to speak for the Americans. If he needs some assistance from the Army, I can help find the right officer for him to speak to."

Cordovan translated. He poured out the charm, going on and on in flowery sounding speech, saying far more then I had. Bonilla glanced at me a couple of times during the translation and then finally locked eyes with me for a long moment. Something told me he had understood my English and the inaccurate translation Cordovan delivered revealed something to him.

Curious, I thought.

Raised voices dragged my attention back to the scene on the slab. The man who had been crying earlier, was now yelling and gesturing threateningly at Sergeant Dodd. Two soldiers grabbed his arms to restrain him but he jerked away from them and took a wild swing at Dodd's jaw.

Crap! We already had a dead body. We didn't need to watch this unit implode on itself because of it, and right in front of an audience of villagers. I excused myself from the group and moved quickly to the scene. Since I wasn't part of the unit and had a separate mission, I had hoped I could stay on the sidelines of this drama. Every step I took toward the fight felt like I was moving toward a place I didn't want to be.

The U.S. maintains a small presence at a Honduran military base; the two countries conduct joint counternarcotics, humanitarian, and civic action exercises. The U.S. troops conduct and provide logistics support for a variety of exercises (medical, engineering, peacekeeping, counternarcotics, and disaster relief) for the benefit of the Honduran people and the Central American neighbors. U.S. forces —regular, reserve, and National Guard – benefit greatly from the training and exercises.

U.S. State Department Profile of Honduras – 1997

Chapter 2

The wild right hook looked slow enough to duck, but somehow the blow managed to connect with Dodd's jaw in a knuckle-busting thud. Dodd swayed a little and took a step back to regain his balance, his hand going to the side of his face where an angry red welt rose on his cheek. He shook his head to clear the effects.

"Reggie, hold on now," Dodd said in warning, his hand up to ward off further violence.

Two soldiers grabbed Reggie, one on each arm, in an attempt to restrain him. They grappled with him, but Reggie seemed determined to strike out at Dodd again. Reggie's red and tear-streaked face made him look vulnerable, but his sudden burst of adrenalin was almost too much for the two solders to handle. Spittle flew from his mouth; his neck muscles bulged in thick cords. He glanced down and got a look at his own bloodied knuckle. He held his hand in front of his face, inspecting it, and then suddenly deflated like a popped balloon. In a voice that came out thin and hazy, he said, "I'm just saying, you can't leave him in there. You just can't." He turned toward the body, tears coursing down his face.

While his demand sounded irrational, to a Sapper, cement usually posed little threat. Their experience with explosives, digging defensive positions, getting rid of obstacles was all part of their normal routine. Even so, the body, and how it got there, complicated things.

Dodd tried to reason with him but his words didn't seem to register.

"Now Reggie, we can't do anything with him till the military police get here. I don't like it anymore then you do."

"But he's my brother," Reggie sobbed. "Oh Bobby, I'm sorry. I'm so sorry." He crumbled to the ground as if drained of the power to stand on his own.

"I want him out of there. Just please, get him out of there."

Soldiers standing around the scene tightened their haphazard circle as if attempting to screen his breakdown from the eyes of the villagers. Some of the soldiers watched what was going on, others looked away as if embarrassed. They were eerily silent and seemed confused about what to do next. I stood on the outside of the group of about sixty men, feeling helpless.

The name tape on Reggie's uniform said Larson. He looked to be in his late thirties. The two chevrons on his collar marked him as a corporal. The low rank for a man of his age wasn't unusual for a member of the National Guard, where unit structure and rank didn't change much year after year. Corporal Larson could stay in the same unit for his entire Guard career and never get promoted if there weren't openings in the rank structure.

First Sergeant Dodd crouched next to Larson. "You can see it's going to take us a long time to get him out, can't you?" He patted Larson's shoulder awkwardly. "You wouldn't want us to do anything that could keep us from finding out who did this, now would you?"

Larson didn't seem to hear. He ignored Dodd, then switched his focus to the two men standing over him as if noticing them for the first time, swiveling his gaze back and forth between them. When he stood slowly, the men tensed, exchanged glances with each other, wary of what Larson might do next.

"What did you see? What did you see?" Larson demanded of them. He was angry again and had found two new places to direct his rage. The men took hold of Reggie's arms in anticipation of another violent reaction. Reggie struggled toward each of them, a strange tug of war going on as the three men shoved back and forth. Larson repeated his question sending spittle flying into their faces. "What did you see, Judd? Porter? What the fuck did you see!?"

"We didn't see nothing, Reggie, I swear it," one of them said, his face wet with sweat. He was tall, slender and blond, with defined muscles in his arms and neck. His face was gaunt and weathered making it difficult to judge his age. He wore the chevrons of a staff sergeant, his name Porter embroidered above his uniform pocket.

Sergeant Judd's uniform was dark with sweat. He was built like a body builder with a large chest and bulging arms. His silver-grey crew cut matched the thin mustache outlining his lip. I always tried to avoid making snap judgments about people, but I took one look at Judd and immediately thought, cop. If someone had offered, I would have put fifty bucks on the hunch. A cop, a highway patrolman, a sheriff maybe, but someone who, when he wasn't serving in the National Guard, carried a badge. Judd merely shook his head as Reggie continued to fire off his questions.

"What do you mean you didn't see anything?" Reggie demanded. "How could you have missed this?" He turned to the mound in the concrete and froze. Slowly, the fight seemed to leak out of him again. He let out a long, slow groan, sank to his knees and sat staring at the body.

I shouldered my way past the phalanx of soldiers and moved closer to Dodd.

"Sergeant Dodd," I said, quietly hoping to keep the conversation between him and me, but evidently I was unsuccessful. At least ten sets of eyes turned and stared at me.

Their expressions ranged from shock to anger, most of them making it visibly clear that my involvement wasn't wanted.

"I understand there's a medical team working in the village somewhere."

He looked me up and down as if I had insulted his mother. "Yeah, so? This looks a little past anything a doctor could help with, don't it?"

The men behind him chuckled. I ignored them.

"I think Corporal Larson is in shock. I think he could use a sedative."

Dodd regarded me for a long moment, then relaxed his shoulders. He spit and hitched up his pants.

"Hank, get over here," he said over his shoulder.

Hank, a tall lanky kid of about 20, stepped up close to his first sergeant.

"Go on up there right quick and see if there's a doctor that can take a look at Reggie, here," Dodd instructed.

Hank nodded, then turned and jogged off through the watching villagers, up a hill and through some trees toward where I assumed the medical group worked.

That done, Dodd looked at me with a raised eyebrow.

"Can I speak to you a moment, First Sergeant?" I asked.

I took a couple of steps away from the group and hoped he would follow me. He glanced at the men clustered behind him, then followed me reluctantly until we were a few paces away from the pack and out of earshot. I understood the experience of being in charge of a situation that left you feeling inadequate. Dodd seemed capable, but if I had been in his shoes, I would have felt grateful to have someone to bounce some ideas around with me. I hoped he would feel the same way, but I didn't want him to think I was sticking my nose in too deep. I crossed my arms over my chest and peered up at him.

"What are you going to do?" I asked him.

He looked over my head at his men, who I assumed were all watching our exchange. Technically Dodd and I were the same rank, but he was a First Sergeant and in a position of command. I didn't have any authority here, but I wanted to offer support. He could take it or leave it.

"It's going to be a while before anyone can get up here," he said, stating the obvious.

"How long do you think?"

"I don't know, but I'll bet it won't be before the rain starts." He squinted up at the dark clouds rolling in.

The forecast I had checked before we left the main camp hadn't called for rain, but there was no denying the thick black clouds drifting closer. I mentioned the clear weather forecast and Dodd chuckled.

"They don't ever get the weather right up here," he said. "Bad part is, when it starts to rain in these mountains, it tends to keep coming down." He reset the cap on his head and spit. "If they don't get up here soon, and it starts to down-pouring, them so called roads we traveled on will become the streams they really are and impassable. We're gonna be stuck with that damn body in the damn cement. Then what are we gonna do?"

"Is there any air support?"

"The medical team has a chopper that comes up here 'bout once a day, but they had some kind of a mechanical problem a couple of days ago. It was one of the reasons we had to go down to the base camp. We brought them the part they needed but I don't know how long it will take them to make the repairs. Course, when it gets to pouring, even the air support is usually grounded."

From this spot, we were almost level with the surrounding mountain peaks that rose slightly higher than our location and were covered in thick jungle forest. The air was sweet and clean but thinner here than at the base camp. Everything seemed more in focus, more vital. On an opposite peak, the simple wooden steeple of a church rose majestically through the trees. On another peak sat a small farmhouse with an equally small herd of fenced-in cattle, their distant bleats echoed between the chasms. The signs of life on the other mountains seemed close, as if you could hello the people living there. Actually getting to them, however, would be hours of travel, first down one mountain and up the next. What looked so close could actually mean days of slow, rough driving.

"Rain or not, you can't move him," I said.

"That's for damn sure," Dodd said. "Course we do have a cop up here. Sergeant Judd over there, he could kind of guide us. Make sure we don't screw anything up."

I took some silent pride in the fact that I had identified the man as police but wished somehow that he wasn't. Something about Judd made me nervous.

"It's a good idea to get some guidance from him," I said. "But won't he be considered a suspect?"

It was like I had pulled a handle that said, "Danger. High Voltage." Dodd's hands went to his hips and he leaned over me. I had to dig in my heels to keep myself from backing up.

"Wait just a damn minute," he said. "It's a little early to be pointing a damn finger don't you think?"

"How many people did you have up here guarding the site?"

Dodd started to speak then stopped, but played the stare-down game with me. I held his gaze, knowing he would put it together on his own.

"Ah, hell." He took a couple of steps away from me and then cursed again with a bit more energy behind it.

"Five of 'em," he said. "And every last one of 'em could be a suspect."

I knew how he felt. It's no fun to realize that people you know and trust, people you have lived with and worked beside, could be murderers. It tilts your perspective in a way that never straightens out again.

"Seems to me, all that standing around over there might be affecting the crime scene," I said, turning and looking at the group clustered around watching us. "Have you got a small tent or a canvas cover you could maybe put up over him?'

Dodd crossed his arms over his chest and looked around the

site. He might have been as much as fifteen-years my senior but, aside from the small belly that hung slightly over his belt, seemed all muscle and hardness. I didn't know much about his experience, didn't know if he was a veteran of the Gulf war, or some other deployment like Panama or Bosnia. His men seemed to like him and so far, considering the circumstances, he had been reasonable. Still, he could easily ignore anything I had to say.

"Yeah," he nodded. "We could rig something like that. And it would mean everyone wouldn't be looking at him anymore. I suppose I'd better post a guard around him too."

"Good idea."

His eyes snapped to me as if to check if I was being sarcastic.

"I stopped that reporter and his photographer from shooting video of the body, but I have a feeling they might try to sneak back here, get the video when our backs are turned."

Dodd seemed satisfied with that answer and nodded.

"I don't suppose it would hurt to get Judd's take on things. See what he thinks we should do," I said.

In unison, we both turned and looked toward the crime scene. Judd and Porter were standing back, quietly talking to each other but seemed to be keeping an eye on Larson, who sat at their feet.

"Cripes, I've never seen nothing like that before," Dodd said. "Bobby and Reggie have been in the unit a few years. I don't know them all that well, but I just can't understand why anyone would want to do such a thing to him." His hand went to his face where a dark purple discoloration had formed. "It doesn't make any sense."

"You let me know if there's anything I can do to help," I said.

"I better go give these boys something to do. They get bored, they'll start getting into trouble." Dodd reluctantly moved back to the group. "Jonesy, go get some of that blue roofing tarp we got back there. We're gonna put up a screen around this whole area right ch'here."

"Okay boss."

"And Pete, you n' Curtis go get some a them rebar poles over there. We'll use those to hold the thing up."

Dodd sent his team bustling around under his instructions. Reggie remained slumped on the slab, looking at his brother's body. I trudged back to my vehicle and poured a cup of coffee from my thermos. It was cold, but I thought the caffeine might help. I made my way back to Larson and hesitated before I put a gentle hand on his shoulder.

"Maybe you could use some of this," I said.

He jerked under my hand and turned his green eyes to me, his face red and puffy. He thought about it for a moment then slowly stood as if his body ached. He took his time about it, but eventually he wrapped the coffee mug in both of his calloused hands and took a shaky drink. I wished I had some brandy to add to it.

"Are you older or younger than your brother?" I asked.

"Bobby's a year older," he said, then thought about it. "Was older."

"Did you join the Army at the same time?"

He nodded his head. "We went to basic together. The drill sergeants got us mixed up all the time. People always said we look alike. Used to really piss the drills off. They split us into different platoons, but..." His voice trailed off as if he didn't have the energy to finish the thought.

I had taken him by the arm and led him to a mud splattered pickup truck with a lowered tail gate, his six-foot height towering over me. He eased himself down, his eyes blank. He moved slowly, as if he had to wait for his brain to fire off the proper signals. He took a sip of the coffee and seemed to taste it for the first time. He looked deep into the cup, then at me. His eyebrows went together as if he were trying to figure out who I was.

"I'm Master Sergeant Lauren Harper. I am from public affairs. I brought the Channel Five News guys out here."

He looked around me to see if the news crew would

materialize. When he didn't see them, he returned his attention to the coffee.

He was broad shouldered and had a large barrel chest. My brown hand on his muscular arm was the same color as his sun-darkened skin. He looked like a man accustomed to working outside. Long, thick lashes circled forest green eyes. He was square-jawed and ruggedly handsome, with a wide mouth and full lips which were parted to reveal even, white teeth. He wore his dark, brown hair cut short on the sides but curled thickly over his head. If Reggie and his brother did look alike, the two of them would have been quite a sight together.

The memory of my last conversation with my sister sprang to mind. We'd had a little tiff. Nothing major, but an argument over the phone, the way sisters sometimes do.

My relationship with my sister made it easy to imagine how Corporal Larson now felt. If I had found my baby sister buried like that, knowing that she had suffered, knowing how frightened she would have been, how terrible the end, suddenly I had to fight back tears. I silently vowed to tell her I loved her next time we talked. Clenching my eyes shut and taking a deep breath, I fought to turn my thoughts in another direction.

"Do you work construction in your civilian job?" I asked him.

"Bobby and me got a little landscaping business," he said. "We started with just doing lawns, pulling up stumps, that kind of thing. Now we design whole gardens and outdoor living spaces. We've been doing real well. The business is really taking off."

His gaze wandered away from my face and took on a vacant look, his shoulders slowly slouching. "Bobby's so smart about business and things. This year we hired some help to take over while we did our Army thing." His voice trailed off and the coffee mug sat forgotten in his hands.

He wasn't paying attention so I stared at him for a while. The large and calloused working hands, the torso of a man accustomed to constant physical labor, the chiseled features and now his open vulnerability. He was raw masculine sex appeal but seemed unaware of it. The image of the handsome Larson brothers, shirtless and sweating while working on lawns, was probably great for business.

I had a pile of questions to ask him but didn't know if I should. The first thing I would want to know, if it had been my sister murdered like that, was who did it. He was still too shaky and I knew, once the investigators got there, he'd have plenty of official questions to answer, but I had to know one thing.

"Was anyone angry with him?"

He blinked slowly, then turned toward me as if only just realizing I was there, taking a minute to focus on me. "What?" he said.

"Was anyone angry with him? Anyone who might want to do him harm?

He shook his head slowly. "He got along fine with everyone. Even with the guys that were up here. We were only gone two days. I brought Bobby some clean uniforms and a book he wanted." He sighed as he realized his brother wouldn't be reading anything anymore.

He suddenly dropped the coffee cup, grabbed my arm and ignored the liquid splashed across the ground. He pulled me to within inches of his face. "I was supposed to be on guard duty, see? I was supposed to do it." He glanced away vacantly. "I didn't want to stay up here. I asked Bobby to stay. As usual, he did what I asked him to do. He always did what I asked him to do."

He stared off into space again. I pried his fingers off my arm. He sat there placidly, his guilt eating away at him.

Porter and Judd must have been part of the guard duty team with Bobby. That would explain why Reggie expected them to know something. Who else made up the five guards I wondered, and why five men? Was there something specific they were asked to guard against?

Dodd and his men applied professional construction

techniques to erecting the protective cover around the murder scene. Thick groupings of rebar fastened together with flex ties made solid poles. Breezeblocks weighed down by sandbags held the poles erect. Ropes lashed the poles to the ground as further support. Sections of plastic blue tarp stretched around the four corners of the square, the grommets from the tarps used to join each section to the poles with flex ties. Since rain was coming, Dodd had the men stretch another section of tarp over the top of the whole configuration to serve as a roof. The makeshift structure was about as secure as any of the tents in the camp.

I was impressed, not only by what they built, but with the speed in which it was going up. This group worked like a team that had been together for a long time. Dodd stood off to the side, giving directions. There was little talk and no bickering. How could a unit that worked so well together end up with such a horrible murder on their hands?

Hank returned from his errand followed by a soldier carrying an olive drab medical bag, the end of a blonde ponytail secured under the floppy brim of her boonie cap. Dodd spoke to her for a minute, and then pointed to where Reggie and I sat. The blonde headed our way, Hank close behind. She wore the gold clover leaf of a major on her cap but looked young. She could have been mistaken for a new private save for her rank insignia.

I stood and saluted her. She returned the salute offhandedly, her eyes already on her patient.

"Corporal Larson, I'm sorry for your loss," she said, while putting her bag down and taking out a stethoscope. Reggie looked at her, but otherwise didn't react to what she said. "I'm just going to check to make sure all this stress hasn't caused you to get sick, okay?"

She moved quickly and gently through her checks, asking him to remove his uniform jacket and telling him to breathe in and out, to look right and left, taking his pulse and temperature, all so smoothly that Reggie barely seemed to move.

"Do you have any allergies?" she asked him. He shook his head no, and watched as she pushed up his t-shirt sleeve, wiped his shoulder with an alcohol swab and prepared the syringe.

"I don't like needles," he mumbled, looking at her.

Before he finished the sentence, she had stuck him, wiped the needle mark with the alcohol swab, and put a small bandage over the site.

"You're going to sleep for a while now, okay Corporal?" She took him by the arm and stood him up. She motioned for Hank to take over. "We want you to get a good rest now."

"Yeah, come on now Reggie. I'll get you to your hooch," Hank said, with a firm grip on Reggie's arm.

"I don't need no sleep. I'm alright," Reggie said. But he followed Hank without a struggle.

"I'll get the sides of the tent rolled up," Hank said as he led Larson away. "You'll have a nice breeze through there. It's almost siesta time anyway."

The young major watched them walk away for a long moment.

"Poor man," she said, watching them. "But Damn. A couple of the nurses told me about him and his brother. They were all gossiping about these two hot guys in the engineering unit. I can see why they were going on about them," she said, shaking her head in disbelief. "Where did he get those eyes? I'd kill for lashes like that." She looked at me for confirmation. I smiled in agreement and she continued to shake her head while she put her equipment back in her bag.

"I thought doctors weren't supposed to get involved with their patients," I said.

"Yes, well. I think there are times when exceptions can be made." She turned to me and stuck out her hand. "I'm Dr. Anne Fordham. We're running the MEDCAP exercise up the hill there."

"Are you reservists too?"

"Yes. Normally my patients are dead." She smiled enjoying the shocked expression on my face. "I work for the Hennepin County coroner's office in Minnesota. I usually volunteer for this kind of Reserve duty every year—gives me a chance to do some good for the living."

"We're lucky to have you here now, as unfortunate as that may be."

"This is the first time I've ever been called on to use my coroner skills on one of these missions. Where's the body?"

I poked my head in the direction of where Bobby lay.

"Do you have any experience with cement?" I asked her.

She turned and stared at the tarp structure in the middle of the school foundation. "Yes, but I had the proper tools and equipment at my disposal at the time. It's in there?"

I nodded. She picked up her medical bag and started walking toward the crime scene.

"Well, so much for the living," she said.

I didn't envy her the job of figuring out how to get the body out of that floor. The doctor seemed to have a different attitude about the challenge. She moved toward the crime scene with a little skip in her step.

Chapter 3

I spotted Cordovan interviewing some of the villagers. The men standing around him, all of them shorter than the tall reporter, had their hats off, as if Cordovan were some important person they needed to show deference to. He ate up the attention while keeping an eye on Dropic who moved around the crowd discreetly aiming his video camera on the scene.

Cordovan wanted me to believe his focus was to produce stories about the Sappers and their humanitarian mission on behalf of the Los Flores villagers. A local news station doesn't spend the kind of money it takes to send a team on location, just to bring back happy, good news stories. Good news doesn't attract viewers. Controversy and scandal attract viewers. Cordovan needed to find a scandal to justify this trip, and I had led him directly into a murder scene. The fact that the reporter had so easily acquiesced in the brief battle to get video of the body told me he was after something bigger. What could be bigger than a body buried in cement?

"What are you up to, Cordovan?" I asked myself.

Clearly, Cordovan and Dropic had worked as a team for some time. The Bosnian presented himself as the friendly one, cracking jokes, acting casual, just the big guy who carried the camera. In practice, he helped the reporter gather information by asking background questions when the camera wasn't on and helped to get the interview subjects relaxed so they would drop their guard. While studying stories the team had produced in the past, I learned they didn't have a problem with using sound bites from interview subjects who didn't realize they were being recorded. I wondered how they were getting the sound bites in the first place so I paid close attention to the way they worked and caught Dropic at his game.

After an interview with a soldier at Soto Cano airbase, the photographer left the camera running and the wireless microphone on while he and Cordovan pretended the interview was over. They complimented the soldier on how well he did, pretended to pack up their gear, but the entire time the camera rolled and the microphone recorded. The solider had no idea he was still being interviewed.

Trying to appear helpful, I unclipped the microphone from the soldier, turned it off and handed it to Dropic. He hid his frustration with a smile.

"Not much gets past you," he said.

"What do you mean?" I asked, innocently.

Now, watching the reporter and photographer working the villagers, I wondered for the gazillionth time what they were after. Cordovan glanced my way and flashed a grin.

Cheeky bastard.

When we first arrived at the construction site, Sergeant Mora, our driver, had taken one look at the body in the cement and walked way. I decided to go looking for him.

I found Mora doing what most young soldiers did when they had a few spare moments. Slumped against a stack of breezeblocks, his rucksack for a backrest, Mora had his legs stretched out in front of him, his boonie cap over his face and his arms crossed over his chest. He appeared to be asleep. My footsteps on the gravel must have alerted him. He peered up at me from under his cap.

"Hey, Sergeant Harper," he said, scrambling to his feet.

"Did you get some rest?" I asked him.

"No. All I can see behind my eyelids is that thing in the floor. I don't think I'll sleep well for a long time."

"Seeing a body does that to you. Keeps you up at night."

"You know this from experience?" he asked.

"Unfortunately. Makes life seem randomly disposable. At least we didn't know him."

Mora narrowed his eyes at me. "Sounds like there's a lot you aren't telling me."

"Not today anyway."

He opened his mouth to ask more, but must have seen from my expression that I didn't intend to add anything further. He changed the subject. "I saw you arguing with Dropic earlier. Have you changed your mind about letting them get video?"

"No way, but the more they hang around doing nothing, the more likely they are to get into trouble. I'm thinking it might be a good idea to take them up to the medical mission in the village. Get them out of this area for a while. Would you mind taking them? Introduce them around and let them get what they need?"

"Sure, I could do that. I'll take my camera too. I need to start working on something for my paper back home."

As a civilian, Mora worked as a junior reporter for a major newspaper in Minneapolis, just starting his career. Writing obituaries had its challenges but like any hungry journalist, he wanted more.

"I'd like to borrow your camera for a little while," I said. "Get some stills of the crime scene. It shouldn't take too long. I'll bring the camera up to you when I'm finished."

"That'll work," he said, as we made our way toward our vehicle.

"Look, I'm not sure what these guys are up to," I said, glancing back at Dropic and Cordovan. "I feel like I won the battle over shooting video of the body too easily. There's something going on I don't know about and I'm at a disadvantage."

"Yeah, the language barrier could be a problem. I'll keep an eye on them. Try to see what direction they're going. No hints of what they might be after?"

"Not so far. Cordovan is a white collar crime guy. I watched a bunch of his stories, usually about some government official that was skimming, or some shaky business bilking people out of money. Nothing that seemed to have any relevance here."

We reached the truck and Mora tossed his rucksack in the back. He patted his pockets, eventually finding a well-worn notebook in a cargo pocket, a pen shoved through the wire rings at the top. He found a tape recorder at the bottom of the opposite cargo pocket and checked to ensure he had a fresh tape in it.

I was always a little jealous of the light-weight equipment a print journalist used. My video camera, tripod, tapes, lights and microphones were cumbersome and heavy. The basic goal, to tell a story, was the same, but our tools were very different. I used images and sound. They used words to conjure their own images. From reading his work, I knew Mora had a good handle on the tools of his trade.

"It would be nice to see my byline on some feature articles for a change," Mora said, climbing into the back of the truck.

"These medical exercises are about as feature-y as it's going to get. And while you're up there, see if you can find out if any of the medical team saw or heard anything interesting last night."

He jumped down from the truck, his camera bag over one shoulder and flashed a smile at me. "Sure, I'll ask some questions. Can't be a journalist without asking questions." He raised an eyebrow at me. "Question for you is, just how far can I go with this?"

"You're the only print journalist here and you're a creative guy. I'll look forward to hearing where your investigation might lead."

I watched his expression as he considered what I'd said. "You don't really care about the articles," he said. "You want to know who did this."

"Of course. One of our own is dead. I'd like to know who did it. Wouldn't you?"

"Absolutely." He glanced toward the crime scene. "That's the nastiest way to go I could ever imagine. Somebody with a sick imagination did that. Someone mean and vicious. Might not be a nice guy to meet."

"Keep that in mind while you're poking around," I said. "And be careful."

Mora launched into a detailed description of his camera and how to use it. It was a large digital thing with lots of buttons and options, lots of menu pages I forgot as soon as he showed them to me. All I really cared about was the big, fat, grey button on top that took the pictures and the screen where they were played back. He showed me everything in the pockets of the camera bag, extra memory sticks, double A batteries, a flash unit, different lenses, lens paper.

With the camera bag slung over my shoulder, Mora and I approached Cordovan. We found him interviewing Bonilla while several others stood around and watched. Dropic had the tripod and camera set up just behind Cordovan. Bonilla, his eyes squinted against the meager sunlight, appeared as if he had given television interviews hundreds of times. He stood calmly in front of Cordovan with a microphone clipped to the lapel of his shirt. The reporter conducted the interview in Spanish so Mora translated for me as we watched.

"This is the third year American soldiers have come and we are very happy to have them here," Bonilla said.

That information grabbed my attention. For the mission to come here, to such a small place, three years in a row, was unusual. I knew it was the first time Dodd's engineers had been here, the first time a construction project had been made part of the mission. Medical teams however, would sometimes go back to villages year after year as a way to build relationships and keep track of patients, but for this small village to get this level of attention seemed out of the ordinary.

"We have never had problems with them coming into our village in the past. We are all shocked that one of them has died. We are very sorry for his family."

"Did anyone in the village want to stop the Americans from coming?" Cordovan asked.

Bonilla glanced around the crowd. His stares prompted many of the people watching to shake their heads no, but I wondered how much of that was forced by his obvious power in the community.

"As I have said, the Americans have come here to help us. We are very happy they are here."

"No one was upset with the Americans, maybe for something they may have done during previous visits here?" Cordovan asked.

Bonilla shrugged. "Each year they come, they have helped us. We are always happy when they come."

Cordovan turned to Dropic and commented in English. "This is going nowhere," he mumbled under his breath, looking frustrated. I wondered how long he had been hearing the same answer to his questions. He finally turned back to Bonilla and thanked him, ending the interview with a handshake and platitudes Mora didn't need to translate.

Cordovan glanced in my direction and I waved him over. He excused himself from the group of curious villagers and made his way to Mora and me. Mora explained the plan, giving Cordovan a vivid idea of what kinds of stories they might find at the medical clinic. Dropic wandered over and listened.

"What do you think?" Cordovan asked the videographer.

"Old people, kids and nurses. What could be wrong with that?" Dropic said with a grin. The reporter and photographer gathered up their equipment and Mora led them toward a narrow dirt path in the direction of a small cluster of mud-brick buildings up the hill and behind a line of trees.

That done, I headed back to the crime scene.

Most professional video camera viewfinders project the image to the videographer in black and white. There have been plenty of times when I was called on to shoot things I didn't want to see. A mass grave site. The aftermath of a terrorist attack. The treatment of wounded in a field hospital. When those missions came along, I would keep my right eye pressed to the viewfinder and my left eye closed. Somehow, limiting the vision to a black and white image seen through a lens, lessened the gore.

What I was about to shoot wasn't bloody but it was gruesome. I knew the pictures I captured on the camera's memory card, which could be erased and reused a thousand times, were going to be seared in my memory far more permanently. I hitched the camera bag higher onto my shoulder and trudged stiffly through the jungle humidity to the body surrounded by plastic tarp.

Chapter 4

The blue tarp walls of the temporary shelter waved gently in and out, as if the structure itself breathed. The plastic walls seemed sturdy enough to withstand the increasing wind and threatening rain. A section of tarp made up the roof and extended down to create a flap for a door. The silhouette of the young doctor moving around inside looked eerily distorted.

What the soldiers had pulled together out of a few sheets of tarp and rebar poles was impressive. Despite their efficiency, Dodd didn't look happy as he surveyed the mess that had been made of his construction project. He stood, hand on one hip, the other holding a canteen. His chest stretched the limits of his brown t-shirt, his arms thick and dark in a farmer's tan. A large dragon tattoo covered one bicep. Rivulets of sweat ran down his face. He pushed his boonie cap onto his forehead and sucked greedily from the canteen.

As I approached, Dodd said something to Hank under his breath, something that sounded like, "Maybe she can do it."

In a company-sized unit, the first sergeant is the highest-ranking non-commissioned officer. The top enlisted guy, which is why most first sergeants are addressed by the nickname, 'Top." The friendly moniker usually helped establish a rapport. Using it might also demonstrate to Dodd that I understood who was in charge.

"Maybe I can do what, Top?" I asked.

He took a deep breath, wiped his mouth with the back of his hand and trained his gaze on me. "Light a fire under them damn people in the base camp to get their asses up here,"

Even if a team had been mounted immediately, and I didn't think that was the case, I knew it would still be well over an hour before anyone of authority could get here. Dodd was getting anxious and that was the last thing this group needed.

"They probably had to notify the embassy and some of the local authorities. That could slow things down."

"The Embassy? What the hell do they have to do with anything?"

"The MPs and CID will investigate, but there will likely have to be some local Honduran police involvement. Who knows what kind of turf wars are going on. I'd bet local law enforcement are arguing they have to be involved for the safety of the local civilians."

"Safety of the locals?" Dodd said. "You're assuming one of us did this? What about one of them?" He gestured angrily at the group of villagers still clustered around the area, watching the drama.

"I'm just trying to point out the diplomatic issues here," I said. "There could be a whole slew of complicated international agreements that have to be considered."

Dodd stared me down for as long as dignity allowed and then cursed under his breath and paced a bit.

"I'm only guessing at all this," I said. "We're here at the invitation of the Honduran government."

"International agreements," Dodd said with a note of scorn in his voice. "That doesn't help us out much does it?"

I didn't have an answer for him.

Dodd shifted his attention to Hank. "What happened here last night, Hank? You see anything?"

But Hank shook his head. "I sure as heck didn't see any of this."

His face flushed bright red. I could have taken his color change for a sign that he lied, but it was obvious the young man was merely painfully shy.

"Sergeant, is Reggie asleep?" I asked him.

His face turned a brighter shade of red. He flicked his head to sweep sweat soaked bangs out of his eyes.

"Was when I left him," he said, his gaze focused on the ground. He shuffled from foot to foot probably wishing I would pretend he wasn't there. I had to stop myself from chuckling at his discomfort and wondered how old he was. It was hard to tell. No more than early twenties and still plagued with some acne problems. Hank stuck to Dodd like he needed a mother hen.

I hitched the heavy camera bag further onto my shoulder. "I thought I'd better take some pictures. Do you think we should see what Judd has to say first?"

Dodd and I both looked toward where Judd and Porter were standing. Most Reserve and Guard units had members who worked in civil service. Police officers, fire fighters, city and county employees usually received several weeks of paid military leave from their day jobs. The extra time and additional pay served as incentive for the weekend military service. For both a cop and a coroner to be along on the mission wasn't a surprise. In fact, it would have been unusual not to have at least one law officer type around. Still, the thought of asking Judd for advice was as appealing as hiking down the mountain barefoot in the coming storm. I'd never spoken to Judd, but I already knew I wouldn't like him.

"We can ask," Dodd said. "But he ain't always very cooperative."

Before I could ask for clarification, Dodd called Judd over and Porter followed him as if they were a two-for-one pair.

"You got any ideas what we should do here?" Dodd asked.

Judd slowly swept the group with a glare, his lips pressed together. When his gaze landed on Hank, the young man jerked as if he'd been slapped. Hank suddenly didn't know what to do with his hands and his acne-scarred face turned crimson. When Judd got bored with making Hank squirm, he switched his focus to me. He looked me up and down. I didn't know the reason for his disdain. It could have been because I was a woman, that I outranked him, that I was black, that I was an outsider. From a guy like Judd, there were too many options. I waited him out. Eventually he turned to Dodd.

"Yeah," he said. "How's this for an idea. Wait for the MPs to get here."

I watched the muscles jump in Dodd's jaw as he gnashed his teeth. Obviously, the tough act from Judd wasn't anything new. The sneer on Porter's face gave me the impression the two enjoyed acting up for each other. The pair grew less appealing by the second.

"That's it?" Dodd pressed.

"I'm just a beat cop, remember?" Judd said. "What do I know about something as complicated as this?"

"We're asking for your professional help because someone in your unit is dead," I said. "It's time to set aside whatever differences you have and do what you can to help."

My attempt to sound reasonable was a waste of time. The pair simply stared at me for a long moment, then turned and walked away. When I started to say something more, Dodd put his hand on my arm, shaking his head.

"Believe me. It ain't worth it," Dodd said. "I didn't think he'd cooperate."

"What is their deal? Why are they so hostile?"

Dodd shuffled about for a second avoiding my eyes. "Long story," he said. "Them two…" But he didn't elaborate further. "This weather is about to change right quick," Dodd said, as he scanned the skies. Directly overhead, there were still small patches of blue, but grey billowing clouds enshrouded neighboring mountaintops and rotated steadily in our direction. The wind had picked up noticeably.

"I don't have any authority with anyone at the base camp," I said. "Where are your officers?" It was a question I'd been wondering for some time. They were a company-sized element, so there should have been at least two or three lieutenants and a captain serving as a company commander. I had done all of my coordination with First Sergeant Dodd and hadn't any dealings with the officers of the company. That wasn't too unusual since I was enlisted as well. Once on the mission however, I expected to see at least one commissioned soldier present. Their absence, especially in this situation, would raise eyebrows.

Dodd reached into his back pocket and retrieved his tin of chewing tobacco. He pinched a large wad of the stuff and shoved it between his teeth and his lower lip. The delaying tactic only served to heighten my interest.

"Well, Sergeant Harper. We got Lieutenant Allen up here," he said. He glanced in the direction of the row of Humvees where a small group of soldiers stood around. A couple of solders had removed their shirts and lay bare-chested on the hoods of their vehicles even though there was little sign of sun left. Their dog tags glinted in the waning light. Others had their headgear off and hands shoved deep in their pockets.

I cringed at the utter lack of discipline. Soldiers never, ever went without some kind of cover on their head. A soft cap, a helmet or a boonie cap was always a part of the uniform. And soldiers never stood around with hands in their pockets. Pockets were for keys or change, never a place to rest your hands. Most offensive, was to see the soldiers without their shirts. It just wasn't done. To see such an open display of skin rubbed me the wrong way especially in front of the large foreign civilian audience. This wasn't the kind of impression the Army wanted to make—not my Army anyway.

"He's only been in the unit a short while. Just come out of OBC," Dodd said. He spit a long stream of tobacco juice, a sign of his opinion of the training given in the Officer Basic Course.

"I don't remember seeing a lieutenant in the group that rode up here with us. Did he stay here last night too?" I asked.

Dodd raised an eyebrow at me in response. "He seems to feel more comfortable up here."

His meaning was clear. The new lieutenant didn't feel comfortable around the men. I glanced over Dodd's shoulder and scanned the crowd of locals still patiently sitting and watching. There was a possibility one or more of them had committed this murder but the more I thought about it, the more I doubted that possibility. The use of construction materials and the cruelty of the method seemed to point to someone who knew the victim well, and had a grudge. Since Hank, Lieutenant Allen, Staff Sergeant Porter and Sergeant Judd were up here when Larson had been killed, they topped the list of suspects, at least in my mind. I wondered if there was anyone else were didn't know about.

"Where's your company commander," I asked.

Dodd chewed and spit again.

"Captain Thomas is back at the base camp," Dodd said, locking eyes with me. "He don't much like sleepin' up here. He's more of a hands-off leader, if you know what I mean."

So, their commander preferred the comforts of the base camp to the more primitive living conditions of the remote village. In Thomas's defense, there was no way for him to foresee that one of his soldiers would be murdered. Still, once the investigators started asking questions, the absence of the commander would be cause for inquiry. It would be interesting to hear how Thomas would attempt to justify it.

"Have you asked Lieutenant Allen to get on the radio? He's the ranking officer here."

Dodd gave me a smirk.

"Hey, Lieutenant Allen!" he yelled at the group of soldiers hanging out near the vehicles. "Can you come over here please, sir?"

I turned to watch as the shortest man in the group turned toward us, pointed at himself in question, then with obvious reluctance, started moving slowly in our direction.

"Sometime this century," Dodd mumbled under his breath.

Lieutenant Allen's chin strap from his boonie cap hung across his throat, the hat hanging down his back. In only his brown t-shirt and BDU pants that were obviously too big for him, he looked like a young boy instead of an officer in the Army. He walked toward us, staring at the ground like a child on his way to the principal's office. It was hard to miss his early baldness, dark curly hair surrounding his now pink scalp. He either wore a thin excuse for a mustache, or maybe it was just dirt around his top lip. His body language broadcast the fact that talking to us was the last thing in the world the young lieutenant wanted to do.

Dodd and I came to relaxed attention and saluted. Allen saluted back with a weak flick of the wrist without meeting our eyes.

"Yes, First Sergeant?" he said. It was the way an enlisted soldier would address Dodd, and I internally cringed at his inexperience.

Dodd looked at me with a raised eyebrow indicating this was an audience I had requested.

I stuck my hand out for a shake. The oddly limp and quick shake he gave me was uncomfortable for us both.

"I'm Master Sergeant Harper, public affairs. I brought the news team up here."

Allen glanced at me briefly, before looking away. "I'm aware of that."

My first impression was that the lieutenant was unsure of himself and covered up his insecurities with attitude. He was not happy about being summoned here. At first, I thought his slow progress toward us was out of embarrassment. After seeing him up close, I got the strong impression he felt it was beneath him to be speaking to us.

"Can I speak to you for a moment?" I asked. Not waiting for a response, I moved away from Dodd and Hank. Lieutenant Allen and I had a thing or two to talk about.

I turned to see him still rooted in place watching me walk away. I reached my intended point, stopped and waited. He glanced angrily at Dodd, then in the same slow insulting pace, made his way to me. He stopped in a wide leg stance, arms crossed over his chest and peered up at me. I let the silence stretch for a moment.

"You asked me here Sergeant Harper. What do you have to say?"

His back was to the rest of the soldiers which was the way I wanted it. I smiled at him. "Put your cover on your head. Now," I commanded.

"What did you say?" He sounded high pitched and whiney.

I continued to smile. "You heard me, Lieutenant. I said put your god damn cover on your head."

"You can't talk to me like that." He dropped his hands to his sides and stuck his chest out. The pink tinge on his cheeks made him look even younger.

"Yes I can, Lieutenant. And you're going to do what I said. Put your cover on your head. Do it now."

He swiveled around, as if looking for help, first toward Dodd, then toward the group of soldiers he had been hanging out with. Dodd pretended to ignore us, but it was obvious he was curious about the conversation.

"That's right, look at that group over there," I said. "Look at 'em!"

He first shot a look at me and stared for a long moment, then turned back to the group. He shrugged.

"And?" he asked, sarcastically.

"Shirtless, standing around without their headgear and with their hands in their pockets. And I bet they all call you by your first name, don't they?"

The color on his checks intensified.

"Now look here …"

"Shut up." I said quietly. "You will start by putting your god damn hat back on your head." I kept smiling at him and gave him a moment to let what I said sink in.

"You can't give me orders," he said. He sounded like a spoiled child.

"That's true. Let's call it a strong suggestion."

He opened his mouth to object again but I cut him off. "When you get your own hat back on your head, you will then tell your first sergeant to make sure his soldiers get back into uniform."

He decided he would stand up to me. With his feet firmly planted, he crossed his arms in front of his chest again, and with a cocky tilt to his head, stared up at me with false bravado. The kid had a lot to learn.

"I will allow them to be without their shirts if I like, Sergeant."

"You'll allow it, huh?"

He nodded. "Yes, it's hot out and..."

"Shut up," I commanded. He opened his mouth again to object, has hands balled into fists at his sides.

"You've got a body buried in the cement, Lieutenant," I said, leaning into him. "And there's about to be a whole passel of people up here; CID investigators, embassy folks, local investigators. First thing they'll think when they see that group over there is that this unit suffers from a severe lack of discipline."

"That's not my fault," he said. "Bobby being dead..."

"That's Sergeant Larson, Lieutenant. Sergeant Larson is the one who is dead. And no matter who killed him, Lieutenant, as the ranking officer here, it's your responsibility, Lieutenant. Yours."

He glared up at me for a long moment, a cruel twist to his mouth as he tried to stare me down. When he suddenly found something interesting to look at on the ground, I knew the gravity of the situation was finally sinking in. He was going to have a lot of questions to answer. If there was a place to lay blame in all of this, he was definitely vulnerable to it. I was sure he was contemplating the possibility of dirt on his brand new record. When his eyes met mine again, his vulnerability began to show. He glanced nervously across the construction site at Dodd, who quickly looked away as if he hadn't been watching the whole time.

"You were here last night, weren't you?"

He continued to stare off, his eyes scanning the villagers sitting around the area. He nodded his head. He had been here as the ranking officer on duty when one of his men had been murdered. His hands went to his hips and he turned to me, ready to defend himself, but I didn't want to hear it.

"Did you see anything? Hear anything?"

"I heard the same thing I hear every night," he said angrily. "A lot of laughing and joking around. Men acting like children. It's amazing how stupid…" He left the sentence unfinished, staring at the ground, shaking his head. He thought the men had been acting stupid, but he hadn't been included in their games and that made him feel left out. The lieutenant needed to get accustomed to the loneliness that came with leadership, because the feeling would only increase as his authority grew.

"You didn't hear any arguing? No one acting out of the ordinary?" I pressed, but he continued to shake his head no.

"I'm not exactly clued into what ordinary is for them, Sergeant," he confessed. "I stay up here because," he shrugged. "I read a lot," he said, as if it were something to be ashamed of. "I stay in my tent. They leave me alone and I read. A lot."

He pulled on the string of his boonie cap so that it slowly slipped up his back. He reached behind himself and settled the cap on his head, peering up at me from under the brim. The golden bar of his rank was bright and shiny. We call new second lieutenants butter bars. He would only wear the gold bar for a few months before being promoted to first lieutenant and swap the gold bar for silver. The first months of leadership can sometimes be the hardest. I felt a twinge of sympathy for him, but brushed it aside. Mistakes officers make affect too many people to let them slide.

"They don't want to be your friend," I said. "They want you to be a leader. They want you to be up to the task. Act like an officer and earn their respect. They may not ever like you, but leadership is not about people liking you. That bar on your cap entitles you to their respect. It's up to you to earn it."

He squinted at me for a long moment, his lips pressed together. He let out a long breath between his teeth.

"Ask Dodd what he thinks you should do," I said. "Listen to what he says. Watch the way he leads these men and learn from him."

"This wasn't supposed to get so complicated. I thought it would be easy," he said.

"Yeah, well now it's not. Now, one of your soldiers is dead. This place is about to be crawling with investigators and you'd better get yourself and your soldiers ready for that. You understand, Lieutenant?"

Part of every non-commissioned officer's job is to train the young commissioned officers they work with. There isn't any official way to get it done. Some officers listen, others don't. I didn't envy Dodd his job.

Allen spent some time consulting the ground, a lengthy internal conversation going on. Finally, he took a deep breath and walked toward Dodd, his shoulders becoming straighter as he made the short trip. I watched as the two exchanged a few words, Dodd looking down at the young officer, an eyebrow raised as he listened. They continued to confer while I made my way back to the concrete slab. When I looked back, Dodd met my gaze and gave me a crooked smile, then turned and shouted to the group of soldiers lounging around the vehicles.

"Is this the goddamn beach or something?" he shouted. "Put your goddamn uniforms on and get your asses over here! You think the clouds are gonna protect you from this Honduran sun? What did I tell you boys about getting sun burned? If I see any red on any of you I'll be handing out article fifteens like Halloween candy." He continued to shout and berate them as they slowly and reluctantly complied with his orders.

Lieutenant Allen walked toward one of the vehicles. I assumed he intended to get on the radio to find out what was holding up the arrival of the investigation team.

I hitched the camera bag securely onto my shoulder and continued toward the plastic shelter and the body. I was a few paces from the safety of the tarp when I heard what sounded like a rapid series of popping noises. It took me a moment to realize it was rain hitting the tarp in big fat drops that sounded like firecrackers. I jumped when a bullwhip crack of lightning ripped across the sky. The intensity of the sound froze everyone in place for a second.

The villagers, who had been squatting in the dirt, rose to their feet and calmly moved back into the tree line. Just as they reached the inadequate shelter of branches and leaves, the skies opened up. Sheets of rain suddenly obscured all vision and in seconds I was drenched.

I jogged the rest of the way to the plastic shelter and visualized the dirt roads we had traveled to get here. The old stream beds and rutted trails would, in no time, be filled with fast moving water. The rocks and ruts that had made our ride bone-jarring, would become mini-waterfalls and in short order, the route would become impassable. Worse, in a storm this strong, helicopters would be grounded as well.

I lifted the plastic sheet and ducked into the shelter. Dr. Fordham knelt in front of the hand, the area around her impressively dry despite the torrent outside.

She peered up at me, her eyes slightly red and tired looking. "I guess this means no one will be coming for a while," she said, a weary note in her voice.

"Yep, probably not for a while."

She turned back to her work. "That's too bad," She mumbled. "I'm going to need some help figuring this one out."

Chapter 5

The odor inside the plastic structure was almost paralyzing. Trapped within the hastily erected shelter, it was thickly sweet, hovering in the small space like a physical thing. Along with the odor, the tarp trapped a horde of flies. The buzz of insects competed with the staccato pounding of rain on the plastic roof. Flies careened off the walls and swarmed around the exposed portions of the body. I groaned to myself, fighting against the urge to run and almost lost the battle. Insects made swooping dives at my ears, the buzz intensifying and decreasing in waves. It was maddening.

I brushed flies away from my face and pulled the camera out of the bag.

"I thought I should take some pictures," I said.

Fordham gestured for me to help myself and stayed focused on what she was doing. She wore plastic safety glasses and thin surgical gloves and I was jealous of the little protection they offered her. As I watched, a fat fly crawled across one lens of her safety goggles. I shuddered at its slow and confident progress. She stayed focused on her work.

"Will it matter if you're in the shots?" I asked her.

She was holding the hand and taking scrapes under the

fingernails. She couldn't move the stiffened appendage, so she was leaning into it, her nose almost touching the grayish white digits. "I'll be done here in just a second," she mumbled.

I stood back, my arms in constant motion in a fruitless attempt to keep the insects away from my face. I pulled my boonie cap down as low as it would go and pulled my collar up to protect my neck. It didn't help much.

Fordham got the scrapings she wanted, gathered her equipment and stood up slowly, her forehead wrinkled in a frown, her lips pressed together in concentration. I didn't want to disturb her ruminations so I began to snap pictures, batting away flies as I went. Eventually their drone became less noticeable.

Muted daylight filtered through the tarp giving everything inside a bizarre bluish tint. To counter the unnatural colors I used a flash, but the periodic shock of brightness from the artificial light froze the scene in gruesome frames.

"How long does it take cement to harden?" Fordham asked.

I opened my mouth to profess my ignorance when she followed quickly with another question. I realized she wasn't expecting answers.

"Was this cement mixed properly or was it done by an amateur? Plenty of flies. No maggots on the fingers. The places where larva usually populate are buried in the cement and there isn't a proper place to take his temperature. It's going to be difficult to determine a time of death. By the time we dig him out, it will be too late. He's been dead long enough to attract flies and animals. Something was eating away at his fingers. Could have been rats. Could have been something else --vultures maybe? It's too hard to tell."

Her description left me feeling wobbly. I shook off the queasiness and kept snapping pictures, realizing that without thinking, I was framing the shots artistically, the way I would shoot any picture. Extreme close-ups of the way the hand hung motionlessly in the air, the angle of the knee rising from the cement, a wide shot taking in the entire scene. It was out of habit that I used the focus to add depth and life to the pictures. I wondered if I were ruining the crime shots in this way, but didn't know any other way to do the job.

Fordham had her hands on her hips and alternated between staring at the corpse and pacing the small structure. She'd take a few steps, stop, stare at it, then repeat her movements.

"Any word on how much of a delay the weather will cause?"

It took me a minute to realize that this time she expected an answer.

"Lieutenant Allen got on the horn to the base camp to find out what's going on."

She'd been at the camp a while so she already knew how impossible travel would be in this weather. She looked up at the plastic roof and cursed.

"Too bad the air support is out too." I said.

"Yeah, those guys have been lounging around here for a couple of days waiting for their part. Someone should probably tell the crew what's going on."

"Does the rest of the medical team know what's happened here?" I asked.

She shrugged. "Some, not all of them, I'm sure. There's about sixty soldiers up there. We had more than eight hundred patients to see today," she explained. "It's like a factory sometimes. It can take a while for news to travel down the line."

She pointed out things I needed to photograph. There were faint boot marks in the cement I hadn't noticed. They appeared to be typical combat boot prints and that wasn't a good thing. Worse was that it appeared to be more than one set.

"See the difference in size?" she asked me, pointing to an average-sized print and another that was much larger, huge in fact.

"They're very faint," I said. "Wouldn't they be deeper if it had been the killer's feet? Deeper because the cement would have been damp?"

"That's what I don't know. These prints could belong to the first couple of people who found him this morning. I just don't know how fast this stuff dries, or if this was quick-dry cement."

She shrugged and then stood, snapping surgical gloves from her hands and rubbing the powdered residue from her fingers. I noticed her nails were broken down to ragged, bloody ridges. She was a nail-biter. Looking at the damage her habit had made to those thin white fingers made my own nails hurt. I resisted the urge to curl my fingers into fists.

"It's obvious the prints are from combat boots, but we can differentiate the brands by their tread marks. That should help us narrow our list of suspects."

Fordham continued to ruminate as I snapped more pictures then, taking a hesitant step closer, used the zoom to get an extreme close-up of the two sets of boot prints.

"Dr. Fordham, if these prints had been made this morning, don't you think there'd be a lot more than just two sets of prints here? There were a lot of people milling around the body."

She grunted something noncommittally and then resumed pacing. She wrapped her arms across her chest, clasping her fingers under each armpit.

I didn't want to jump to any conclusions, but looking at the difference in the size of those boot prints I immediately thought of the two soldiers who had been on guard duty with the murder victim. Sergeants Porter and Judd. One was large and muscular, the other average-sized. They had both been in the area when the murder actually happened and they didn't seem too surprised or shocked. One thing was certain. Dodd's wish that this didn't involve one of his soldiers wasn't going to come true.

It was growing increasingly uncomfortable inside the tarp. I waved flies away from the things I was photographing and from my eyes, nose and mouth. You'd think, over time, you'd become accustomed to the smell but it only grew worse, as if it coated my nose. The clamor from the rain. The mound where his head was outlined. His hand with the partially eaten fingers. The angle of his knee with the splatters of dried cement. The trowel markings where someone had bothered to smooth the surface. It was a horror. I needed to get the hell out of there.

"Two makes sense," Fordham said, under her breath.

I jumped at the sound of her voice and then was grateful for it. I realized I had been getting myself worked up, lost in my own gruesome thoughts. Her matter-of-fact voice quickly brought me back down to the present. I shrugged off the creepiness and focused.

"What do you mean?"

"There had to be at least two of them," she said. "One to hold him down, the other to pour the cement. If Bobby was built like his brother, he was probably a pretty strong guy. It might have been a violent struggle to hold him down, unless they incapacitated him somehow."

"You mean like, drugged him?" I asked.

She shrugged and fished a bandana out of her cargo pocket and wiped the sweat from her face. She folded it neatly and shoved it back into her pocket.

"Drugged, beaten to near unconsciousness, drunk maybe," she said. "I won't be able to tell until we get some lab results back. I don't have all the equipment I need for the tests but I can make do, at least try to rule out a few things."

"How are you going to get him out of there?" It seemed impossible. Dr. Fordham didn't seem too daunted by the task.

"First a jackhammer, then picks, chisels and finally, brushes to wipe away the powder. It will take time, but there's no way around that."

"Do you think they should start with the jackhammer now or would it be better to wait?"

"I'm not sure. It's obviously important to leave the scene unaltered for the investigators, but leaving him in there for too long, this humidity, the rain?" She shook her head. "It's not a decision I can make on my own. We'd better get on the horn with the investigators and ask them what they want us to do."

I showed her the pictures I had taken in the digital playback mode on the camera.

"Looks like you captured everything we need in here. There's a cement mixer and some equipment outside I'd like you to get some shots of. Once you're done, can you make copies and get them to me in my lab?

"Of course. I'll bring you a CD. "

I followed Fordham as she ducked under the plastic door and stepped out into the deluge of rain. We both stopped, appreciating the sweet freshness of the air and the lack of buzzing flies. I took a couple of deep breaths. Despite the gloomy weather, everything outside the tarp looked vibrantly alive, pulsing with energy, the rain refreshing. I tilted my head back and let the drops course down my face and felt my body unclench a bit.

"It feels good to have a pulse," Fordham said. When I glanced at her, she explained. "Something I say every time I leave a crime scene." She took a deep breath. "Well, I'll get on the radio. See what the investigators want me to do. Maybe you should find the helicopter crew. See how their repairs are coming. It would make things a lot easier if they could fly down and pick up the investigators. But hey," she said, nudging me. "Looks like one of the pilots found you."

I turned, just as I heard my name called.

"Harper?" He shouted over the rain.

"Oh no," I mumbled, as I watched him splashing his way toward me. Rain poured off the brim of his soft cap. He carried a metal briefcase.

"Do you know him?" Fordham asked.

"Harper, I can't believe it!" he said as he took long strides in my direction.

"Fletcher," I said.

"I guess you do know him," Fordham said. "Interesting."

Warrant Officer Four Fletcher Mayes stopped right in front of me, his dark chocolate skin glistening from the rain and his familiar brown eyes staring at me. He set the case down and, ignoring the fact that I had a huge camera hanging on my shoulder, wrapped his arms around me, lifted me up and spun me around.

"Harper, I can't believe you're here." he shouted over the rain, his wide grin defined by those memorable full lips. I always found it hard not to stare at his mouth.

"Put me down, Fletcher," I said, wondering why rocks are never around when you so desperately want one to crawl under.

"How cool is this, Lauren?" He plopped me back down on the ground with his big hands clamped on my shoulders. He bent down so he could peer at me under the brim of my boonie cap.

"I'm not sure I would describe it that way," I said.

Fletcher ignored the comment and stood up, wrapped an arm around my shoulders and pressed me into his side as if I were his best buddy. He was performing for Dr. Fordham now, all smiles and hearty laughter.

"Harper and I go way back, don't we Harper?" He squeezed me into his side until I was balanced on one leg. I wanted to slam my foot down onto the top of his boot.

"Well, I'll let you two catch up," Fordham said, grinning at me without the slightest idea of my inner turmoil. She waggled her fingers at me and walked off toward the hospital, leaving me alone with the pilot.

There was a time when I had long speeches planned for what I would say to Fletcher if I ever had the opportunity. Speeches where I would tell him how he had made me feel, but of course all of those well thought out words had flown out of my head the minute I came face to face with him again.

"Damn it, Fletcher. Would you let go, already?" I shrugged out of his grasp and straightened my uniform.

"Come on, Lauren. Don't be that way. You're glad to see me, right?"

I watched his mouth form every word and wanted to shout, "No. No, I'm not happy to see you. Not one little bit." But I didn't say anything.

I was stuck in a remote mountain village in the jungle with a dead body, a torrential downpour, a murderer, and to top it off, a man who had broken my heart. There simply wasn't anything appropriate to say.

Chapter 6

You can't fool me, Lauren. I know you're glad to see me." Fletcher's wide grin produced deep, perfect dimples. I used to love seeing his dimples. Now, they made me want to run away.

"What the hell are you doing here?" I asked, shrugging out of his grasp.

He chose to ignore my obvious discomfort, employing his ability to remain eternally positive no matter the circumstance. "I've been stuck on this mountain for three days. You being here now makes it almost worth it. It's great to see you, Lauren."

I clamped my mouth shut, afraid if I responded, a slew of inappropriate stuff would spew out.

"Is that a sat-phone?"

He held up a large aluminum-sided suitcase. "I heard you guys needed one."

The satellite phone would make communicating with the base camp easier, but I wished someone else had delivered the goods.

"Great." I mumbled "I'll take you to the First Sergeant so you can get it set up." I started toward Dodd, intending to hand Fletcher off as soon as possible. He walked beside me, firing off questions.

"How have you been? What have you been up to? I can't believe you're here. You know, I was just thinking the other day that it was around this time last year that we were in Bruges. Remember that? You ate all that chocolate. Remember that hotel with the tiny little bathroom…"

His whimsical trip down memory lane stretched my patience. I stopped, my hands on my hips and took a deep breath, counting to ten. "What's wrong with your chopper?"

He took a few more steps before realizing that I wasn't walking beside him.

"It's red-lined. One of the warning lights isn't working properly, and we found a bad bolt, if you can believe that. Crew chief says we're not flying until we fix whatever it is. The engineers were supposed to bring the parts back with them. I guess they've been a little distracted."

"How long will it take to fix it?"

He walked back to me and stood too close. "Not long, I don't think. A few hours maybe, but now we have this weather to contend with. I hear these rain storms can hang around for days." He playfully punched my shoulder. "But that would give us a chance to catch up, right Lauren?"

When he reached up to brush a wisp of hair from my forehead. I stepped back. "Stop it, Fletcher. Just stop."

"What?" His wide-eyed expression, the quizzical gap between his full lips and the charming dimples on his dark face, screamed innocence, but I knew better. Fletcher's self-awareness included his knowledge that he was attractive. He never hesitated to use his good looks when it suited him. Once upon a time, his honesty and innocence were appealing to me, sexy and desirable. Now, I knew it was just a crafty tool he used to manipulate. I'd been a victim of it before. I refused to be manipulated by him again. I turned my back on him and headed toward Dodd and Allen.

"Lauren, wait. Would you just wait a second?"

When I kept going, he eventually followed, a curse mumbled under his breath. Thankfully, I found Dodd and Allen easily and made introductions.

"Where do you want us to set up the satellite phone, sir?" Fletcher asked.

"You can put it in the command tent," Allen had to crane his head back to look up at Fletcher.

Dodd quirked an eyebrow at the young lieutenant. He'd made a quick, logical decision. An easy decision, but still, you had to give Allen some credit for exercising his authority for the first time.

The apparatus took only minutes to install with Fletcher giving step-by-step instructions. They placed the umbrella-looking receiver outside the tent and plotted coordinates to the satellite the signal would bounce from to eventually connect us with Soto Cano. In short order, they were crowded around a table, surrounded with the smell of moldy canvas and damp uniforms, ready to make the first call.

Since they were all busy with the new toy, I ducked out of the tent and left them to it. They didn't need me in there, and I wanted to put some distance between myself and the pilot. I still had pictures to take and other business that was becoming more urgent by the second. I went looking for the latrine.

I headed in the direction I thought most logical to put a latrine, away from the worksite and living areas but still within the perimeter. I found the latrine tent at the end of the road, about 50 yards from the nearest living quarters.

There were only men on the team, but they had hung a wooden sign across the door with "Men" written on one side and "Women" written on the other. I helloed the tent, and when no one answered, flipped the sign to indicate a female was inside. I pushed the flap aside and entered the darkened interior.

A wide wooden bench sat in the middle of the structure with four positions, two on each side of the bench, back to back. Each position was separated from the next by a couple of feet of space and upright plywood walls, giving each seat at least the illusion of privacy in the make-shift toilet. You wouldn't be able to look your neighbor in the eye, but you'd know they were there.

Porcelain seat covers and short wooden poles stacked with

plenty of toilet paper made the latrine one of the nicest I'd ever seen in a jungle. I always kept wads of toilet paper in the cargo pockets of my uniform just in case, but the rain had rendered my supplies into a damp wadded mess. It was a relief to see the clean and dry paper waiting. All of the toilet seats were closed, which was a good thing. No telling what critters might crawl in there and cause trouble for an unsuspecting person.

Still, from experience I knew it was better to be safe than sorry. I lifted one of the seats and used the small flash light on my belt to make a quick check inside to be sure there weren't any surprises. I was impressed with the depth of the trench they had prepared and noted they regularly used lye to control the smell and to encourage decomposition. First Sergeant Dodd had a latrine to be proud of and that was no small thing in my book.

I sat down to relieve myself but kept thinking about something I'd seen in the trench during my brief inspection. When I was finished and had buttoned my trouser pants, I lifted the toilet seat to check inside again.

In a far corner inside the trench, I saw something, pale and pink mostly buried in the muck. It looked like cloth with printing on it. I moved around to the other side of the bench and looked inside again. It was underwear, the word Hanes written on it. The most disturbing thing about the find, the underwear looked child-sized.

I searched for something to use to fish the underwear out of the hole and didn't see anything handy. I went out of the tent and walked into the tree line, where I found a long, sturdy stick, took it back into the latrine and used it to try to bring the pink fabric out. It took some time to retrieve it, and I was grateful that no one came to request the use of the facilities while I was at it. Eventually I was able to pull the thing from the hole.

I didn't want to touch the pale pink undies. Much of the fabric was soaked through and covered in muck. They'd been ripped down one side so that only one leg hole remained intact.

How could the panties have gotten down there? It was unlikely any locals had used the latrine. If one of the locals hadn't put them there, who did?

I'm not sure how long I stood there, staring at those torn panties, my hand, white knuckled around the stick where they dangled, and my thoughts growing darker by the second. I knew what sexual assault did to the psyche. In the short time of my own recovery, I'd managed to shove the memories to remote recesses of my mind, places I avoided. When I wandered close to them, a molten rage burned there, one I feared I wouldn't be able to staunch if I touched it.

It would be so easy to just drop the panties back into the hole. Forget about them. Forget about the memories they conjured, but there was no way I could do that. I wanted to know who killed Larson, but I also wanted to know who had torn this little girl's panties from her. What happened to this little girl? I didn't bother trying to convince myself that I was jumping to conclusions. I knew in my gut something violent had happened.

The rain picked up in intensity, the sound hollow in the almost vacant tent. Wind forced its way through a gap somewhere in the canvas, producing a low, undulating whistle that made me shiver.

There was no way I could talk to Fletcher or Dodd about what I'd found. How could I talk to them about the possibility of a little girl's sexual assault? It felt wrong to bring it to any of them.

Fordham was the only person I could show them to. She'd understand the need to find out what happened here.

Settling on that decision, some of the tension between my shoulders released. Now, what to do with the evidence?

Sergeant Mora kept his spare batteries in a Ziploc bag in his camera kit. I dumped the batteries in a side compartment of the camera case and stuck the underwear in the plastic baggie sealing it tight. I looked at that tiny pair of panties through the plastic bag and had a very bad feeling about what they meant. Did someone drop them in the latrine to try to hide them? Who did they belong to?

I didn't think I'd like the answers to any of those questions. I shoved the evidence in the cargo pocket of my uniform pants.

I left the latrine and headed directly back to the construction site, thinking about the panties. Who put them down there? How did they fit into what had happened to Larson? Was there any connection?

By the time I made it back to the construction slab, rain ran off the sides of my boonie cap in a steady trickle. I ignored it and set to work. I wanted to get the pictures done quickly so I could bring the new evidence to Fordham. Having the panties in my pocket made me feel anxious.

I found the small cement mixer Fordham had asked me to photograph. Next to it was a wheelbarrow, a shovel and a half-empty bag of cement mix. Everything had been shoved to the side of the foundation frame, as if discarded, no longer needed and forgotten. Cement was left to harden in the wheelbarrow, in the mixer and on the shovel. That neglect didn't fit. I glanced around the rest of the site, at the neatly stacked cement blocks, the supplies and equipment securely protected by sheets of tarp, the tidy way a small dozer was left parked near a stack of gravel.

Everything stowed in its proper place, except the implements used for murder.

I took a few more pictures, feeling doubtful that, even with the right equipment, anyone could get fingerprints from the tools left out in the torrential rain. The cement had been purchased locally, much of the writing on the bags written in Spanish, but like many things that could be found outside the U.S., the labels were in English too. The most important information being that it was quick-dry cement. I wonder how that fact would affect Dr. Fordham's time of death calculations.

At what time in the night had Bobby Larson been killed? What led up to that moment? The moment when someone decided to drown him in cement?

The brutality of it dragged my memory back to Bosnia, to Specialist Virginia Delray and the day I had discovered her body. I'd been avoiding thinking about her. Avoiding reliving that moment when I realized she had been murdered. Once the investigators started, they simply looked to the person closest to her and decided I had killed her.

A loud growl of some kind of predatory animal sounded in the distant jungle. The guttural noise startled me. I realized I'd been standing still, frozen for a long time. Remembering. The memory still fresh. Even the rain reminded me of Bosnia, of the gloom that had settled over my head the moment I had found her body. I'd felt the way Reggie Larson had looked, vacant-eyed and confused, until the terror set in. Had it only been four months ago?

The investigators had been wrong and had wasted so much time making my life miserable, they'd almost let the real killer get away. Their stubbornness at their accusations against me had almost allowed an evil man to get away with murder, and much worse.

Well, I could be stubborn, too. I didn't know Larson or anyone in the unit, but I knew what it was like when the wrong person stood accused of murder.

I knelt down, stuffed the camera into the bag, shoving in the stray bits of strap, snapping the clamps closed, feeling clenched up again, angry.

Once CID got here, my role in the investigation would end. They'd probably think I'd done too much already. If Fletcher's forecast was right, and it did rain for days, any chances of catching the killer could be washed away.

A couple of days might be all the time I needed to ensure they were at least pointed in the right direction. And if I needed any more encouragement, the pink panties in my cargo pocket were a reminder of another victim. Someone CID probably wouldn't care about in their search for a murderer.

The rain suddenly shut down. One moment it was a downpour, the next, only random drops hit the tarp roof. In the near silence that followed I heard someone calling my name.

I stepped around the wheelbarrow and saw Fletcher outside the command tent waving at me to come. I walked toward him, taking my time, and despite myself, admired him in his flight suit.

Chief Warrant Officer Four Fletcher Mayes had sat down uninvited at my table in the Post Exchange bookstore in Heidelberg Germany, a steaming cup of cappuccino in each hand

and that knee-weakening smile on his face. His skin looked silky smooth and flawless. His bald head and caramel-colored eyes made me think some storybook hero had leapt off the page of a novel. He'd been wearing his flight suit then too. I have always had a weakness for that uniform. Something about the way the form-fitting jumpsuit drapes down from a set of broad shoulders makes me want to tug on the long zipper and see what's underneath.

That day in the coffee shop, Fletcher made small talk for exactly five minutes before asking me out. We had dinner and danced and against all of my dating rules, I invited him to my apartment. Sleeping with someone on a first date was verboten, but I couldn't resist Fletcher's charms. Not that night anyway.

I watched him as I approached. He paced impatiently while I took my time getting there. When I'd met him, it had been years since I had allowed myself to be open to a relationship. Fletcher somehow managed to coax the feelings from me, constantly seeking to please until I'd given up. I'd dropped my guard. I hadn't said the 'L' word to him, but I'd been close to that. Close to thinking he was the one for me, until he proved me totally and completely wrong.

Now, here he was. Mr. Charming, with his warm banter, his super white smile and the dimples, the ones that made me want to melt even when I was ready to wring his neck.

Sometimes the world is just too freaking small.

"Would you come on already?" Fletcher said.

"I'm coming. Jeeze."

"There's someone on the phone who wants to talk to you." Fletcher strode into the tent, picked up the receiver and held it out to me.

"Harper, here."

"Master Sergeant Harper?"

"Yes?"

"This is Chief Santos, from CID."

"You're kidding."

"No, Sergeant. It appears we have another murder which

brings us together."

"Is Ramsey there too?" I was almost afraid to hear the answer.

"No. Chief Ramsey is not with me on this trip. I will be the lead investigator on the case."

First Fletcher, now Santos. I silently cursed, wondering why men from my past couldn't stay in my past where they belonged.

Chapter 7

It had been Chiefs Ramsey and Santos who had accused me of murder in Bosnia. The pair had grilled me for hours and had almost arrested me for something I didn't do. They'd been idiots, the pair of them. Ramsey, with his icy blue eyes and his refusal to listen to a word I said. And Santos, the overly formal speaking Puerto Rican who sat like a silent sentinel in the corner, typing away at his notes. I mostly remembered seeing the top of his dark head bowed down over his keyboard, as if he didn't want to see that the entire investigation was pointed in the wrong direction.

"Sergeant Harper. Are you still there?"

Realizing how tightly I gripped the phone, I glanced at Fletcher and saw the quizzical expression on his face. I was sure he wondered why I reacted the way I did to the investigator.

"I will need your help, Sergeant Harper," Santos said.

"My help? You want my help?"

"You and Chief Fletcher must be my eyes and ears. You must begin to question witnesses. I know that you have excellent instincts and I believe they will be most helpful during the first hours of the investigation. Those first hours are crucial."

"You've got a lot of damn nerve, asking me to help you."

"I understand why you would be reluctant."

"Reluctant? Are you getting good reception on your end of this conversation?" I asked, fully aware that my volume was increasing. "Because this is not reluctance you hear in my voice."

"Sergeant Harper, it is necessary. It will be too many hours, too much time will have passed by the time we can arrive. I believe you, along with the assistance of Chief Fletcher, will be able to conduct the necessary interviews to set the groundwork of the investigation. I am putting my trust in you."

I glanced at Fletcher. Something about the grin on his face told me that he already knew what Santos was telling me. He obviously wanted to get involved, which made me wonder what was more alarming. The fact that I'd be working with the pilot or that I'd be working for Santos, the man who almost ruined my life.

Even reminding myself that, only a few minutes before, I had decided to start asking questions on my own, wasn't enough to cool my anger. Working for Santos? The mere thought of it turned my stomach.

"How can you say you have trust in me, when you almost arrested me for murder?"

"But you did not kill Specialist Delray."

"No, I didn't. That didn't stop you and your partner from trampling my reputation and almost ruining my career."

He cleared his throat, then remained silent. I listened to him rustle about, the whistle of his breathing, the shuffle of paperwork. He cleared his throat again and I let the silence stretch. There were things I could say to ease his discomfort, but he didn't deserve that. He deserved to feel as uncomfortable as possible.

Eventually, he spoke up again.

"I realize an apology from me would be inadequate," he said. "The investigation we conducted combined with the outcome of the case and what you went through subsequently, have only served to convince me that you are an extraordinary soldier. I am fully convinced that Specialist Larson will be best served if you start the interviews as soon as possible."

"And what if I refuse?"

"Master Sergeant Harper, this is not a request."

Oh, the expletives I wanted to hurl at the little investigator. My body vibrated with pent up anger. I pictured him sitting there, unmoved, still as stone, the way he'd been in the interrogation room.

An order. He was ordering me to help him.

Counting to ten wouldn't help. I'd have to go for fifty or a hundred. One thing I knew about Santos. He'd wait me out. The guy had the annoying capacity to sit silently forever.

Thinking about that made my pressure gauge go up another notch. I searched for something good, some positive thought to release the built up tension. I'd already convinced myself that I needed to help the investigation along. Santos was just giving me an excuse to do what I'd already decided to do. Those thoughts were enough to relax my shoulders a bit, but not enough. Not nearly enough.

Cool and calm. Try to sound cool and calm, I told myself.

"Yes, sir. Your eyes and ears." The sarcasm dripped from my voice.

Silence on his end. He hadn't expected me to agree. I smiled.

"Then you will do it?"

"Of course, sir. Happy to help." I said as I flipped the bird at the receiver.

Then I glanced at Fletcher who stood with his mouth hanging open, his eyes wide. Something about his expression struck me as funny. I covered the receiver with my hand to keep Santos from hearing me struggle to keep it together. I had my silent belly laughs, my head thrown back, my stomach suddenly tight as a fist.

The "what the hell" expression on Fletcher's face made me laugh even harder. He looked almost fearful. Santos remained silent. Stony silent.

My rational brain knew I was acting on nerves and stress and one shock after another, but that didn't stop me from feeling as if I could wig out completely if I didn't get it together. Eventually I settled down and thought about Larson, the cement, the nasty person who'd done it. And the nerve of this guy for ordering me to help him.

The mirth of the moment disappeared. I took a deep breath and listened to Santos waiting me out.

"I need to let my sergeant know that I've been reassigned," I said. "He'll have to take over my mission."

"Understood."

"I'll go do that now, if you don't mind. You can brief Chief Fletcher on how you think we should proceed."

"That seems prudent."

Fletcher's quizzical expression made me feel a bit sorry for him.

"Chief, you may want to tell Fletcher what happened in Bosnia," I said. "He doesn't know what happened and I'd rather not go into it."

"Ah, I see." Santos cleared his throat. The first sign that he was uncomfortable. "Again. Understood. I will brief him while you attend to your duties. We shall speak again soon, Sergeant Harper."

I handed the phone to Fletcher. Santos wouldn't expect any friendly goodbyes and I wasn't prepared to give them to him.

"Chief?" Fletcher said.

"Fucking Santos," I said to myself as I left the tent. "Un-freaking believable."

A few villagers remained sitting under a tree near the construction site, their heads all turning as I passed, probably wondering why the crazy lady was talking to herself.

I trudged my way up the hill and into the village. The tiny mountain town consisted of a handful of mud brick buildings scattered on either side of a small dirt road. The road, now a river of mud, was where all of the clinic patients stood, waiting their turn. The line snaked for a couple hundred yards down the middle of the village. I looked for the end of the line and couldn't see it from where I stood. I wondered how far some of these people must have walked to take advantage of the free services. It was still early. They all had a long day ahead of them.

Children darted between legs, splashing in the mud. Men held umbrellas over the heads of elderly women. Young girls fiddled with each other's hair and whispered behind their hands at my approach. A young boy, obviously with Downs Syndrome, sucked his thumb and hid behind his mother's skirt. An old woman, her eyes white with cataracts, clutched a young woman's arm and smiled at something she heard, her mouth a mass of broken and rotted teeth but her smile still bright.

I spotted Dropic near the front of the line. He was down on one knee, oblivious to the mud, his video camera now covered in a canvas and plastic water repellent bra. A small group of children stood in front of him, laughing and jockeying for position in front of his camera. They smiled and stared at their own reflections in the camera's lens. Dropic tilted his head away from the viewfinder and said something to them in Spanish. The children all squealed in laughter. Adults laughed as well. I visualized the image he was capturing—the innocent smiles of the children, the squeals of laughter. He was getting good video.

As I got closer, I noticed Sergeant Mora and Cordovan standing nearby, talking to a woman in the line. Cordovan asked the questions, but Mora listened and took notes, tossing in a question now and then.

"I didn't understand that last part," Mora said to Cordovan.

"She says, they were required to pay with money or with livestock, and the price kept going up," Cordovan translated.

"Ah. Livestock," Mora said, nodding his head and scribbling in his notebook, flicking a drop of water off the paper that had rolled down from the boonie cap.

"She says now, with their own schoolhouse the children won't have to walk as far, and they can save money."

"Where will they find a teacher?" Mora asked.

Cordovan translated the question. The woman shrugged and smiled and answered him. This time Mora understood her words and didn't need help with the translation.

"What did she say?" I asked.

"She says they will have to pay for a teacher, but they hope the teacher they get will be more honest than the one in the other town and not keep demanding more money," Mora explained. "The village will provide food and a place to live to make him or her a part of their community."

I waited while they continued the interview. It was hard to judge the woman's age. Her hair was jet black with thick silver streaks. She wore it pulled back tightly in a braid that hung down her back. She tucked stray hair behind her ear with the hands of a woman accustomed to hard work. She was thicker and taller than the man standing beside her. I assumed he was her husband. It was impossible to tell if the lines on their faces were from age or just from the challenges of life in this remote place. The husband listened and nodded his head in agreement, his eyes on the woman as she spoke. Her high cheekbones, full lips and wide dark eyes revealed the beauty she must have once been.

Sergeant Mora thanked her for her time and said something that made her blush and giggle. Her husband said something teasing, and she smacked him playfully on the shoulder. They both dissolved in giggles, her head resting briefly on his shoulder.

"Are you getting what you need?" I asked Mora as he flipped a page of his notebook and finished his incomprehensible scribbling. He gave me a wide grin of perfect teeth.

"Are you kidding? My problem will be trying to figure out what not to use, there's so much here."

"Good, because it looks like I'm going to be tied up with other things."

That got his attention. I pulled him aside and explained the situation, that help could be days off and that I had been given new orders.

"I've talked to some of these folks," he said. "The farmers say it will probably rain for several days. They've been having dry weather for some time, so they're happy about it."

"I'm glad someone is."

Mora pointed in the direction of a group of men standing

nearby under a tree. "Have you met the mayor?" he asked, putting air quotes around the word mayor.

"Bonilla? Briefly. What do you think of him?"

"Well, he comes off all polite and such, but I get the impression a lot of these folks don't like him."

"What makes you think that?"

When I glanced at Bonilla I found him staring back at me, the smile he wore at our initial greeting, long forgotten. He seemed watchful, vigilant, as if he didn't want anything to get by him. I wondered how long he had been staring at me.

A small, stooped man standing next to Bonilla talked, gestured, seemed to plead with his palms up, his forehead wrinkled in worry. Bonilla kept watching me, ignoring the man and his pleas. Finally, he turned and give a brief but sharp look at the man, who froze for a moment and almost recoiled under Bonilla's glare. Then the man dropped his hands, and with shoulders slumped, turned and walked away.

Bonilla turned his attention back to me, as if signaling that he knew I watched the entire exchange.

"It's like they all have to deal with him, and he just says no all day," Mora said. "I haven't seen one man walk away from him looking like he got what he asked for."

"Do you know what they want from him?"

"I haven't the slightest idea. Approval? Permission? Who knows. Whatever it is, they're not getting it."

So the power guy in town wasn't a nice one. How many times had I seen that in remote places around the world?

I talked with Mora some more about the clinic and what footage Cordovan and Dropic wanted to get. "Cordovan asked what happens when the people run out of the antibiotics, lotions and the other stuff the doctors are dispensing. He says it's all just temporary fixes, and then we leave."

It was true. The U.S. Army wasn't a never-ending source of charity. The truth was, we came to places like this for training, real world training. Soldiers gained the opportunity to treat patients, maybe run across the occasional exotic disease. The Sappers built stuff and met the challenges of construction in an isolated area. It appeared to be charity, but it was self-serving. It was nice to be able to provide what little support we could for these folks, but in reality, Cordovan was right. Once we left, they'd have to fend for themselves, at least until we came back again.

As I removed the memory card from the camera, Mora gave me a rundown on what he had learned in his interviews. He had plenty of extra memory cards and a laptop to download pictures he captured, so I kept the card I had used for the crime scene photos. I'd email the pictures to Santos using the satellite phone and dialup internet access.

I gave him the camera bag. "I'll be in the headquarters tent at the construction site if you need me."

"Oh, I almost forgot," Mora said. "When Colonel Scaporelli saw Dropic and his video camera, he got kind of upset. He says he wants to talk to the public affairs officer who authorized them being here. I told him that was you."

"Is he the commander of the medical team?" I asked.

"Yeah. He's inside. Like I said, he was kind of pissed."

"He's probably just camera-shy. I'll talk to him." It wasn't unusual for military types to get uptight once they saw cameras. Plenty of careers had been impacted, or halted permanently, because of something said or done in a media interview. Medical exercises like this one were some of the best and safest stories the Army had to offer. No matter how safe I thought it might be, the guy in charge could have a different take on the matter.

I reminded Mora that we had a case of MREs and bottled water in the back of the Humvee.

"We've been invited to eat with some of the villagers," he said, smiling. "I'll take a home-cooked meal over an MRE any day."

"Alright, but just be sure everything is cooked, sergeant. No raw vegetables and only drink bottled water. I can't afford for you to get sick."

"No worries, Sergeant Harper. I'll be careful. You be careful with Colonel Scaporelli. What are you gonna say to him?"

"Probably the same thing I tell most people who object to

media coverage. Shut up, salute and smile for your close up."

Mora laughed. "Good luck with that."

I walked away knowing I would need every ounce of that luck.

Chapter 8

I walked past the long line of waiting patients and through the front door of the medical tent, ducking down through the entrance to make my way across the uneven plastic flooring.

Once through the door, I recognized that I wasn't in a typical clinic. The medical team had come to this mountain village with a hospital-in-a-box, a concept developed by the Army to bring medical care to remote areas when needed. The series of tents and equipment provided the services of a complete hospital including operating rooms, laboratories, radiation and pharmacy, all transported in one large shipping container. They'd probably delivered the whole thing to the mountain village by Chinook helicopter.

I passed into a large open space. Windows in the tent walls illuminated the room. The walls flapped quietly in the breeze. Light rain sounded muted against the canvas. It reminded me of the hospital I'd spent time in while in Bosnia. They weren't pleasant memories.

Two long tables fronted the space where soldiers greeted patients and directed them to different areas. The medical assistants checked temperatures, took blood pressure readings and started charts on each visitor. Despite the long line outside, and what had probably already been a busy morning, the soldiers were taking their time with each patient.

I asked one of the soldiers where I could find Colonel Scaporelli and was directed to go through an adjoining tunnel and turn left. Once through the tunnel, signs in Spanish and English guided people to various exam rooms; laboratory, dental, optometry and pharmacy. I followed the directions and found myself in another large tent which was divided into examination sections. Curtains separated exam areas, three on each side of a wide center hallway. I asked the first soldier I came to where I could find Colonel Scaporelli.

"He's with a patient right now, right over there. You can wait if you like. He should be done in a few minutes."

Trying to stay out of the way, I stood outside a curtained exam area waiting for the Colonel. I waited and watched as nurses, doctors and patients moved about.

Several minutes later, a father carrying a young boy accompanied by a tearful mother stepped out from behind a curtain. The child rested his unusually large head, with a swollen and distorted face, on his father's shoulder, his arms and legs wrapped tightly around the man. I didn't need a medical background to tell that this kid was very sick. I couldn't tell what was wrong with him, but whatever it was, it appeared to be something far more serious than this remote clinic was equipped to treat. Colonel Scaporelli, with a hand on the mother's shoulder, spoke to an interpreter telling the family to be sure to leave good contact information. He gently stroked the face of the boy as the translator relayed the words. The father, fighting back tears, thanked the doctor and then led his family down the hallway of the large tent.

Colonel Scaporelli made notes on his chart, shaking his head. "Call Dr. Rogers at Doctors Without Borders. They might be able to find him a bed in Tegucigalpa. Once Rogers sees the chart, he'll understand what needs to be done."

Scaporelli handed the chart to the nurse, then he turned to me.

"Kidney disease," he said. "Poor kid. With his blood type and the advancement of the disease, the most we can hope for is to keep him comfortable."

"You can't do that here?"

"We're not authorized to provide that kind of long term care."

Scaporelli watched the family, accompanied by the translator, as they moved slowly through the clinic. He looked deeply saddened by the diagnosis. I wondered how he lived with the daily tragedies of his profession. His dark salt and pepper hair was trimmed close to his head. Olive-colored skin and the dark shadow around his jaw line made me think he probably had to shave a couple times a day. Thick dark lashes lined large brown eyes, which betrayed his emotions.

He took a long deep breath and slowly blew it out through pursed lips. It was something I imagined he did often to move on from such moments. With his hands on his hips, he turned to me and raised one perfectly arched eyebrow.

"Are you the PAO, then?"

I nodded in confirmation and we introduced ourselves, shaking hands. His palms were dry and smooth, his handshake firm.

"That body in the cement couldn't have made your job any easier," he said.

"It does complicate things."

"Well, let me make your life even more complicated. I'm all for freedom of the press, but not here. That reporter, what's his name?"

"Tony Cordovan."

"Right. That guy. He called my office in Minneapolis before I left home. He told me he was coming here and that he would want to interview me when he got here."

"He did?" I was surprised. Cordovan hadn't mentioned the exchange and hadn't asked me for an interview with Scaporelli. "Did he mention what he wanted to talk to you about?"

"No, and it doesn't matter. I'm not talking to him. I've seen his work in Minneapolis, that Action News team thing he does. I don't want anything to do with him."

"Okay," I said. I had seen Cordovan's reports. Even though Dr. Scaporelli was doing good work, it was possible Cordovan would twist things. It was one of the reasons why I had been ordered to babysit him.

"I don't want a single camera or reporter anywhere near this clinic," Scaporelli went on.

I started to respond but he cut me off.

"I'm an oncologist by trade, but I've led this mission here once a year for the last three years. My military career is secondary to my civilian work. I come here because I want to, not because I have to. Keeps me on top of my game, if you will."

"And to help people," I offered.

He waited a moment to see if I were being sarcastic.

"Yes, to help people. It was my idea to train with the hospital-in-a-box up here. We bring them the best medical care available, perform minor surgeries, they see dentists, have their eyes examined and in some cases, we even save lives. But I get paid a lot of money for my services in Minneapolis. I don't need my patients seeing me on TV or in a newspaper giving free services to people. Besides, knowing that guy, he'd make this look negative somehow."

"Sir, how did Cordovan get in touch with you?"

"His wife is a patient of a colleague of mine. I bet he didn't tell you that. I've consulted on her case several times. I can't discuss it, of course, but she's ... well, she's very sick."

"Why wouldn't he have mentioned that?"

"Because he's sneaky," Scaporelli said. "I treat his wife, but that doesn't mean I like the guy."

If she was that sick, why would Cordovan leave her to come here? Not many people, no matter how ambitious, would knowingly leave a very sick spouse to come to an isolated location like this. If I needed proof that Cordovan was after something negative, sensational or tawdry, I'd found it. It was worrisome.

"Sir, I'm not going to try to talk you into an interview with him," I began but Scaporelli interrupted me.

"Good, because this is not up for discussion." He spun on his heels and began to walk away. I followed him and struggled to keep up with his long strides.

"You're right, sir. This is not up for discussion. Army public affairs have approved these journalists and it's my job to see that they get the stories they came here to get. Cordovan has to be able to interview patients and soldiers working in this clinic."

He stopped abruptly. I almost ran into him. He spun toward me, his lab coat brushing across my legs as he turned. His handsome face was red and pinched in anger. He towered over me, leaning down to make sure I understood who was boss.

"Last time I checked, I was the Colonel and you were the Master Sergeant. I get to say what happens at my clinic."

"Sir, with all due respect, please don't confuse my rank with my level of authority in this matter. The U.S has spent millions of dollars to send your unit on this mission. Part of our job is to keep the public informed about how we spend that money. These journalists are helping us tell that story. It's not up to you or me to say they can't be here. This goes way above either of our pay grades."

He stared at me for a long moment, simmering with rage. I didn't look away. When he spoke again, his words came out between clenched teeth.

"If other doctors want to talk to them? Fine. But keep them away from me."

"Okay, sir. I can do that." But I was speaking to his back. He strode away, his lab coat billowing behind.

Chapter 9

The unpleasant conversation with Scaporelli taken care of, I asked the next soldier I passed where I could find Dr. Fordham.

"She's usually in the lab, Sergeant. Just down that way."

I followed the directions, knowing that Fletcher would be growing impatient for me to return. It didn't make sense to go to my meeting with him without dropping off the evidence I'd found first. He'll just have to wait, I thought.

Soldiers stood behind a table at the front of the large pharmacy tent, filling prescriptions for villagers who stood quietly in line. A translator explained dosages and answered questions. People walked away with their hands full of plastic vials and tubes.

In the rear of the tent, Dr. Fordham sat bent over an old fashioned microscope. Fordham didn't notice me standing next to the table, her attention riveted on whatever she saw in the microscope. Eventually, she glanced up and saw me.

"Sergeant Harper."

"Hey Doc. I was in the neighborhood. Thought I'd bring you the pictures," I held up the camera's memory stick.

"I'm kind of a luddite," she said, pointing at her laptop. "Could you download them for me?"

The laptop sat on a table positioned in front of a heating vent. I plopped down, and the sudden warmth washed over me, making me moan in pleasure. Occasionally, drops of water from my uniform plunked onto the floor around my seat. The heat, the sound of rain tapping on the canvas and the buzz of the overhead florescent lights made the lab feel almost cozy.

It didn't take me long to download the pictures to a file, but the warmth felt too good to leave it right away. I leaned my elbow on the table, put my chin in my hand and let my tension drain away like a leak in an air mattress, the release almost audible.

I slowly clicked through the shots. The images of Larson's body weren't any less gruesome on Fordham's computer screen than they had been through the lens. The pale fingers, the exposed bones, the cement splatters on his uniform. The grisly images almost ruined my relaxed mood. Almost. As I closed the file, another folder on Fordham's desktop caught my attention.

"Dr. Fordham, I don't mean to be nosy, but this folder on your desktop. Is this an abbreviation for child assault?

"Yeah. Go ahead and take a look. That poor girl."

The first picture was of a young girl's back. From the date stamp, it had to be a girl from the village because it had been taken a couple of days before. There were large bruises along the girls back and down her legs. Bruises in the shape of fingers striped across her arms. There were close ups of the bruises. Then pictures of the young girl's hairless genitalia, also purple with bruises.

"This is horrific," I said. My voice came out shaky and quiet, much more quiet than I had intended. I glanced down at my hands and noticed a slight tremble. I clasped them together.

"I thought so too, and I've seen child assault before."

"Do you know anything about the attack? Who did it?"

"Since we've been here Colonel Scaporelli has examined two different girls, eight and ten years old. Their mothers brought them in. When Scaporelli tried to question the women, they wouldn't talk. He asked me to step in and see if I could get them to cooperate. I was able to convince one of the mothers to allow me take pictures of her daughter, but that was it. Neither the mothers nor the girls would say anything. I'm not even sure the fathers of the girls knew they were seeing a doctor, the mothers were that secretive. No way are they going to press charges or accuse anyone."

I stood and fished the baggie out of my cargo pocket, taking a deep breath as I made my way to Fordham. My legs felt shaky. I hoped she wouldn't notice and ask questions. The attention she paid to her microscope saved me the embarrassment.

"You should see this," I dropped the baggie on the table next to her.

She picked it up, examining the panties through the plastic. "Holy crap. Where did you find these?"

"In the latrine trench down at the construction site."

"Well, that can't be good." Her forehead wrinkled at the evidence, rolling it around inside the bag to get a better look at it. "Definitely children's underwear. Doubtful I'll be able to pull any useful evidence from them. Evidence-wise, where you found them is about the most significant thing about them."

"I wish I hadn't found them there."

She slowly put the baggie on her lab table, stood and started pacing. She watched her boots as she walked and seemed fascinated by the mud squishing from the sides of each step.

I took a seat near her and interrupted her ruminations.

"Major, this along with a dead body..."

She put her hand up to silence me. "Let's not get ahead of ourselves. You found them in the area where the soldiers live. That area happens to be where someone was murdered. The two things may be connected, but also may not."

"Maybe a family member suspected a soldier and killed Larson as some kind of revenge or something," I said, moving back to my seat. The pictures of the little girl were still visible on the laptop. I closed the lid, not wanting to look at them anymore.

"You'd be accusing that dead soldier of rape and worse."

"I suggested a family member could have suspected a soldier did it. That doesn't mean Larson actually did anything. You said both girls came into the clinic in the last couple of days. The bruising in the pictures isn't old. That means those assaults happened sometime during this mission. The villagers could have blamed the assaults on Larson for some reason, maybe because an American was an easy target. Or maybe someone wanted revenge and Larson was the unlucky guy."

"Possible. Also possible that the rapist is someone local. Those mothers were scared for their daughters. That leads me to believe that the person who raped the girls is still around here, and will still be around when we leave."

"Or they were afraid that by bringing the girls to be examined they'd be implicating the people who did the revenge killing."

Fordham stopped in front of me, shaking her head. "You see, this is why I don't like detective work. I'd rather just let the science solve mysteries for me. All this speculation makes my head hurt."

Judging from the bruising, the little girl had suffered horribly. The fact that she was so young made the attack all the worse. Just thinking about it made me angry.

Suddenly my own memories played through my head. The smell of the barn. The helpless feeling of having my hands bound. The lingering stench of my own filth, the sounds, the pain. Sweat and tobacco. The scratchy feel of hay against my skin.

I squeezed my eyes shut, clenched my fists and tried to push the images away, my breath short. The language I couldn't understand, the fear that made my insides feel like liquid, the desperation, the humiliation, the very real understanding that I would never forget, never be the same. And the anger. The acute desire for revenge, to inflict some sort of punishment on the men who'd changed my world in profound ways.

Eventually, the sound of my own whimpers drew me back to the present and I realized Fordham had her hand on my shoulder. She leaned down to me, saying my name over and over.

"Sergeant Harper, are you okay?"

I couldn't speak, just shook my head and took in a trembling breath. When I exhaled, it came out in a shudder that racked my whole body, but it helped. A few deep breaths later, I felt better.

"I'm fine."

"You kinda' zoned out there for a minute."

"I'm fine. Really."

"I'm sorry. If something like this happened to you, then I'm very sorry."

"Don't be." My words came out more curt and angry than I meant them to, but I wasn't ready to talk to her, to anyone about it. She was being kind, but I wasn't ready for kindness. Somehow it felt as if I might never be ready for it.

She stared at me for a long moment, but must have realized she wouldn't get anything else from me. She moved back to her table and changed the subject.

 "Thanks for bringing me these," she said, holding up the baggie containing the panties. "There will be too many DNA types to sort through, but the investigators might be able to do something with the scientific analysis. Even if I can find any useable DNA on Larson, we won't have any results until we get it to Soto Cano. Have we heard anything from them?"

I clenched and unclenched my hands. No more shakes. I took another deep breath and felt almost normal. "About that," I said. "The weather reports don't look good and the lead investigator doesn't want to lose any time. Chief Fletcher and I have been assigned to start the interviews of the unit, the villagers, anyone we think might be helpful. Then we're supposed to report our findings to the head investigator, Chief Santos. You should let us know if there are questions you want us to include in our interviews."

"I see." She hesitated for a long moment, looking at the evidence bag on the table.

"What's wrong?" I asked.

"Well, I'm just wondering if you're up to it."

I pressed my lips together and stood. "Yes, Major. I'm up to it," I said, not bothering to keep the irritation out of my voice.

"It's just that, I'm concerned. For a minute there you seemed …"

"I know how it seemed, but I'm fine. There's nothing to be concerned about. Besides, if the two things are connected—what happened to the girls and Larson's murder, then believe me, I have every motivation to find out exactly what happened here."

Fordham scrutinized me, probably deciding whether or not I was going to flip out on her. My words may have sounded like bravado, but I meant them. I'd been kidnapped and brutalized, but I had survived. The rest of my life would not be defined by that experience. At least, that's what I told myself each time I woke up with the shakes.

The worst possible scenario would be that the two things—the murder and the rape of the girls—were connected in some way. I didn't want that. I wanted complete separation between the dead body in the cement and the young girls with their bruises. If not, then the ugliness factor of Larson's demise had just grown into a large stinking pile of crap.

"Have you managed to find anything in the evidence you were able to collect so far?"

She threw her hands up in frustration. "Nothing. Nothing! No prints, no trace evidence, nothing. I'm sure I won't be able to get much of anything until we get him out of that cement. We'll have to use a wet saw to cut around the body and bring the whole slab out. Then I'll just have to start chipping away at it."

"We're lucky to have you here, Dr. Fordham. It could be days yet before any official investigators are able to get up here."

"We don't have days to wait, I'm afraid. We're losing evidence, if there is any, the longer he's in there. I'll have to get that first sergeant…what's his name?"

"Dodd,"

"Yeah. I'll have to get him to give me a couple of people to work on getting the body out of there."

She took off her lab coat and started gathering supplies and tools for her evidence kits.

"Doc, I'd rather not be the only female living down on the construction site. Is there any chance there's an extra cot around here I can use?"

She stopped and looked at me curiously. "You're not afraid of them, are you?"

"Of course not."

She stared at me for a long moment. I started to feel like whatever it was she'd been examining under her microscope. "It's just easier," I explained. "Easier for everyone if I stay with other women. If you have the room, I mean."

She had more questions, but she kept them to herself. "Sure, there's plenty of room for one more. The ladies and I have got a nice little set up."

Fordham gave me directions to the women's sleeping area, then turned back to the task of gathering her equipment for the return trip to the murder site. I headed toward the door and then, with a deep sigh, turned back to her and blurted out what I had to say.

"I'm sorry I was so short with you, ma'am."

She stopped her preparations and fixed me with a serious look. "It's okay, Sergeant Harper. But if you need to talk to someone, no matter when, you come to me. Do you understand?"

"Yes, ma'am. No matter when. But I'm okay really. It's just, those pictures."

"They triggered a memory. Triggers come at unexpected times and in unexpected ways. Until you deal with the trauma, whatever that is, you're going to have fears and moments like that. It can be overwhelming. Keep that in mind."

"Yes, ma'am."

I shouldn't have felt embarrassed, but I did. I'd completely zoned out mentally, got lost in those horrible memories. But I had things to do, a mission to complete. I brushed the episode off as being understandable considering how tired I was, all the work I still faced, finding the body, Fletcher, everything.

Yeah, I probably should have listened to the doctor a little more, but at the time, I felt like everything would be fine.

Chapter 10

In a back corner of the hospital, the women occupied an entire tent section, each of them staking out their own hooch using poncho liners, clotheslines and sheets to create the illusion of privacy. Towels hung from hangers to dry, small mirrors were suspended from cords tied to the tent walls, duffle bags were tucked neatly under cots, creating a wide open and clutter free area. I found the makings of a cot stacked against a wall and put it together, then picked a corner to call home.

I've made temporary homes throughout much of the world. A cot in a corner, a sleeping bag on the ground, a poncho liner and rucksack for a pillow in the back of a truck served as home sometimes for days, weeks or months. I'd camped out in so many places, some cold, some scorching hot and others damp and full of bugs, that I'd stopped worrying about the suitability of a place to lay my head. The corner in the hospital was better than most.

Thinking about camping reminded me of the first time Fletcher asked me away for a weekend. He'd wanted to pitch a tent in some remote area of Northern Italy, made it sound romantic, but I was having none of that. I spent so much time in a sleeping bag for work, I never wanted to spend my off-time roughing it. Once he knew my preferences, he only took me to four star or better hotels that offered fluffy towels, room service and huge soft beds we used as play areas.

For our first trip, we took a train to Monte Carlo. He wore a tuxedo. I wore an evening gown. We drank champagne, we played roulette and didn't care that we lost. On another weekend, we went to Rome, where we ate pasta at an outdoor restaurant near the Spanish Steps and tried not to stare at the movie stars sitting at the next table. Then we went to Spain and made love on a beach, waking up the next morning to a breathtaking sunrise.

I no longer trusted Fletcher. That didn't mean my attraction for him had vanished. He was a confident, intelligent, romantic, movie-star-handsome man. I looked down at the cot I'd be using later and figured Fletcher must have found a woman who thought camping was the most romantic thing it the world. Well, she can have it. And him too, I thought.

I shook my head hard, as if to flick off the memories, then checked my watch. Fletcher was bound to be getting frustrated with my absence. I'd never seen him angry. If I messed about much longer I might get the opportunity.

Turning to leave, the sound of someone crying stopped me. I thought about leaving her to her privacy, but the sobbing sounded desperate. I couldn't ignore it. I followed the sounds, looking behind a blanket strung up with laundry pins along a nylon cord

"Are you okay?" I asked.

The crying grew louder. I walked around the curtain and saw a soldier lying face down on her cot, her shoulders heaving. I sat on the edge of the cot and rubbed her shoulders, and figured there was only one reason to cry that hard.

"Did you know Bobby?" I asked her.

"I can't believe he's dead!" she sobbed. "I just can't believe it."

I let her cry for a while, rubbing her back. Eventually the sobbing slowed down. I looked around the area and found a box of Kleenex next to one of the cots and brought it over to her

"How did you know him?"

She sat up, wiped her face with the tissue and wrapped her arms around her knees. Even with the puffiness around her eyes, she was a beautiful young girl with golden brown irises, high cheekbones and flawless, tan skin. She wore her dark hair pulled back and tightly bound in military style.

"I just met him on this exercise. I didn't know him very well, but he was such a good guy, you know?"

"Were you dating?"

"No. Like I said, we just met." She went on to describe a typical Army Reserve romance. They had met at the start of the exercise. They started hanging out. They discovered that they didn't live too far away from each other in Minnesota but as yet, hadn't said if they would meet up when they got home.

"I think he really liked me," she said, and the tears started up again.

"Do you know why anyone would want to kill him?" I asked.

She got quiet for a second and I thought she was about to tell me something, but she shook her head. "No. I mean, everybody loved Bobby. Who would do such a thing to him?"

"That's what I'm trying to find out. Anything you could tell me might help us find his killer."

She suddenly seemed to be cried out, avoided looking at me. "I don't know anything," she said. "Look, I need to get back to work." She got up, and put her uniform jacket on, straightening it and wiping her eyes. She was a Staff Sergeant and the name on her uniform was Paulson. She blew her nose, then checked herself in a mirror hanging near her cot. She glanced at me quickly, then made for the exit.

"Well, if you think of anything, look for me. I'm Master Sergeant Lauren Harper," I said to her retreating back.

She turned at the doorway, gave me a nervous smile and left. She had something to hide. I wondered what it was.

I thought about that as I made my way out of the hospital, moving past mothers with wailing babies, old people with bottles of medicine clutched to their chests, and people wearing glasses who more than likely had lived with failing eyesight for much of their lives. I was just about to leave the clinic when a group of people caught my attention.

Sergeants Porter and Judd were talking to few a soldiers, the group huddled close together as if they didn't want to be heard.

Porter's face looked red and wrinkled. The veins in his forehead and his long, thin neck appeared taut and pulsing. His mouth moved fast as if he had lots to say and little time to say it. Judd towered over the group, his arms folded across his large chest. He stood slightly behind Porter as if providing protection for the smaller man.

I tried to get a look at the three other soldiers, but couldn't see them all clearly. My curiosity was piqued, so I wandered over.

"Sergeant Porter, Sergeant Judd," I said.

Porter stopped mid-sentence and turned an angry glare in my direction. When he realized who had interrupted him, he strangled off the cuss word forming on his lips. He instantly flashed a grin, then tried to appear relaxed by putting his hands in his pockets, then decided against that posture and took them out again. His antics just made him look all the more shifty.

"I was telling these guys about Larson," Porter said. "They ah, they hadn't heard about it."

It was a poor attempt at a lie and Porter knew it. I lifted an eyebrow at him. He turned a bit pink but didn't back down. I turned my attention to the men standing around him wondering why these guys had been the focus of Porter's anger. They each wore medical unit patches on their uniforms, so I knew they worked in the hospital somewhere. I read their names on their uniforms, but ignored the information and forced the introductions to make my own eye-to-eye assessment of each of them.

Private Paterson was rail thin with curly brown hair. I said my name, and held my hand out to shake. He took it reluctantly, his handshake awkward, limp and uncertain.

"And your name is…" I asked.

"Ah, Paterson, ma'am," he said, his eyes going to the man next to him as if seeking approval."

"You don't have to call me ma'am, private. I'm a working stiff, just like you," I corrected him. He shifted his weight from foot to foot and wouldn't meet my gaze. I shifted my attention to the man next to him.

Private First Class Granger was a short, thick young man with skin that matched my mocha color. He wore his head shaved. Granger boldly stared at me as he shook my hand with a strong, steady grip. His confidence was probably why Paterson sought his approval. When I introduced myself, he didn't need prompting.

"Private First Class Granger, Sergeant. Are you finding your way around the clinic alright?" he asked politely.

"Yes. I'm impressed. You guys are doing good work here."

"Thanks, Sergeant. We try." His grin seemed open and genuine. I wondered what he was doing with the motley-looking crew.

The third guy, Private First Class Burke was a pretty-boy, dark-haired kid with big blue eyes, rosy cheeks and a bold look that said he knew he could make the young girls blush. He shook my hand with a cocky smile, then tilted his head to the side and made it obvious he was checking out my ass. When his eyes met mine again, he realized by my look that he had taken a liberty he shouldn't have. I continued the handshake and held his gaze, my eyebrows drawn together. I let the silence hang for long enough to ensure he got the point.

"And your name is…"

"Private First Class Burke, Sergeant," he said.

"You look at all your NCOs like that, Private?"

"No, Sergeant. But not all my NCOs look like you." He gave me a big toothy grin, proud of himself. Porter chuckled. I ignored Porter and pulled Burke closer. He stumbled forward, almost falling into me. I was taller than him, so he was forced to look up. His smile disappeared.

"You see any reason why looking at me like that would be insulting, Private?"

"I guess so, Sergeant." A pink flush rushed up from his neck and he tried to release my handshake, but I wouldn't let go.

"If we were the same rank, that would have been sexual harassment, Private. Since I outrank you, Private, it's not only sexual harassment, it's also insubordination, Private. Do you understand?" The other men held their breath and Burke didn't look so cocky anymore.

"Yes, Sergeant. Sorry."

I dropped his hand. "For a young private, you just displayed an alarming lack of respect and very poor judgment. It's still early in your career. I suggest you figure out what's more important; being a good soldier, or," I turned my gaze to Porter, "impressing your friends."

"Yes, Sergeant," he said. "Thank you, Sergeant."

I wondered again why Porter and Judd, two sergeants from the engineering camp, were having an angry conversation with soldiers who were far younger and junior to them. I raised an eyebrow at Porter, not saying anything, but letting him know he had sparked my curiosity.

"Nice to meet you all," I said, glancing around the group.

Paterson, Granger and Burke. Now that I had the names, I added them to our list of people to interview. I felt their eyes on me as I left the clinic.

I glanced at my watch and knew Fletcher would be furious by now. I'd been gone far too long, but I had one more thing to do before I headed back to the construction site.

I found Mora right away and asked him to come with me while I talked to Cordovan. Cordovan and Dropic were interviewing people who waited in line for the clinic. I called them over and got down to business.

"I understand you already tried to arrange an interview with Colonel Scaporelli while you were still in Minneapolis."

Cordovan exchanged a look with Dropic then flashed his Ken-doll smile. "Sure. I knew he was going to be here and I figured, what the heck. I wanted to get some background ..."

"Why didn't you tell me?"

He ran his fingers back through his hair. The action left a thick lock dangling attractively in front of his face. He narrowed his eyes at me. "I didn't think it was any big deal. Did he change his mind? He seemed adamant that he didn't want to talk at the time."

"That hasn't changed. I hope you'll respect his wishes."

He exchanged another look with Dropic who suddenly consulted the ground. "I figured once we got here he might change his mind." Cordovan's smile faltered a bit.

"Well he hasn't. I would like your assurance that you won't try to interview him."

He shrugged. "Okay."

"And you won't chase after him trying to get some quick comment."

"Would I do that?" he asked, a false innocence in his voice.

"I've seen your tapes."

He exchanged another look with Dropic.

"Let me put it this way," I said. "You've asked for an interview with the Commander of this medical unit. He has refused your request. You will not go anywhere near him. You won't get any video of him. You will respect his wishes."

Cordovan crossed his arms over his chest and wrinkled his forehead at me as I laid out the restrictions.

"I was just trying to get some background tape—what he does when he's not in uniform, something to round out the story."

"If there's something specific you want from Colonel Scaporelli," I added, "perhaps I can find someone else who could speak to you on the topic. Just exactly what did you want to interview him about?"

Cordovan obviously wasn't ready to reveal what he was up to. Again, his gaze flicked to Dropic, who was now scanning the skies in his attempt to look uninterested. These guys were really starting to get on my nerves.

"At some point I'll have to talk to someone in charge to get the meat and potatoes of the mission," he finally said.

"Okay, done. Anything else?"

"Nope, not right now."

I knew there was something more, but further questioning wouldn't do any good.

"Sergeant Mora will schedule an interview with the senior hospital NCO or another one of the doctors."

"Okay, sounds good," Cordovan said.

I wasn't fooled by his friendly acceptance.

I backed away from them, motioning for Mora to follow me. "I don't know what they're up to, but he's got something hinky up his sleeve. It's not like we can stop them from doing anything, but it would be nice to at least be aware of what they are after."

"Okay, I'll see what I can do. So far, they've just been asking the usual questions you would expect about the clinic and the treatments."

"Pay attention to anything they ask that strays from those topics. I'm completely in the dark here. I'm counting on you to see if you can figure out what this is about."

Mora grinned. "Don't worry Sergeant Harper. I'll be watching them. One thing's for sure. Whatever they're after, it must be something worth dragging them all the way here to stand around in the rain. It has to be something interesting."

"Yeah," I said. "That's what I'm afraid of."

I walked away, wondering if I should have said something to him about the young girls and my suspicions that they might have been sexually assaulted by someone local. I decided I would talk to Fletcher and Chief Santos about it first before I discussed it with anyone else.

The thought of having to speak to Santos again wasn't sitting well with me. I had too many unpleasant memories of being interrogated by him and his partner, Ramsey. I trudged through the village and downhill to the construction site, all the while dreading what would come next.

Chapter 11

I crouched in the back of our Humvee, moving bags and equipment around, searching for our case of MREs when the distinctive clanking of a Humvee engine starting split the air. As I tossed the case out the rear of the truck, the vehicle passed me, giving me only a glimpse of a man behind the wheel, his dark hair plastered damply to his head.

That fleeting look should have been enough to concern me. Safety regulations are very specific. You never drive a military vehicle alone, you always have an assistant driver and you don't drive a Humvee without wearing a helmet. That lone helmetless head should have been enough to tell me something was wrong, but I ignored it.

Fletcher was waiting for me and I was preoccupied with getting back to the command tent, the upcoming conversation with Santos, everything I'd learned while at the clinic. I didn't wonder who was in the truck or where they might be going. Later, I would remember that fleeting glance and feel guilty about not saying anything, but at the time, I was too wrapped up in my own stuff to care.

I found my rucksack and dug out my overshoes and rain jacket which were buried in the bottom of the bag, climbed out of the truck, and propping myself for balance against the tailgate, struggling to get my overshoes on. The light green and bulky boots were hard to walk in, but I'd only brought one pair of combat boots and wanted to keep them dry.

The case of MREs was brand new, so I cut the plastic ties

holding it together, slipped off the rectangular, cardboard wrapper and opened the case of twenty-four meals in large brown plastic wrappers, the name of each meal written on every package. The menu ranged from chicken tetrazzini to beef stew to southwestern style chicken. Most of it sounded tasty, but the main dish isn't the most important part of an MRE. It's the extras that come with it that make each meal desirable. Some soldiers know exactly what is in each and every packet. I hadn't memorized all the extras so it was always a guessing game. I sifted through the meals feeling lucky that I had first pick and decided on beef ravioli.

My boots made squashing sounds in the mud as the constant rain and foot traffic had reduced the one road in the camp to a flooded, gooey, mess. By the time I reached the command tent, I was covered in mud spatters up to my knees and feeling a little smug that I had donned my overshoes and jacket.

Despite the rain, the air felt warm and muggy the way jungles tend to be, so Fletcher had rolled up the heavy canvas sides of the tent to expose the mosquito netting surrounding the room. As I approached, I watched him moving around inside, arranging chairs and tables.

He had placed a laptop on one of the tables, the satellite phone sitting next to it. He stationed a folding chair in front of the laptop, then spent some time deciding where to put the other chairs. He seemed to carefully consider the exact placement of the seating. He was only a silhouette to me, a dark shadow inside the netting, and there was something voyeuristic about watching him when he didn't know it.

My emotions remained in a turmoil over having to work with him. When we were dating, it only took a few months to realize that, while he made me feel like the center of his world when we were together, I didn't really know him. He never introduced me to his friends and never told me much about how he kept himself busy when we weren't together.

I had kept my relationship with Fletcher to myself, except for my sister Loretta, who I always tell everything. Despite being eight years younger than me, and the fact that I'd raised her since she was sixteen, Loretta somehow remembered all of the wise life lessons our mother had often bestowed upon us. Over frequent phone calls, she tried to warn me about Fletcher.

"Girl, what do you really know about him?" Loretta had asked.

"Not much, I guess. I know his mother and sister live in New York. He's never been married and doesn't have kids."

"Doesn't have any he claims anyway."

"Loretta, I don't think he's like that. He's not that devious."

"Do you at least use protection?

"Of course we do. He's very careful about that."

"I bet he is. Has he introduced you to any of his friends?"

"No."

"Have you ever even been to his house?"

"Well, no, but that's because he's always taking me to romantic places."

"Lauren, you don't know what he's like in real life. You've been so busy getting swept off your feet, you don't know what your prince charming does when he's not riding you around on his white horse."

"But the times we've been together, it couldn't be fake. It just couldn't."

"Honey, you don't know what you don't know. But I suggest you'd better find out."

Loretta's advice made me rummage around in my own feelings, and I didn't like what I found. I had convinced myself that it didn't matter that I only heard from him occasionally. We were both soldiers. Long trips to places without regular phone service were routine. I tried not to question the gaps between seeing each other, tried not to ask for more than what he was willing, freely, to give. Maybe I didn't ask the questions because I didn't want to know the answers.

I'd always prided myself on my independence and scoffed at the women I knew who looked for a man to change their world, the women who needed to be desired above all else. I felt contempt for them. Contempt for the female character that used cleavage and giggles to render a grown man into putty simply to fulfill her quest to be wanted. Contempt for the women who practiced manipulative dosages of flirtation and helplessness that twisted men into a tight-fisted need to respond and rescue.

When I realized Fletcher couldn't be trusted, I told Loretta the relationship was over. Just like that. Done.

But at times, I'd still remember the feel of his hands brushing a hair away from my cheek, or the deep rumble of pleasure I conjured when I gently sunk my teeth into his flesh. I missed it. Any contempt I'd felt for the other women he may have manipulated, I felt ten-fold for myself. He'd sought to fulfill my most intimate desires and he'd succeeded. I missed it more than I wanted to admit.

Standing out in the rain wasn't going to change the fact that I had to work with him. As I approached the tent, Fletcher sat down and struggled to open an MRE. He tried to pull the bag open and when that didn't work, tried using his teeth.

I pushed the tent door aside and stepped in. He gave me an embarrassed look.

"I can never get these damn things open," he said.

I dropped my rucksack and sleeping bag, then gave him the Swiss Army knife I always kept in a holder on my belt. He smiled at me, then his smile disappeared.

"Where the hell have you been?"

"I'm sorry. It took a lot longer than I thought."

"What took a lot longer?"

"I'll tell you everything, but right now, I'm starving. Can we eat first?"

He handed my knife back, and dumped all of the items from his packet out on the table.

"What'd you get?" he asked.

"Beef Ravioli. You?"

"Ham slice."

I cringed.

"Hey, don't knock it," he said smiling. "It comes with," and he held up the items as he gloated over his bounty, "cheese spread

AND pound cake."

The crackers that came along with cheese spread were like civil war hard tack ... stiff, dry and tasteless, but the cheese spread made up for it. Eating MREs always reminded me of a school cafeteria lunch when everyone opened their bags and compared, shared and exchanged what they found there.

"Hey, jalapeno cheese," I declared happily.

While our entrees warmed up, I took out my notebook and started scratching out some notes. I'd learned a lot of little things on my trip through the hospital, and needed to make sure I didn't miss any details when I related them to the investigator.

When I glanced up, I caught Fletcher staring at me, his expression illegible.

"What?"

He looked away, cleared his throat and fidgeted.

"What's going on, Fletcher?"

"Nothing. I just...I mean, you. Santos told me, well...he said that you..."

"He told you about Bosnia." Now I recognized the expression on Fletcher's face. I'd grown accustomed to it in the weeks since I'd returned. Men couldn't look me in the eye. They acted embarrassed, some even fearful. Women wanted to hug me and cry and tell me their own stories. The looks of pity and sympathy pissed me off the most. People may have heard the story, but they didn't know what had happened. They didn't really know. Only a handful of people knew the entire story, knew what had been done to me, what I had done to the men in that barn. Santos was one of the people who knew the details. Now he'd told the story to Fletcher.

"Fletcher, don't you dare feel sorry for me. Let's get that clear right now."

"Pity? No, I...that's not... I mean, look at you. Most people wouldn't have survived that. Most people would have been broken by it."

My shoulders relaxed some but not completely. I had asked Santos to tell Fletcher about it, mostly because I didn't want to do it myself. The subject was bound to come up at some point in the investigation.

"I can't afford to be broken by it, can I?"

"Santos said you were the strongest, most brave woman he'd ever met. From the story he told…"

The description made me cringe. "I survived Fletcher. I got through it. That doesn't make me brave. It was just survival. I just did what needed to be done." Santos wouldn't have thought my reaction in the lab was anything brave. Like a quivering ball of pathetic was how I had felt.

Fletcher tilted his chair back, balancing it on two legs, then looked out of the tent, his gaze wandering over the camp. "And saving those men? That was survival too?"

"Fletcher…"

"He said the British government is giving you some kind of medal."

"That's the first I've heard of it," I mumbled. Just the mention of anything British had my thoughts turning to Sergeant Major Harry Fogg. If I hadn't been called away on this mission to the jungle, Harry and I would have been cavorting on a beach somewhere, drinking fruity cocktails with umbrellas in them and finally taking some time out of uniform to "properly get to know one another," as Harry would say. I wondered if the big special operations soldier, with the cocky smile and the green eyes had anything to do with talk about an award. I missed Harry.

"What are you grinning about?"

"Was I grinning?" I asked.

"Yes, rather wickedly. What were you thinking about?"

There was no way I would tell Fletcher about Harry. He already knew too many details about me. I collected our meals which were plenty warm enough by then, dropping Fletcher's on the desk in front of him.

"We're done talking about Bosnia, Fletcher. Clear?"

"I don't see why…"

"We're done," I said. "If you want more details, ask Santos for the official report. There are a couple of versions out there, both classified, but if you really want to know everything that went down, Santos can probably get you access. I'm not going to talk about it."

I shoved a bite of food into my mouth and almost had to spit it out, it was so hot. I waved my hand in front of my mouth, in a ridiculous attempt to cool it off, but it was no use. The pasta had been hot enough to leave a blister.

He chuckled at me. "Careful, hero chick. Don't ruin the image I have now."

"Shut up and eat your lunch."

We settled down and ate. I scribbled a few more notes. While I scribbled and ate, Fletcher wrote his own notes, stopping long enough to prepare a cracker with cheese on top and handed it to me, nudging my shoulder to get my attention. The gesture felt strangely intimate. Not quite like dropping a grape into my mouth, but leaning that way. I smiled in thanks then quickly looked back at my paper to cover the heat that rushed to my face.

We munched and worked on our notes in comfortable silence. I thought about what evidence we had seen, what I had heard, what concerned me, filling several pages. When I thought I was finished, I went over it once more.

I noticed that Fletcher had made two lists. One titled, people to interview. Another list titled, questions to ask. I gave him the names of the three soldiers I'd met at the medical unit who had been talking to Porter and Judd and the name of the female soldier, Paulson, who had been crying in the women's bunk area. He added the information to his lists.

Finally, he wiped his mouth with a paper napkin, dialed the number for Santos, and put the call on speaker phone. We both listened as the phone rang once and was picked up immediately.

"Santos," he said.

"Mr. Santos, this is Chief Mayes calling. I have Master Sergeant Harper here with me."

"Chief Fletcher. We have been waiting well over an hour for your call."

The words came through clipped and heated.

"That's my fault, chief," I said. "I've been at the medical clinic …"

"We'll get to that," he interrupted.

Great, I thought. I've already pissed him off.

"Let me introduce the other people in the room."

Fletcher and I exchanged a look as Santos ran down the list of names and titles of the people assembled to assist in the telephonic investigation. Military Police, the forensic specialists who would analyze Fordham's evidence, even a Chaplain who wanted to ensure the dead man and the dead man's brother were provided spiritual assistance.

The introductions complete, Santos fired questions at us, demanding an accounting of what had happened since the convoy had arrived and we discovered the body. I did most of the talking at first, with Fletcher chiming in when necessary. I mentioned Dr. Fordham and the work she had already done.

"You're lucky to have a coroner there," Santos said. "We need to get her on the horn with our forensics people here. They've got some ideas about how to extract the body."

"She's concerned about getting him out as soon as possible," I told him.

"I concur," Santos said. "What else do you have?"

I told him that Larson had a brother, Reginald, who was a member of the unit. "I was there when Reggie first saw the body. He was hysterical and we had to sedate him. He did a lot of raving, but he said one thing that was notable. He said," and I flipped through my notebook until I had the exact words I thought I had heard. "He said, 'It should have been me.' After talking to him, he told me that he was supposed to stay back with the group who were assigned guard duty, but his brother pulled the duty for him. We might want to consider whether this is a case of mistaken identity."

Fletcher spoke up then. "He was in shock at the time. Obviously, we'll need to talk to him in a more formal interview."

"I concur," Santos said.

"We won't be able to do that for a while," I said. "Fordham

gave him a sedative. He'll probably be out for a few hours."

Fletcher gave a description of the crime scene, and noted the boot prints in the cement. That there were two definite sets of prints but it was impossible to tell when they had been made.

"At this point, we know, in addition to Robert Larson, Staff Sergeant Porter, Sergeant Judd and Lieutenant Allen and Specialist Hank Kendrick were all here. Allen was the only officer. Judging from their sizes, I would bet Porter and Judd's boot prints will match those found in the cement."

"If they were at the scene when you arrived, the prints could have been made then and not during the murder," Santos observed.

"That would depend wouldn't it?" Fletcher asked. "On how long it takes for the cement to dry and when Larson was killed."

"I took pictures of the crime scene," I said. "The cement bags indicate it's quick dry cement so, what? Twenty minutes or so for it to harden? Unless the heat and humidity have anything to do with the drying time."

There was discussion among the investigators in the room. While they went back and forth, Fletcher and I shared more crackers and cheese. He took a bite of the jalapeno cheese spread. "Wow, this is good," he whispered.

"What was that, Chief?" Santos asked.

Fletcher responded with a mouth full of cheese and crackers, covering his mouth and making faces at me in a silent laugh, "Ah, nothing. Sorry to interrupt."

I hit him in the shoulder. He pretended I'd really hurt him. Santos brought us back to business.

"I've looked at First Sergeant Dodd's two-oh-one file," Santos said. "He's been around a long time. You'll have to be the judge as to how much you can trust him. I can tell you that he was active duty for a decade before going in the Reserve. His entire military career has been exemplary. I've also looked at the young lieutenant up there with you, first lieutenant Allen. He apparently had some issues during his OBC training. His very first OER wasn't exactly stellar. Have you met this guy?"

I thought about the little man with the confidence problem and wasn't surprised about the status of his Officer Evaluation Report. As inflated as those evaluations usually were, anyone would be hard pressed to fill Allen's with platitudes.

"Yes, we've met," I said. "He told me he preferred to stay up here. I get the impression the men don't like him much. He's a bit defensive. Unfortunately, there aren't any other officers here, aside from the medical unit leadership."

There was a long moment of silence from Santos's side. I rode it out.

"Okay, noted," he finally said. "What else do you have?"

I told him about the torn panties I found in the latrine and that two young girls had been examined in the clinic who may have been sexually assaulted, leaving out the way looking at that evidence of violence had made me feel. When I looked down, I realized my hands were clenched together, my knuckles white. I felt Fletcher staring at me, leaning close as if willing me to leech some of his strength from him. He cleared his throat and looked at the speakerphone.

"This is not a secure site," Fletcher said. "Anyone could have put those panties there."

"Agreed," I said. "But we have to consider the possible assaults as part of the investigation. A vengeful family member immediately comes to mind."

Again, there was a long silence from Santos's side of the phone, some murmured conversation around the room.

"Excellent observation," Santos said.

Fletcher made a funny face and mouthed the compliment back at me. I stifled a laugh and punched him again.

"Where is the evidence now?" a voice in the room asked.

"Dr. Fordham has it," I said, attempting to sound as if I wasn't laughing under my breath. "It was covered in grime. I doubt she'll be able to get anything useful from it,"

More discussion followed. We waited for the experts to finish. Fletcher doodled on his paper and I watched his hands.

They were large and strong hands with long, slender fingers

and I had always found them sexy. Suddenly I was flooded with memories of how he would direct me with his hands. A gentle push on my back, a pull on the back of my neck, a guiding tug across my shoulders.

I gasped at the memory and when I glanced up, Fletcher was watching me. Our eyes met and I felt as if he knew exactly what I had been thinking. My face grew hot. He smiled and cocked his head to the side in question. I shook my head in the negative and looked away.

Santos finally interrupted the quiet.

"I haven't been able to review all of the personnel files from everyone in the unit, but we're working on that," he said. "We're also gathering civilian criminal records. It would help if you got me the names of everyone who stayed to guard the site. I can ensure those names are run through as quickly as possible."

"It's more than just the engineering unit, Chief. There's a medical team up here too, and all of them were here over the weekend," I said. "The missions are only a couple hundred meters apart. If all the engineers that were up here are suspects, so should the medical teams be."

"You're correct. I'll get JAG to request their civilian records as well. You say all of them were in place at the time of the murder?"

"They didn't leave to go to the base camp like the others," I said. "There of course could be alibis we don't know about."

"Noted," Santos said. "If we should come up with anything significant in their records checks, we'll let you know immediately."

"Good," Fletcher said. "We'll start our interviews with Dodd since we know he couldn't be involved. I thought we'd just start by getting each of them to tell us what they might have seen, find out if there were any conflicts, get some background. Does that sound okay to you, Chief?"

"Yes. How are you going to handle interviewing the villagers?"

Fletcher and I exchanged looks. Judging by his expression, we had the same thought, which was, "How the hell should WE know?"

"What do you suggest, Chief?" Fletcher asked, shrugging his shoulders, and shaking his head at me.

Again, there was a long silence. I remembered how Santos acted during my interrogations in Bosnia. He rarely said a word. When he did speak, it was usually to say something significant. While partnered with Chief Ramsey, who did most of the talking, the long silences weren't noticed. Here, on his own, the pregnant pauses made me feel fidgety, with that uncomfortable notion that silences had to be filled.

"You will have to begin slowly with the villagers," he finally said. "You obviously can't interview everyone. Look to those that have been working with the engineers. You should know that an American embassy attaché told me we will be able to conduct our investigation without much interference from the Honduran government. However, we still need to be discreet. Very cautious. Especially when it comes to the sexual assault victims."

Great, I thought. We could spark some kind of international incident out here in the jungle on our own. Fletcher may have had experience with flying by the seat of his pants, but I was never comfortable with winging it. What I was comfortable with, was working with the media. I knew I was headed for a battle, but the subject had to be broached.

"Chief, I'm sure you're aware of the investigative news team I escorted here."

"Yes, we're aware."

"My plan is to allow them to get some shots around the camp. We've erected a shelter around the body…" but Santos didn't let me finish.

"No, absolutely not. We can't allow the media access to the site." For someone who used as few words as possible, Santos seemed to have plenty to say against letting the media do their job. I had been prepared for resistance, but this was my area of expertise. If Santos wanted to fight about it, I was ready for a battle.

"Chief, I respect your position, however it makes more sense for us to allow them to get footage that will help them tell their story without compromising the investigation. Better to feed them something I can control, then to deny them everything and have them claim we're attempting a cover up."

My statement was met with silence from Santos but lots of discussion throughout the room, most of it negative. Investigators, police, intelligence people, they would all rather keep everything a secret whether it needed to be or not. Fletcher rolled his eyes at me while we waited out the discussion. When two people in the room started shouting at each other, I figured it was time to step in again.

"Gentlemen, if I could interrupt for a moment," I said. More grumbling followed but they eventually quieted down. "This news team is here after some kind of investigative news story. They were not expecting to find a murder scene any more than we were. Frankly, I'm not sure what they originally came here to find but, whatever it is, it must be major. I'd rather give them some limited access to the murder than wait to find out what they're really after."

"A bird in the hand, so to speak," Santos said.

"Exactly."

A gruff voice from the room piped in. "How do you know the murder isn't the worst of the two?"

"Because, they haven't been interested in it."

"Ah," Santo said. "Which means, whatever they are after is more sensational than a murder."

"Fucking media," someone close to the phone mumbled. General sounds of agreement circulated the room. Fletcher and I exchanged looks. They could all think poorly of the press from their safe location at Soto Cano. Fletcher and I were the ones in the juggernaut's path.

Finally, Santos interrupted the discussion going on in the room.

"Master Sergeant Harper, I will leave the decisions about the media to you. I'm sure you are aware of the sensitivities here."

Further objections were raised in the room, but Santos ignored them. He continued by reminding us to be cautious. His advice was like telling a guy in a canoe to be careful while he approached

Niagara Falls. The only thing that was going to help us survive this ride was luck.

A sudden loud clap of thunder made me jump. I glanced at Fletcher, and he smiled at my skittishness. I thought it impossible, but the rain started coming down even more intensely. The weather was a perfect reflection of my mood.

Chapter 12

Santos wrapped up our conversation with a weather report. Days of rain. Heavy cloud cover. No flights, no convoys on the rain-drenched roads, no help for at least a couple of days.

"FYSA," he said, tossing out the acronym that meant, 'for your situational awareness.' His use of the term made me chuckle. Alphabet speak, a symptom of a life lived in the military, is like a secret handshake one learns if you're part of the club. My ability to translate the jumble of letters confirmed my own infection with the ailment. Most of the time, knowing the word associated with each letter isn't necessary, as long as you get the gist. And if you really don't know what all the letters mean, it's better to pretend you know and hope no one asks you to clarify.

I shook my head to reorder my thoughts and tuned into what Santos was saying.

"There's a Honduran special operations squad on a training mission in the mountains near you accompanied by NATO advisors. They're moving on foot through areas very close to your village on a drug interdiction mission. Problem is, these guys tend to stay hidden, and are outside our communication net. They may come through there though. One never knows."

I wasn't sure if I liked the idea of a special ops team lurking about in the jungle, or that they were looking for drugs in the area. It was yet another complication we didn't need.

"Okay, Chief. We'll keep an eye out for them," Fletcher said, signing off. He added a promise that we would call again in a few hours. He hit the disconnect button, stood up slowly and stretched his arms over his head, with a long, low groan. I slowly rotated my head on my neck and realized how tightly wound I had been throughout the conversation.

Fletcher sat down, leaned back and balanced his chair on two legs. "Dodd, then the brother if he's awake, then the L-T, then the other guys who were left here." he said.

"That's Porter, Judd and at least two others whose names we don't know yet." I said the last few words while trying not to yawn, then finally gave into it, long and noisily covering my mouth with my hand. Fletcher raised an eyebrow at me.

"Sorry," I said.

He turned his attention back to the tent ceiling, stretched his arms up then folded them behind his head, rocking his chair gently back and forth.

I sighed, then laid my head down on my arms on the table, turned to look through the mesh of the tent walls, knowing we had a long and exhausting afternoon of interviews ahead of us. I wondered how cooperative any of the men would be considering we were a couple of inexperienced people assigned to investigate the murder of someone they knew. Cooperative or not, the list of questions I had seemed to grow instead of shrink.

But first, by silent agreement, we both needed a couple of seconds to relax. I watched the rain sheeting down and allowed the constant drumming on the tent roof to seep into my awareness, the steady noise helping to soothe and calm. Lightning lit up the area, then several seconds later, thunder rumbled over us. Despite all the noise and pyrotechnics, it was peaceful. There was something cozy about watching the torrential weather outside while we stayed dry and quiet inside.

"I could use a treadmill right now," I said. A good long, sweaty five miles would help take some of my tension away and help me focus. The sound of Fletcher's chair plopping down hard made me jerk my head up to look at him. I didn't like the dark stare he directed at me.

"What?" I asked him.

He shook his head, then snatched up his meal and poked at it as if thinking about taking a bite of the entre that had surely turned cold by then. "You're always running away, Lauren," he mumbled, shaking his head.

"What are you talking about?"

"Just what I said. Running from your problems is never the answer."

"I could use a good workout. How do you tie that to running away from my problems?"

He shrugged noncommittally, but I didn't like the body language and didn't understand what he was getting at. I should have left it alone but didn't.

"No, you started this. What problems have I run away from?"

He tossed his food on the desk, his eyebrows drawn together. The level of anger seemed out of proportion to my simple desire to take a run. He narrowed his eyes further and paused several beats, then finally blurted it out.

"Me. You ran away from me," he said, as he poked a finger into his own chest.

I must have looked like a fish tossed onto shore the way my mouth opened and closed in silent shock. After several long moments while I searched for something to say, what actually came out didn't sound like me.

"I have no idea what you're talking about."

"Lauren, I thought we had something special."

"You thought… wait, what?" I said, in a voice several octaves higher than normal and wondered if we were talking about the same relationship.

"And believe me," he said. "Any doubt I may have had about your feelings was completely cleared up by the way you reacted when you saw me this morning."

"But Fletcher,"

"But Fletcher," he mimicked, in a childish falsetto.

Mocking me. He was mocking me and that pissed me off. "If

our relationship was so special, why were you dating all those other women?"

He responded with clenched teeth, a wrinkled forehead, flared nostrils. "You made it clear you didn't want to be exclusive. What did you expect me to do?"

I'd never seen him angry before, had never seen the intense look in his eye, as if he'd been holding this back for some time. "I made it clear? How the hell did I do that?"

"We dated for almost eight months. In all that time, you never called me, not once. You never asked me to do anything. Every time I asked you out, I felt as if I was begging for your company." His voice shook as he slung the words at me. He stood, and came around the table, towering over me.

"I called you," I said weakly. "Didn't I?" But couldn't remember if that were true. I stared up at him, shocked.

"Then when we did get together," he went on, "it was like you kept me at arm's length, never letting me close. Stupid me, I kept trying and you kept running away!"

"That is so not how I remember it." I shook my head and found it hard to breath. Could I have so thoroughly misread his intentions?

"You don't remember? Or is it because you were just a big tease? All those trips we took. That kind of treatment must be so common for you that it didn't mean anything. I was just another sucker bending over backwards to please you."

"Now, wait a minute…."

He took another step closer. I backed away from him and stuck my arm out straight, palm up to stop him. He still towered over me, his physical presence beginning to feel like a restricting band around my chest. I gasped for breath. "I thought you wanted the space. You never said you had any real feelings for me. I didn't think you…"

My voice sounded thin and whiney and I hated the way his anger frightened me. Fletcher had hurt me, not the other way around. He was conveniently altering the history of our relationship to justify how he had treated me.

I wouldn't let him turn the tables on me. I clenched my hands into fists and planted my feet. "Do you know how I found out about you?" I almost whispered it, low and forced, too ashamed of it to say out loud even to the person who'd humiliated me. "My hairdresser. My hairdresser told me about all the clients he had who couldn't stop talking about the hot pilot who took them on romantic trips. Evidently, there were so many of them, all I had to do was mention your name to him and the stories came tumbling out. I even heard a woman talking about you in the locker room at my gym. If I had told you that you were the subject of locker room gossip, would you have denied it, or been flattered by it?"

It took me a minute to realize the deep rumble in his chest was a chuckle, one with a razor-sharp edge to it. When he stopped laughing, he put his hands on his hips and shouted at me, "Did you think I gave a shit about them? That I saw any one of them more than once or twice?" His voice boomed around me as he stalked back to the desk.

"How was I to know that?"

"You could have asked!"

"Look, this is not the time or the place to be getting into this. I'd better give you some space to calm down." I stepped back intending to move toward the door, feeling uncomfortable about turning my back on him.

"And I prove my point. You're running away again!"

He came toward me. In my rational mind I knew he would never raise a hand to me, but I began to tremble none the less, a reaction I seemed to have little control over. It reminded me of a cat my mother had rescued from an animal shelter, a scrawny, abused thing that cringed every time you raised a hand to pet her. No matter your good intentions, her first assumption was that you meant to do her harm. This instinctive need to shrink away was new to me. Bosnia had done that to me, and I hated it. I grabbed my jacket from the back of my chair, threw it on and fought against my instinct to cower. When I shouted at him, I felt the harsh rasp in my throat from the volume I produced.

"I am not running away from you. You obviously need some

distance. We've got a job to do."

"You think I don't know that?" he bellowed. This was a Fletcher I didn't recognize. I felt as if I had been holding a defective firecracker with a very short fuse and never realized it was burning.

The vein in his temple throbbed as he took another step toward me. I grit my teeth, and had actually planted my feet so that I'd have some leverage to shove him away, when someone cleared their throat in a loud and pointed way.

First Sergeant Dodd stood just outside the mesh walls of the tent. His shoulders hunched against the pounding rain. He grinned, his gaze bouncing back and forth between us.

"Ya'll know everyone can hear you hollerin' at each other, right?"

It was like someone had pulled the plug on a drain. My breath leaked out of me, leaving me feeling wobbly in my relief but mortified to realize that the scene had been witnessed by everyone.

Dodd walked around and shoved his way through the tent flap. I backed up to let him enter. He took a long, hard look at me. I felt as if he saw the fear and vulnerability Fletcher hadn't noticed. I squared my shoulders and stared right back at him, having no desire for his sympathy. He glared at Fletcher then, mentally assessing the fault of the argument.

"I was about to take some bets," Dodd said, shaking off some of the rain. "Odds were even that you'd either be tussling soon, or doing what me and the misses do after we've had a good blow-out." He'd made a joke, but I knew he wasn't convinced anything was funny.

Fletcher and I exchanged a look, my face instantly hot. I had to turn away. Fletcher chuckled, the deep rumble more genuine this time. "Don't worry, Top," he said. "Just a little spat between old friends. Right, Lauren?" He raised an eyebrow at me, no hint of a smile on his face.

"I need to go to the latrine," I announced and, before he objected, ducked out of the tent.

My head pounded. The shuffle of my feet kicked up huge splashes as I stumbled forward, trying to put some distance between myself and the tent. After several paces, I stopped, feeling breathless. "What the fuck?" I mumbled to myself. Their voices drifted out to me, an unintelligible jumble of words and laughter. The mirth felt like a knife in my gut. I put my head down and scurried away.

I should have felt gratitude that Dodd had happened along to break up the shouting match, but he had come too late. If he'd heard us, everyone else in the camp had too, and it wouldn't be long before the gossip began. The two outsiders investigating the murder either hated each other, or had something more going on. If I was the murderer, I know which rumor I'd try to spread around.

Chapter 13

I walked in the direction of the latrines with no intention of actually going there. Replaying the argument with Fletcher in my head, I kicked myself for all the things I could have said and kicked myself harder for dwelling on it. How could we have seen things so differently? Had he revised history or had I?

I walked past the latrine not knowing or caring where I actually went. I simply needed to be gone. I followed a wall of vegetation at the edge of the jungle and after a few yards, found myself on what might have been a narrow road if the heavens hadn't opened and turned it into a gushing torrent. Water flowed over and around large rocks forming impromptu waterfalls. Tire ruts were now deep pools. The rushing water reinforced the unpleasant knowledge that travel was impossible. We were stuck on this mountain in the jungle. Perhaps for a long while.

I stayed to the side of the road and out of the water, making my own path in the grass and mud. My only thought was to put some distance between myself and Fletcher. He said running away from my problems was a habit of mine. In this case, he was right.

The rain slowed and suddenly, as if someone had flipped a switch, it stopped. The silence felt alien. I halted my progress and listened as fat drops plunked off soaking leaves. Dappled light around me changed subtly as the clouds thinned, allowing a bit of sun to fall on thick, jungle foliage.

I tilted my head back, turning my face up to the sky and

breathed deeply, listening to the gradual rising cacophony of insects and birds as the sounds of the jungle grew in volume, no longer overpowered by the deluge. The wind shifted and the strong, earthy scent of animal wafted by. The heavy clang of a bell, the bray of a cow, low and slightly panicked, along with several voices in Spanish and English all speaking at once, drifted my way. The voices were almost drowned out by the high whinny of a horse.

It seemed natural to turn in the direction of the sounds. I followed them until a wide field of tall grass and shrubs stretched before me, the start of a small path cut by human movement. I followed the path and the sounds grew louder.

An animal pen, with large gates on each end, stood on a small patch of field, surrounded by a thick grove of trees. A sizeable crowd of men and boys, some balanced or sitting on the rungs, circled the corral. Several horses chomped grass, their reins merely dropped on the ground. A few boys surrounded a group of cows, periodically nudging the animals to ensure they stayed together. One man stood under a tree, holding ropes connected to two large, pink and mud-splattered hogs.

The crowd was soaking wet, most with mud splatters liberally decorating their clothing, but there was camaraderie in the group, smiles and laughter, despite the restless stomp of hooves and the nervous twitch of tails.

A cow struggled inside the small corral, its wide, frightened eyes and flaring nostrils peeking out between the rungs. A brass bell hanging from a leather strap around the animal's throat banged loudly.

Balanced on a rung of the pen, a soldier, his brown t-shirt and boonie cap dripping from the recently stopped rain, pulled the cow's lips back and examined its teeth then looked in both ears.

"Let me know when you're ready for the vaccines, Dr. Reece," another soldier said.

"Any time," Reece said, still propped on the corral wall. One by one, his assistant handed him syringes as he expertly injected the animal. In the middle of the process, he glanced down and saw me watching.

"It's okay," he said. "You can come closer."

I pulled myself up onto the pen. The cow's nostrils flared, eyes white in fright. She huffed and stomped her disapproval at being restricted inside the wooden gate.

Reece, mid-thirtyish, slender, leaned over the walls of the pen and seemed comfortable there, as if he had spent plenty of time in just such a position. His dripping wet t-shirt was covered in grim. There were streaks of dirt across his nose and cheeks, his blue eyes bright against sun-darkened skin. The bright smile on his face served as testament to how much he enjoyed himself.

"We give them some vaccines against common diseases and an injection of a de-worming liquid," Reece explained. "This one looks pretty healthy." He ran an appreciative hand down the cow's back, making calming sounds.

I reached out and stroked the cow and marveled at the depth of her huge, brown eyes. Reece spoke to the farmer in rapid Spanish, asking questions, nodding his head at the responses he received.

"We'll give her the de-worming fluid now," he said. Reece grabbed the cow by the nostrils and I stared at a large pink tongue and massive teeth. He inserted a long tube attached to what looked like the nozzle of a gas pump down the cow's throat. One quick pull of the trigger and the fluid was coursing into the cow.

"That's it," Reece said. "She's good to go."

The cow brayed loudly, but seemed to have a short memory as she ambled out of the corral, following the farmer placidly.

"You can hang around all you like," Reece went on jokingly. "We can always use another set of hands. I'll let you give it a try if you want."

"Thanks for the offer," I said. "But I've got to get back." Just saying it made me remember the tension I would face when I confronted Fletcher again.

The idea of staying to help, of getting dirty and smelly around the animals and this easy group of farmers and cowboys appealed. But I had a mission to do, like it or not. For a few minutes, my mind had been on something other than murder and old romances and interrogations.

I didn't want to think about the anger that had flared so rapidly with Fletcher. Worse, I wanted to avoid thinking about the fear that had come on so unexpectedly. I had cringed. Sure, Fletcher was a womanizer. That I was convinced of, but there wasn't any reason to think he would ever harm me physically. Why had I flinched?

The pile of emotional crap I had to wade through was too high and I didn't have the time or desire to start swimming. Clearly, I had mental wounds that needed healing and Bosnia was at the heart of them. Would Fletcher think I was running away from that too?

I jumped down from the railing. "Thanks for letting me watch," I said.

"No problem," Reece said. "But hey, can I ask you something?" Without waiting for a response, he turned to the crowd and said something in Spanish. They all nodded their heads and responded amicably. The men who had been perched on the fence climbed down and many lit up hand-rolled cigarettes.

"I told them I needed a break," Reece said. He leapt down from the corral rungs and followed me as I walked away from the pen.

"I wanted to ask you if it was true one of those Larsons is dead." He leaned in conspiratorially, a smirk on his face.

On this side of the camp, Reece wouldn't have seen the body. If he had, I hoped he would have realized the inappropriateness of the question. Evidently, I didn't have to verbalize that I disapproved of the inquiry.

"Don't bite my head off," he said, holding his palms up to me. "I just heard, that's all. Is it true?"

"Did you know them?"

"Everybody knows the Larsons out here," he said. "Which one was murdered?"

"What do you mean, everybody knows them?" I asked, mentally noting that he not only knew that someone was dead. He'd known they were murdered.

Reece peered at me with a smirk for a second. "You're

interrogating me, aren't you?"

We stood that way for a long moment, staring at each other and wondering if we knew what the other was thinking.

"It was Bobby," I said and waited to see what, if any, reaction he would give me. His eyes wandered away from my face.

"Huh, Bobby" he said, not showing any disappointment or surprise.

"What did you mean, everybody knows them?"

"The game," he said. He pulled a rag out of his pocket and wiped grime off his hands. When he saw that his words hadn't registered with me he went on. "The poker game. No one's told you?"

"Why don't you tell me?"

"Not much else to do out here. We play Texas Hold'em. The Larsons ran the game. Sure made the nights go faster, I can tell you that. You ever play?"

I shook my head no. "I thought only Bobby stayed up here this weekend. Reggie came up with us from the base camp today."

Reece shrugged then scanned the crowd of farmers and ranchers. The Hondurans were crushing out finished cigarettes, and some began to climb back onto the corral rungs. Reece looked at the activity as if he wanted to get back to the animals, but he had more to say.

"Evening comes pretty quick up here. When the sun goes down, the work stops and sometimes the nights feel very long. Most every night for the last week, we've been playing poker. The Larsons were kind of hosting the game. Getting more people to play, making sure things were honest and friendly."

The soldiers on this mission were under General Order Number One, which prohibited drinking, sex with locals and gambling. It was a pretty standard order imposed on soldiers when they were sent to remote regions of the world. Drinking, sex and gambling tend to be reasons for conflict. Ordering soldiers to avoid such activity had proven to help maintain good order and discipline. If the Larsons were organizing poker games, they were in violation of the order and could be in serious trouble. I wondered how much Dodd knew about the activity. As the senior leaders, both he and Allen could suffer consequences for the violation.

"They were making money at it?" I asked.

Reece, shrugged. "I never paid them anything. It was just a social thing. We play for money, but the Larsons weren't charging a fee, just kind of being the hosts, I guess."

The farmers watched us, probably wondering when the doctor would be coming back. Reece took a couple of steps toward the corral, restless to return to his work.

"Ask any one of the guys. They all played."

"You're part of the medical unit aren't you?"

"Yeah. So?"

"What's your name?

"Reece, Jeremy, Captain, one each," he said, with a flirtatious smile and wink.

"Master Sergeant Harper. Lauren Harper.

"Well, it was good to meet you, Master Sergeant Harper."

"You too, and thanks for the information."

Reece tossed a casual wave at me and climbed back onto the corral, reaching out for the horse next in line.

The only thing I knew about poker was that the pots grew very large, very fast, which meant that someone won big and many more lost. Since the games were large and involved soldiers from the medical unit, our pool of potential suspects had swelled significantly. Not to mention that anyone playing the game could be brought up on charges for illegal gambling while on duty. Reece seemed casual about it, but I'd bet Dodd and the rest of the engineers understood that word of a nightly poker game could spell trouble for them.

Thunder rumbled in the distance and I felt a few drops of rain plunk down on top of my boonie cap. Seconds later, the steady beat of rain drummed down. I shoved my hands in the pocket of my rain jacket and shivered, despite the humidity.

Chapter 14

Bobby had fought his attacker and had been buried alive in wet cement. Someone or maybe more than one, had poured that cement on him, sealing him in a suffocating tomb and then, after committing that horror, had expertly smoothed the floor around the body. Whoever had done that had a deep sadistic streak, maybe even found humor in the cruel and twisted method of the murder. Interviewing a long list of people who could all potentially be that sick twisted person, wasn't on the top of my list of things I wanted to do, but it had to be done. I'd messed about long enough. I had a mission and it was about damn time I settled down and got it done. Fletcher and I had a killer to find.

When I ducked through the tent flap, Fletcher ignored me and continued typing. I took off my jacket, draped it over the back of the chair and sat down in front of him. He continued to ignore me.

"Did you interview, Dodd while he was here?" I asked.

He paused in his typing for just a second, then continued, while he talked. "I didn't think it prudent to wait. I'm typing up my notes now." he said.

His words were clipped, the anger still evident. I ignored that.

"Learn anything interesting?"

He stopped typing and shot a look at me that glared his unwillingness to forget about our argument. In the next moment, he thought better of that and took a deep breath, scrubbed his face and bald head with his hands.

"No. Hell, I don't know," he said with a sigh. "He gave me the guard duty list. Bobby Larson, Porter, Judd, Hank Gunderson and Lieutenant Allen. Those were the five left here over the weekend. Then he just went on and on about how the Larsons are good soldiers. Said most of these people have been together in the unit for years, that they're a tight-knit group. He said they do a lot of barbequing and socializing outside their weekend meetings." Fletcher shook his head in frustration. "They sound like a perfect, happy family."

"But you don't believe that," I said.

"No, I don't believe that." He shrugged and went back to typing, his fingers hitting the keys a little harder.

"Did he tell you about the poker games?"

Fletcher stopped and gave me a quizzical look. "No. Should he have?"

I told him what I had learned from Reece. "I didn't get many details, but he said everyone played, money won and lost. He said poker was the only social thing going on around here in the evenings."

"Then we need to check that out," Fletcher said.

"It's interesting that Dodd didn't bring it up."

"Yes, very interesting."

We locked eyes for a long moment.

"Fletcher, I need to …," I started.

"You don't need to apologize, Lauren," he said, holding up a hand to stop me, as if he had the right to be benevolent about it. I could have let that piss me off a little, but I didn't.

"I wasn't going to."

"Oh." His eyebrows went up and his mouth formed a perfect "O," as a bit of moisture broke out on his forehead. I wanted to enjoy his discomfort for a moment, but that would have been petty.

"Santos told you about Bosnia, right?"

Fletcher nodded, then tilted back in his chair and listened.

"Well, Santos and Ramsey almost arrested the wrong person. Me. All I kept thinking about when they targeted me was that they were allowing the real murderer to get away with it. Ever since then, the idea of that, of a killer going free, well it just doesn't sit right with me. I have no idea how to go about this, but I want—no, I need to figure out who did this to Larson. And I don't want to let the personal crap between us get in the way of that. It's too important."

Fletcher let his chair plop down and regarded me for a minute. "Okay. I get that."

"So…truce?"

"Truce," he said, as he stretched his mouth into a grim smile then stood up slowly. From the look in his eye, I was pretty sure he was going to hug me. I didn't want that. My hands were going up, to shove him away if I had to, but shouting from outside the tent drew both of our attentions.

Hank was running down the road, yelling for help.

"Top, TOP!" he yelled. "You gotta come! He's about to drive off the cliff! He's gonna do it, Top."

Soldiers wandered out to the road, wondering what the commotion was. It was hard to miss Hank's mad dash into the area, his face red from running and screaming. Fletcher and I watched through the mesh walls of our office as Dodd came out and listened to Hank's near hysterical explanation.

"I thought he'd be sleeping from that shot the doctor gave him, but he was gone!"

I couldn't make out what Dodd said, but whatever it was only seemed to make Hank more frustrated.

"But he's out there on the cliff, Top. He's gonna drive over it, I'm telling you. He's gonna drive over."

Hank was practically wailing now, pointing in the general direction from where he had come.

Fletcher and I exchanged looks, then took off at a trot toward Hank.

"Where?" Fletcher asked.

Hank took a moment to look from Fletcher to Dodd in indecision. While Dodd seemed to want more information before he made a move, Fletcher wanted action.

"Just show me where."

"Come on." Before the words were out of his mouth, Hank took off in his loping gate, up the small hill, toward the village, then took a right and headed, first down the main road, then down a narrow foot path. The curious followed. I noticed Porter and Judd were among those that wanted to see what was going on. Lieutenant Allen, though separated from the main body of followers, came along as well.

Two village men stood on the foot path and, as we approached, anxiously waved us in the direction we were headed. They trotted alongside Hank, pointing and explaining as we made our progress down the path.

It was easy to recognize that a Humvee had been driven in this direction. Deep mud tracks from the fat tires marred the grassy expanse. The ground, soft and muddy from the rain. You didn't need to be an expert tracker to know the vehicle had been moving quickly. Fast enough to slip and slide through the saturated earth, leaving huge muddy mounds of dirt in its path.

The metallic rumble of an idling Humvee grew louder as we approached, the engine noise revving in a steady pulse as someone pushed the gas pedal over and over.

The entire gang of us dashed through the edge of the jungle, then through waist- high shrubbery, a clear path of the Humvee in front of us. Finally we came to a clearing and stopped several meters away from the edge of a cliff. To our left, the vehicle sat, its nose pointing toward the chasm. Someone was sitting in the Humvee looking straight ahead.

"Everybody stay back a ways now," Fletcher said. After a brief hesitation, he slowly walked toward the vehicle.

"Wait a minute here, Chief," Dodd said. "You don't even know him. Maybe I should go talk to him."

Fletcher hesitated, then agreed. "Okay, but don't rush it. Take your time. And don't startle him." Dodd made his way around the back of the vehicle, slowly, quietly, his eyes on the occupant of the vehicle. He approached the driver's side.

"He should be talking to him, not sneaking up like that," Fletcher said to me in alarm. I agreed. It was a bad idea. Our opinions were confirmed when Reggie revved the engine loudly, then yelled at Dodd.

"Don't you come near me, Dodd. You stay away!"

"Alright, Bob..., ah, Reggie. It's alright. No one's gonna hurt you," Dodd said.

"I'm Reggie. I'm Reggie, god damn it! Bobby's dead!" he wailed.

"I know, I know. I'm sorry. I just sometimes get your names confused." He continued talking, but it was impossible to hear him over the engine noise and the distance. He bent down to have a better look inside the vehicle, his hands out is if he were trying to ease a wild animal.

"Can you hear him?" Fletcher asked.

I shook my head no. Fletcher, with a glance at me, eased closer to them. I didn't know if he was trying to sneak up on them or just trying to get close enough to hear. Whatever the reason, Reggie saw the movement and reacted badly.

"You stay back! You all better stay back," he hollered.

Everyone froze. I looked to my front where the cliff dropped off. Lush jungle foliage surrounded us. Exotic-sounding birds sang in the tress and insects buzzed around our heads. A few fat rain drops struck my face and I cursed that the weather was going to start up again. In seconds, the drumming of rain on top of my head increased in pace and obliterated any hope of hearing what was going on inside the vehicle.

I didn't have any idea how far down that drop would be. Part of me wanted to see, but part of me didn't. My head swam with the notion of sailing off that edge inside a vehicle. I realized I was panting; my heart raced from the tension in the air.

Dodd continued to talk to Reggie. I couldn't hear the words, but his voice sounded soothing, calm. Reggie sobbed, the weight of his sorrow shaking his shoulders and echoing off the hillside around us.

Then everything changed. "No!" Reggie screamed. "There's nothing you can say to fix it! Nothing! He's gone and you'll be sorry when I'm gone too!"

The metallic spring of the released hand-break echoed across the chasm. The engine roared, drowning out Dodd's scream to stop. Mud shot up behind the vehicle as the tires fought for purchase. Fletcher sprinted toward the truck but his effort was useless.

The Humvee went straight ahead, then tilted forward as it tipped off the edge of the cliff and disappeared. For several seconds there was silence. We all stood there, slightly dazed and open-mouthed, the rain hitting the top of my head sending rhythmic jolts to my thoughts. Dodd and a couple others raced to the edge to look over. Then a horrendous crash, a deafening roar, ushered up from the chasm and seemed to ricochet around the mountain tops. The echoes went on for several seconds as if the vehicle had tumbled several times, or maybe it was just the sound reverberating over and again.

"Holy shit," someone said. I covered my face with my hands and stifled a sob, my entire body tensed, waiting to hear the whoosh of an explosion, but it never came. Someone put their hand on my shoulder and I nearly jumped out of my skin, breathless and a little frantic.

"Are you okay?" Fletcher asked.

I wanted to roll my eyes at him, and ask how anyone could be okay after witnessing what had just happened, but I nodded my head with the answer he wanted and looked toward the cliff where everyone peered.

One of the village men pointed below and said something excitedly in Spanish. Then, Dodd and the rest of the men leaned over, staring.

"Oh, good lord!" Dodd said. "He's moving!"

Chapter 15

He couldn't have survived that," Fletcher said, his eyes wide. After a brief hesitation, he dashed to have a look for himself.

Despite my desire to see what was going on, I was a little slower to approach. I have what I like to think of as a healthy fear of heights. I do not enjoy looking over the edge of things. Sheer drops, cliffs, tall buildings and bridges, the long drops make my stomach do funny things and my head swim. After watching that truck sail over the edge, the last thing I wanted to see was the results.

I eased my way around to the outside of the crowd. I didn't want anyone near me when I looked over, anyone who could mistakenly stumble, or push me accidentally, or on purpose, over the edge. That was all part of that healthy fear I had. Before I looked over, we all heard the moan. A deep, rumbling noise, illustrating pain and fear. The moan echoed and rolled up to us eerily amplified. Goose bumps sprang up on my skin and I froze in place.

"Oh my god," Hank whispered near me. "He don't even sound human."

Allen spun away from the cliff shaking his head and cursing. "Holy Christ!" he bellowed. "What the fuck are we supposed to do now? What do we do now!?"

Up to then, Allen had stayed on the sidelines, watching and

observing and taking as little responsibility for the things going on around him as possible. To hear him say "we" as if he were part of some team that had to deal with the situation, surprised me. It felt out of character. I wondered what made him claim a sudden investment in the situation.

He paced and cursed under his breath for a time then glanced up and froze. I followed the direction of his stare and realized he was looking at Dodd. Dodd's body language was like a coiled animal ready to strike. He glared at Allen. The two of them locked eyes for a long moment. Allen put his hands back in his pockets as if to restrain himself and Dodd refocused his attention back down the hill.

Curious, I thought. Was that a First Sergeant attempting to keep his lieutenant in line, or something else?

I glanced at Fletcher who leaned over the edge of the cliff, looking left and right, maybe trying to assess how they could get down there.

He said something to Porter and Judd that I couldn't hear, but they were both shaking their heads in the negative. I still hadn't seen for myself what we were dealing with and like it or not, I had to look.

I edged closer to the cliff, my heart thundering in my chest. Another moan, this time turning into a high pitched shuddering wail, didn't help to ease the goose bumps already dotting my arms. From the nervous murmuring I heard around me, everyone on the cliff seemed affected by the precariousness of the situation.

I made it to the edge and slowly leaned my body forward to peer over the drop. The grassy cliff we were standing on gave way to dirt, rock and sand as if the front of the hillside had simply given way. The continuing rain sloshed down the hillside, bringing mud and rock with it, and leaving the feeling that, at any moment, the very ground I was standing on could give way and send me and all of the observers sliding down into the chasm.

The vehicle wasn't anywhere near as far down as I expected. That explained how easily his moaning rose to us. The canvas-topped Humvee rested upside down just over a hundred feet down, but that seemed far enough to have killed the man. The steel roll bars on the truck had provided the protection needed to save Reggie's life. Reggie lay underneath the vehicle, halfway out of the driver's side, just behind the hood of the truck, his face to the ground. I watched as he tried to push himself out from under the truck but his arms gave out and he collapsed there. Another moan rose up from below and bounced around the hillside.

If he had taken a running start from further away and built up some speed, the truck would have sailed further and landed hundreds, maybe thousands of feet below. As it was, his hesitation and his last moments spent staring over the cliff had cost him the fatal dive he attempted. I wondered how aware he was of his situation, if he regretted going forward or regretted more that he had botched the task.

Allen, though under more control, paced back and forth behind the crowd. He mumbled the same question over and over again. "What are we going to do? What the fuck are we going to do now?"

The crowd seemed torn between looking over the edge at the gruesome wreckage or watching the near breakdown of their Lieutenant. Everyone directed nervous glances in Allen's direction. To my untrained eyes, his movements and frantic mumblings seemed slightly psychotic as if he had missed taking his medications. He was asking questions to the air but appeared to answer them as well.

Unlike everyone else, whose gaze seemed drawn to the lunatic murmurings, Fletcher ignored the display and grabbed a couple of the men gawking at the wreckage.

"Double time over to medical and tell them what's going on here," he ordered. "Be sure to tell them it could be over 100 feet straight down. Get moving!" The soldiers nodded their heads and took off in a sprint.

The two local men who had led us to the site were having a lively discussion, pointing and gesturing at the cliff and the tree line behind us.

"Anyone here speak Spanish?" I asked.

One of the soldiers stepped forward and apparently had been listening in already.

"They're saying the cliff is weak. This ground has been crumbling away for some time now and with the rain, they expect more to give way. The old guy is saying it's not safe for all of us to be standing here."

As if to demonstrate their distrust of the ground, the two men backed further away from the cliff, gesturing at the rest of us to follow their lead.

I didn't need to be convinced. I backed away and thought that if the ground gave way beneath me, it would only confirm everything I had always feared about cliffs and heights and all things that had to do with shear drops. My heart rate shot up and I barely stifled the need to scream like a child and run for the trees. After getting a few feet away from the edge, however, I began to feel a little better. Still my fear included watching other people look over edges and that's exactly what everyone was doing, what everyone continued to do despite the warning to back off.

"Alright, everyone back up," I said in a voice that seemed a few octaves higher than normal. I cleared my throat and tried to summon up my command voice. It was hard to do when my knees felt so rubbery.

"Alright, all of you. Back up!" I said. "Now!"

My words rang with authority. Some of the men shot angry glances at me, but I stood up straight and motioned for them to back up. There are advantages to having several chevrons on your collar. People tend to do what you say.

"We don't want any of you joining him down there," I said. "Now back up!" The more I went at it, the more confidence I felt, and seeing fewer people peering over the precipice helped to slow my heart rate. Some grumbles continued, peppered amongst the murderous looks from Porter and Judd, but the crowd began to back away from the edge.

Fletcher and Dodd, the guys in charge, stayed where they were. Someone had to keep a watch out and try to come up with some options.

For several minutes, we stood around like that, Fletcher checking his watch, wondering how long it would take the medical team to arrive. Dodd pacing back and forth and looking down below. Then, as if to confirm the danger, a sizeable chuck of earth gave way under Dodd. At least a foot of ground simply began to slide away under his feet. He backpedaled but wasn't quick enough. He went down on his butt with a startled yell and clawed the ground to prevent a fatal slide down the hill.

It was confirmation of everything I fear. The ground gives way. The earth moves. To lean over a cliff was stupid. Heights were dangerous and there was no value in going near them.

Dodd continued to slip over the edge. Both arms, muscles stretched taunt, were flung behind him, his fingers digging in to prevent the slide. His legs kicked into air as he tried to move back from the danger.

The earth under Fletcher began to give way as well and I watched in horror as he started to lose balance. He tottered out of control for an agonizing second, then he crouched and leaped, kicking his legs behind him to land on his belly. He stretched out and, grabbed Dodd by the back of his collar, halting them both.

Several soldiers in the crowd rushed to help, but more weight on the cliff would only spell more trouble.

"Stop!" I yelled. "Don't make it worse than it is. He's got him. They're okay." I said, breathless from the near disaster.

Fletcher crawled backwards and pulled Dodd as he went, each of them mumbling expressions of relief. When they felt safe again, they stood slowly and wiped dirt and mud from themselves.

"My lord, that was close," Dodd said.

Fletcher, bent at the waist, hands braced on his knees, and nodded his head. "Yeah, no kidding."

"Thank you."

Fletcher flapped his hand at Dodd, shaking his head, still trying to catch his breath. "Rope," he said. "I think we need some rope."

As if in answer to his request, a Humvee carrying a handful of people from the medical unit came through the forest following the tracks Reggie's vehicle had used. Soldiers piled out of the truck with medical bags and equipment. One glance at them was enough to confirm what I had feared. We weren't prepared to deal with this disaster.

Two soldiers had small coils of hemp rope, probably meant for bracing tents, not designed for rock climbing. No way would that rope be enough to get anyone down to the crash site, let alone bring the victim up. Dr. Fordham, with her medical bag, her blonde ponytail swinging back and forth, led the pack of medics and emergency techs. Fletcher held his hands up to slow the group.

"You've got to be careful, or the ground will give way," Fletcher said. "I almost went over myself."

She slowed her pace, shaking her head. "We don't have the equipment or the skills to get down there. We're not equipped for rescue operations."

I turned to the soldier who had done the translation before. Indicating the villagers, I said, "Ask them if they know a way down."

I didn't need translation to understand the negative head shaking. The two men put the palms of their hands up as if to say that none of us should expect them to risk their necks going down there. I didn't blame them.

Fordham and her medics approached the cliff slowly and cautiously. They took a quick look over, then backed away and discussed the options amongst themselves.

By this time Fletcher had had enough of Allen's frantic pacing. The lieutenant's mumbling, mixed with the occasional moan echoing up from Reggie's precarious position, kept everyone on edge. He couldn't do anything about Reggie at this point, but he could do something about Allen.

Fletcher grabbed Allen by the arm and led him roughly away from the crowd to the edge of the clearing. I was pretty sure Fletcher would tell the junior officer that he had better settle down and try to help figure out what to do next. At least that's the conversation I hoped Fletcher was having with Allen. But Allen stared at Fletcher with a vague, slack-jawed expression. I had little faith that anything was getting through.

The exchange attracted the attention of Judd and Porter who inched closer to Fletcher and Allen, attempting to hear the conversation. I figured having those two lurk around, wouldn't help. I stepped into their path to block their progress.

"Someone's going to have to climb down there," I said. They chuckled thinly, and narrowed their eyes at me.

"Why should we risk our necks to save that asshole?" Porter asked. Judd nodded his head in agreement.

"We should stand around and listen to him die?"

"It would serve him right," Judd said. "Selfish bastard doesn't deserve to be rescued after what he did."

I let that comment hang in the air for a long moment and watched him twitch uncomfortably. His gaze eventually slid away from me, his lips pressed together as if forcing himself to keep quiet.

"What do you mean, after what he did?"

Judd opened his mouth, but Porter cut him off. "Judd's just talking about the fact that the man drove himself off that cliff, for Christ sake. Now, we got to risk our necks to rescue him. Not only that, but we'll have a mountain of paperwork to do for the report of survey on that fucking vehicle. There ain't no end to this shit."

Porter rolled his eyes dramatically to emphasize how easy it should be for me to understand their attitudes. A report of survey was not a fun piece of Army business. It involved hours of paperwork, interviews and investigations to determine how expensive pieces of equipment were lost or damaged. The experience is never pleasant. It was interesting that the inconvenience of paperwork rose to the top of Porter's priorities.

"I thought you said Larson was a friend of yours."

"He is. That don't mean I'm willing to jump off a cliff for him."

Porter took out a pack of gum and offered me a piece, squinting at me. I shook my head at the offer and cocked my head at him curiously.

He was a liar and he was forcing Judd to lie. Whatever they had to hide, they were both in on it or protecting each other.

Dodd had claimed the unit was tight-knit, like a family. If that were the case, rescuing their family member would be a top priority. Instead they all seemed to hoard a pile of secrets, banding together for no reason other than to obscure the truth.

I ruminated on all of that, when I glanced at Fletcher and Allen and saw movement in the jungle behind them. A second later, a well-armed, fully camouflaged soldier appeared. The rain helped to obscure him, but it was plain that we were only seeing him because he had decided he wanted to be seen. He held an automatic weapon, and his finger rested over the trigger guard as he swung the barrel left and right. Bandoliers of ammunition crisscrossed his chest.

Slowly, one by one, similarly armed and ready commandos appeared just behind Fletcher and Allen. One moment it was only jungle. The next, a small army had silently emerged from the trees like a photograph in a basin of film developer.

My heart rate picked up. No one said a word. Fletcher's hands slowly floated up, waist high, palms out and fingers spread in the universal sign to display he was unarmed. We all copied his movement.

For long moments we stood staring at each other, my group on the hillside, wondering who the intruders were who stealthily appeared out of nowhere. They weren't wearing American uniforms and I didn't see any patches, names or even ranks that might identify them. It felt as if a collective breath were being held, a pregnant moment of hesitation as we all waited to see if what our eyes told us was true. Did men just appear out of the forest?

I glanced behind myself and realized that the band of warriors surrounding us were blocking our only exit away from the sharp abyss to our rear. The engineers, the villagers, we all began to shift around nervously, wondering what, if anything we should do or say.

One of the commandos stepped forward cautiously, divorcing

himself from the camouflage of the forest. He was taller and broader than the rest, powerful in build, his chest and shoulders thick and beefy. His low boonie cap shielded his eyes. Stripes of black camouflage paint slashed across his face. He wore his automatic rifle slung high across his wide chest. He crouched slightly, as if ready to spring, and despite his size, made me think a sudden movement from any of us would result in an instant, lethal response. He looked menacing, dangerous, like violence ready to be unleashed.

His gaze slowly swept the crowd sliding past me. For a moment, I felt relieved to be ignored, invisible, and I relaxed. Suddenly, his gaze snapped back to me, his body going taut.

He stood slowly erect and smiled, his teeth flashed white in the darkness of his war paint. "Well, hello luv," he said.

Chapter 16

Harry?"

"At your service," he said, with a slight bow and a grin.

My heart rate, already tripping along nervously, hiccupped a bit and went right on racing, now for a different reason.

"What are you doing here?"

"I was supposed to be on bloody holiday, but my date canceled and I figured, what the hell. If I can't lay on a beach on the Italian coast, I might as well go to the jungle and run around with this lot." He indicated the killing force arrayed along the jungle behind him as his eyes crinkled to slits by the smile playing on his slightly blistered lips.

He was just steps away from me now. I had somehow moved closer to him and he to me as we chatted, the gentle rain the only thing separating us. Every inch of me wanted to touch him, to run my fingers over the cleft in his chin and the square hard edge of his jaw. His soaking wet boonie cap slanted down over his green eyes. I felt them gently sweep over my face appraisingly. His smile dazzled me, starkly white against the paint on his plump and peeling lips. Then I noticed he'd had his tooth capped, the one that had been broken when I met him in Bosnia. I'd thought his damaged tooth added to his charm but the repaired appearance made him all the more handsome. I heard myself say his name again in a sigh and felt my face flush brightly. I knew I must look star struck, which was exactly how I felt.

He leaned down and kissed me on one cheek and then the other. He stood back and looked at me.

"Now I've done it. I've left traces," he said with a chuckle. He licked his thumb and rubbed at my cheeks where some of his camouflage paint had come off. As he gently cradled my chin in his palm, his eyes bored into mine. "It's good to see you, Lauren," he said in a whisper. He leaned in again and sniffed the air around me. "I've missed the sweet smell of you."

The men standing behind him began to chuckle, locker room mumblings and quiet catcalls leaking in our direction. I let out my breath and tried to pretend the earth hadn't moved under my feet.

"Ah, Master Sergeant Harper," Fletcher interrupted with a fake clearing of his throat. "Do you care to make introductions?"

I didn't care to. I didn't want to take my eyes off Harry, but I also didn't want to be the center of everyone's attention.

I took a step away from Harry and tried to clear the buzz in my head. "Chief Fletcher Mayes, this is Sergeant Major Harry Fogg," I said, with halfhearted gestures between the two, my eyes still locked on Harry's face.

"That's Fogg with two G's," Harry said. "Of Her Majesty's Army." He reluctantly directed his gaze at Fletcher and snapped his heels together, brought the back of his finger tips to his forehead in a brisk British salute that was somehow both respectful and mocking at the same time. After the salute he casually stuck his hand out for Fletcher to shake. The two men sized each other up in the way that men do as they silently shook hands and looked hard into each other's eyes.

"You're not just Army, are you Sergeant Fogg?" Fletcher said. "You're SAS."

Harry's eyebrow quirked up. "If I confirmed that, Chief, I'd have to kill you."

Fletcher laughed nervously, trying to assess if the big man was serious. Harry simply smiled. I noticed fingers squeezed together and a visible tightening in Fletcher's jaw. I wondered what assessments they made of each other.

Sergeant Major Harold Fogg had saved my life in more ways

than one. We had met in Bosnia and he had been my friend through some of my darkest days. To recover from all that had happened there, we were to have taken a long, leisurely vacation together starting in London where I looked forward to meeting his mother. Then we were to have flown to Milan, and after an overnight stay and some shopping, catch a train to Cinque Terra for a week or more in the quaint Italian coastal village of Monterosso. The plan was to eat plenty of seafood, drink lots of red wine, roast our bodies on the beach, hike the olive groves and as Harry put it, "properly get to know one another."

The getting to know one another part had been a source of nervousness for me, but also an acute source of longing. I hadn't seen Harry in months, not since I'd said goodbye to him from a hospital bed in Bosnia. Since then, we'd been emailing and calling each other almost daily prior to my leaving Germany. Still, I hadn't realized just how much I missed him, how much I wanted to see him until he pointed that cocky grin in my direction. I had forgotten how good the deep rumble of his voice sounded, how much I liked the way he looked down at me, how his presence made me feel safe.

My orders to Honduras had put a screeching halt to our vacation dreams. I had clung to the hope that we could still do all we had planned when I returned from my unexpected Central American mission. After the excruciatingly long flight from Germany to Tegucigalpa, by way of Atlanta and Mexico City, followed by a two-hour long bus ride to Soto Cano air base and days at the dry and dusty base camp, all of my dreamy vacation images had faded away.

To look at Harry now was a total and pleasant shock I felt in the curling of my toes.

Harry finished his introductions to Fletcher. "And this handsome devil is Sergeant Jesus Gutierrez." Harry expertly rolled his Rs as he indicated a grizzly, dark brown little man who stood next to him. Gutierrez stepped forward, rendered a salute that mirrored Harry's, then snapped to parade rest, his feet shoulder-width apart, one arm bent behind him, the other hand gently resting on the sleek-looking weapon securely strapped across his chest.

A shuddering moan followed by a call for help put an abrupt end to our introductions.

"I can't move my legs," Reggie wailed from far below. I bit back on the anger that suddenly flashed in my head and glanced around at the crowd to see if anyone else felt the same way. There were head shakes and hands thrown up in frustration.

"God damn idiot," Dodd mumbled.

"That's what brought us," Harry said. "We were on patrol Northeast of here when we heard a right, bloody bang up. We had to come see for ourselves. How'd he get down there then?"

I opened my mouth to speak but realized it was too complicated to answer in full. Fletcher didn't hesitate to fill the void.

"Drove off the cliff. Long story," he concluded.

"Right. How far down?"

"'Bout a hundred, hundred fifty feet."

"How many down there?"

"Just one."

"Well then," Harry said. "Right. We'll just have a look then."

Harry strode forward, then stopped. He motioned for Gutierrez to approach. They consulted with each other, then swung their weapons around to rest on their backs, and dropped to their bellies to low-crawl. They slithered forward by digging and pulling with elbows and knees to made quick work of the yardage.

It was apparent the two men had established an easy partnership. Their heads rotated back and forth in synch as they evaluated the situation. They passed a small set of binoculars back and forth as they checked the eroding hillside and focused on Reggie, who still moaned from his dangerous position on the large outcropping below the cliff. They discussed, made decisions and began a low-crawl back in my direction.

I watched them and thought, I didn't know Harry could speak Spanish. And, look how much larger he is compared to Gutierrez.

And, how can I get him alone for at least long enough to kiss him, to really kiss him? And, how can I concentrate on all of this crap going on around us with Harry so near me?

By the time all of this flashed through my head, Harry stood in front of me again. We stared at each other for a long moment. He took a deep breath in, then dragging his gaze away, issued orders.

He traveled with a large squad-sized element, at least a dozen men or more. They quickly organized the equipment they would need, rappelling harnesses, clamps and lengths of black nylon rope. I looked at the coils of rope they had and didn't think it would be enough to reach the injured man.

Fletcher seemed eager to point out the shortcoming. "That'll get you about halfway there," he said, his arms crossed over his chest and a scrawl on his forehead.

"It's all we'll need, mate," Harry said, and didn't stop to explain.

The medic on Harry's team consulted with Dr. Fordham. They modified a stretcher with a couple of blankets and straps to ensure Reggie would be secured before they hauled him up the hill.

By this time, more villagers had arrived to watch. Most stood around in the tree line eyeing the Honduran special forces soldiers suddenly in their midst. Bonilla and his horde cut a path through the watching group and established themselves at a point central to the action. Bonilla eyed the soldiers and mumbled to the men around him. He seemed to give instructions, and pointed in a couple of directions. A few men ambled away, as if sent on a mission but didn't want to be noticed.

I noticed, and so did the Honduran soldiers. The tension in the air between them and Bonilla's group was palpable. I wasn't sure what it was about, until I saw one of the soldiers grab a leaf from a nearby shrub. He rolled the leaf between the palms of his hands and inhaled deeply, his dark eyes scanned and scrutinized the village men who looked away discreetly. The gesture made me take a closer look at the shrubbery around us. All along the open area between the jungle and the cliff were scores of the chest-high shrubs.

I've spent my share of time in woods and jungles, but I've never been any good at learning the names of trees, or understanding the medicinal purposes of roots and plants. Hell, most times it was hard for me to tell the difference between a plant and a weed. I hadn't noticed how similar all of the shrubs were, how they grew in such straight rows, or the five points on their abundant leaves. On closer inspection, one thing was clear even to my untrained eyes. The marijuana plants were healthy and plentiful.

Bonilla and the villagers watched the soldiers and the soldiers eyed the villagers. I wondered what would happen to this private crop once all of the rescue drama was concluded.

And speaking of drama, Cordovan, followed closely by Dropic and Sergeant Mora, stepped through the foliage. Cordovan hesitated for a moment then made a straight line in my direction. A strange sense of relief settled over me. At least the reporter and photographer were problems I knew how to handle.

I anticipated that Dropic's camera wouldn't go over well with these special operations soldiers. They often got touchy about their faces plastered in the news.

As predicted, the sight of the large camera got some of the Hondurans agitated. They moved in Dropic's direction, their hands up to block his efforts to capture what was going on. Cordovan and Mora inserted themselves into the group and a lively discussion ensured. I moved closer and watched the back and forth exchange. Finally they seemed to reach some understanding. When the Hondurans walked away Cordovan wore a triumphant smile.

"What was that about?" I asked, Mora.

"Some of them do undercover work," he explained. "They don't want their faces shown. Dropic has agreed to obscure their faces in the editing process."

"And they agreed to that?"

"Cordovan can be charming when he's not being a dick," Mora's sly grin toward the reporter a sign that the men had bonded.

Cordovan slapped a hand on Mora's back and chuckled. "Such a joker, this one,"

I looked away from them for a moment to watch the progress of the rescue preparations. When I turned back around, Dropic had the camera on his shoulder and Cordovan pointed a hand held microphone in my face. Dropic, his feet spread wide, his arms hugged close to his body to steady his shot, nodded his head at Cordovan to start. The red tally light on the camera went on immediately and I knew the tape rolled. I glanced at Mora whose smile had turned into an angry glare.

"Can you tell me what's going on here?" Cordovan asked me.

I didn't want to do an interview. Didn't want to talk about the fact that one of the soldiers on this mission had just driven a vehicle off a cliff in an attempted suicide, but the camera would capture me refusing the interview and that looked just as bad as saying the wrong thing. I dredged up my on-camera interview appearance, relaxed my facial muscles, parted my lips, raised my eyebrows a bit to appear interested and willing to be informative.

Inside, I seethed.

"We are in the process of rescuing a soldier who is injured and trapped on a ledge about one hundred fifty feet below us. Honduran soldiers and our American medical team are working cooperatively to conduct the rescue," I said.

I clasped my hands behind my back until I was white knuckled and looked at Cordovan.

"How did the soldier get down there?"

"The soldier went over the cliff in an American military vehicle, we call a Humvee."

"He went over the cliff. And just how did that happen?"

"A full investigation of the accident will be conducted. Right now we are concentrating on bringing him up from the ledge and making sure his injuries are treated."

Cordovan wasn't happy with that answer.

"Isn't it true that he drove off the cliff? That he attempted to commit suicide?"

"It's too soon to tell how it happened. Rest assured we will conduct a full investigation to discover the cause of the incident so that we can prevent such accidents from happening in the future."

"Ah, cut it," Cordovan said. The tally light went off. Dropic pulled the camera away from his face and stared at me darkly. He allowed Cordovan to express their combined displeasure with my performance.

"You know exactly how this accident happened," Cordovan said, putting little air quotes around the word accident.

I smiled and responded in a quiet but firm voice. "You ever stick a fucking camera in my face again without asking my permission first and I'll have your ass out of this village if I have to walk you back to Soto Cano through the fucking mud myself. Do we understand each other?"

He sputtered for a moment." You can't do that!"

"Try me. You are here at the courtesy of the U.S. Army. You abuse that privilege again and you are done."

"I'm just trying to get the truth."

The one thing I knew for sure, was this news team was after something sensational. I didn't know what that something was and that was bothersome. Now, they not only had a murder to talk about, they had an attempted suicide. Add that to whatever their intended story was and this whole thing was turning into a cauldron of excrement.

"That was just plain rude, Cordovan. You want an interview? All you gotta do is ask for one. You want to shoot some footage of this team effort to save the life of a man in a perilous situation? I don't have a problem with that. But you go out of your way to try to put me on the spot in the hopes of making the Army look bad, and you'll find yourself off this mountain."

"Harper, I don't have to try to make this look bad. It couldn't get much worse and you know that." He snapped off a leaf from a nearby shrub, sniffed it and raised an eyebrow at me.

"You're right. It's a fucking mess," I said. "But when you use ambush tactics, all you'll ever get from me is the canned party line. You want a real interview about this, you can have it. Just not right now and not on your terms only. I get to play a role in deciding when and where."

"I'm only trying to do my job," he said.

Photographers and reporters always said the same thing. I'm just trying to do my job. Problem was, doing the job sometimes meant shooting video with little explanation of what was really happening, telling a complicated story in 60 seconds or less, and oh-by-the-way, earning brownie points for displaying someone else's mistakes in a truly sensational way. Just doing a job could be destructive.

"And you're proud of that job aren't you?"

Cordovan shook his head and chuckled, flashing his teeth. "A man is buried in cement. Another drives off a cliff. Now, here are Honduran special troops who are not known for soft hands, especially when it comes to a large crop of marijuana. If you think you can keep me tied to this nice story about the Army helping poor villagers, you are mistaken."

I sighed. It's usually better to shut up when you know you're losing.

"Sergeant Mora, please help Mr. Cordovan and Mr. Dropic get the video they need. This rescue operation is dangerous and must be done quickly. They are to get what they need without interfering with the operation in any way. When the injured man is brought up, they cannot shoot his face. His identity is protected by law ..."

"Yes, yes, we are aware of the law," the reporter said.

"They are to let us know who they want to interview. We will ask permission before they roll tape." I waited while Cordovan considered the demand.

"Of course," he said with a slight bow.

"If they interfere, if they attempt to interview any American or Honduran military member without asking permission, I will revoke their privilege to be here and they will be escorted off this mountain."

"Yes, Sergeant," Mora said.

"Is that understood Mr. Cordovan?"

"Yes. Understood."

"And when they are finished here, you can take them back to the construction site. As long as they don't shoot the body, they can get video of that area. I hope to have a statement about that for them later this afternoon."

Cordovan raised an eyebrow at me. "That's a different tune than you played earlier today."

"No, it's the same tune. Just played when I'm ready."

He chuckled. "And one more thing. You won't attempt to take my video or prevent me from telling this story in the way in which I choose?"

"It's your journalistic integrity at stake, Cordovan. By the way, Sergeant Mora is a journalist too. He's writing a print story. For which paper was it again, Mora?"

The sergeant cleared his throat. "Ah, the Tribune."

I smiled. "Yes, the Tribune. That's a major paper isn't it?" I asked, even though I knew the answer. "It might be interesting, based on the facts mind you, what kind of stories you both tell."

Cordovan raised an eyebrow at Mora who kept his mouth shut; a sly grin played at corner of his mouth.

"I understand your terms, Miss Harper, and I agree." Cordovan bowed again, this time a little deeper.

"It's Master Sergeant Harper, Mr. Cordovan. I worked too long for these stripes to lose them to you."

He flashed his white teeth and nodded. "If nothing else, Sergeant Harper," he said, emphasizing the sergeant, "I respect your style."

"Thank you. That means so much," I said, letting the sarcasm drip from my words.

He opened his mouth to say more, then realized the rescue operation was moving along and he was missing it.

"If you will excuse me," he said politely, and they trotted away, Dropic's camera on his shoulder already.

Mora started to follow them, but stopped. "Did you really mean that? He can shoot what he wants?"

"As long as it's not that body in the cement or the face of the man on the stretcher, yes. As far as interviews go, we'll see who he asks for. Their problem with getting video out still exists. It could be days before we have a way out of here. By that time, it won't be news."

Mora looked at me like he didn't agree. I scanned the scene, the marijuana plants, the quiet villagers, the special forces soldiers armed to the teeth and the complicated rescue operation, and shook my head. Who was I trying to kid? This was history making fucked-upped-ness. I decided I needed to call Colonel McCallen and tell him --or rather warn him, about what was going on here. I kind of looked forward to hearing what he would think about Harry showing up.

"Right, Lads," Harry shouted. "*Vamanos!*"

The sound of his voice put a smile back on my face. I went to watch him in action.

Chapter 17

Come along, lads. It's not like we haven't trained for this," Harry shouted. He wasn't smiling, but his energy betrayed his enthusiasm for sending men down the mountain. He switched to Spanish and Gutierrez joined him to issue commands to the men as they completed their specified tasks.

Some of the men concentrated on the correct placement and configuration of complicated anchors for each line that went down, the anchors serving as the insurance that those doing the rappelling wouldn't plummet down the cliff. Much attention was devoted to them. Others linked lengths of rope together with complex knots, carabiners and clamps. Everyone had a job to do and they all seemed to do it with little discussion. Gutierrez and Harry moved among them double checking the work. After checks and re-checks, and only about a quarter of an hour of preparation, four men were ready to head down the cliff.

The men wore thick gloves, their feet planted on the edge of the cliff, the ropes fashioned into harnesses that gripped their waists and thighs. They faced Gutierrez and Harry and nodded their readiness. Gutierrez used hand signals and verbal commands to synch their efforts and when the men acknowledged the commands, Gutierrez flashed a final hand signal. The four men pushed off. One minute they were there. The next second they had dropped away, as silent as if they had simply vanished. My breath caught in my throat as I watched them disappear. The idea of voluntarily stepping off from a great height, no matter how many safety checks were made, did not seem like a good idea to me.

Harry and Gutierrez lay on their bellies and watched. I wanted to tell Harry to stay back but that would have been silly. I was feeling a little silly.

My attention had been on so many other things since Harry arrived, I hadn't had time to let his presence sink in. I took a minute to simply watch him. To absorb the information that he was really here, just yards away from me. I had an urge to find a mirror. I looked down at my mud-splattered uniform, the deformed-looking green overshoes on my feet and the black crusty mud under my fingernails. I sighed. There wasn't anything I could do about it.

I tried to convince myself I didn't need to worry about how I looked. I hadn't been wearing a dress or even makeup when I first met him. Instead, I'd been carrying an M16, wearing a helmet and flak vest and covered head to toe in mud from a different country. It struck me then that he had never seen me in civilian clothes, hadn't yet seen me with my hair down or wearing lipstick. I am a soldier. I live to soldier. Harry had met me the way I usually am and somehow, had seen past the mud and the uniform to the woman inside and wanted her.

"What are you smiling about?" Fletcher asked me, from a position closer than I expected. I jumped a little and felt foolish.

"I, oh, was I smiling?"

"Yes. You've been doing that since he got here," Fletcher said, as he turned to look at Harry.

My face flushed. I looked down. My heart did a tap dance. I shrugged, shuffled around, kept my mouth shut. Fletcher stood there for a few long seconds, watching me squirm.

"We're wasting our time here," he said. "We should be interviewing people. Preparing our report for Santos when we call him again. And it's getting late."

The one thing I agreed with was the waning of the hour. It

wasn't threatening to get dark yet, but the thick cloud cover that had brought the rain would mean loss of light sooner rather than later. They had to get Reggie up before it got dark or the dangers of the rescue effort would multiply.

"You're not suggesting we leave, are you?" I said.

"Yes. We're not doing any good here. We have a job to do."

"Everyone we need to talk to is here. You want to drag them away to come answer your questions?"

"Yes, that's exactly what I want to do. And when did they become my questions?"

I glanced around the area. Everyone was focused on what was happening at the cliff. Everyone except for Dodd, Porter and Judd. They stood huddled together and seemed to be arguing but were keeping it quiet. Dodd talked while he poked his finger at the other two. Judd glared, while Porter talked over Dodd and pointed at the cliff. Porter's face was red, and he leaned into Dodd until they were almost nose to nose. I wondered what that was about.

Lieutenant Allen stood several paces from the group and switched his attention back and forth between Dodd and the rest, and the rescue operation. While he watched it all, wide eyed and fidgety, he chewed on his fingernails like they were lunch and dinner.

Then there was Bonilla and his group. The Honduran had is arms crossed, while he leaned against a tree and watched the rescue effort, intense, as if he didn't want to miss a thing. The men with him stayed a few feet away, whispering to each other as if they were afraid to disturb Bonilla and become the focus of his attention.

"I think we might want to see what happens when Larson comes up from that cliff alive," I said.

Fletcher started to argue with me, then stopped. He glanced around and began to see what had stirred my attention. The anxious looks from the people we wanted to question. The way they all focused on the rescue. It could have been anxiety for the man below, but I didn't think so.

Fletcher studied them all for a long moment, Dodd and his men, Allen, then Bonilla and his group.

"Larson knows something," Fletcher said.

"Yep."

"What?"

"Maybe he knows who killed his brother."

"Why would he try to kill himself then?" Fletcher said. "Why wouldn't he want to make sure the ones who did it were punished?"

"Maybe he was punishing the guilty man," I said.

Fletcher shot a look in my direction. "You think Reggie killed his own brother?"

"No, I think he thinks they meant to kill him."

Fletcher tisked me. "You watch too much television."

"Well he's at least feeling guilty. Maybe he did something someone might want to kill him for."

"Wild speculation. The only person I've questioned so far is Dodd. We don't even know if these other people have any connection to the crime at all. You're basing all of this on…"

"Observation." I counted off on my fingers. "The way they've acted, the things I've heard them say and the things I've heard Reggie say."

Fletcher gave me a look to say there was one I was forgetting.

"Okay, maybe some wild speculation," I added.

Harry motioned for Dr. Fordham to join him at the cliff. "We could use some direction over here," Harry called. "These men are only first aide trained."

Fordham took a few steps in his direction but Harry motioned that she needed to get down on the ground. She hesitated, looking down at her white lab coat. She took it off and tossed it at a solder, then gingerly lowered herself to her hands and knees. She crawled a few paces that way, but Harry wasn't satisfied.

"You need to distribute the weight, doctor. It's nothing that won't come out in the wash."

She hesitated again. "Oh, hell," she muttered, then lowered herself to the ground and low crawled like an infantryman.

"That's better," Harry encouraged.

When she reached him, he gave her the binoculars. She focused down on the group and shouted instructions to the men below while Harry translated when necessary. Fordham called for a neck brace, a hard backboard, additional straps and bandages. The Honduran soldiers strapped the supplies onto the board and lowered it all down the cliff. Fordham pantomimed how things should be done from her prone position. Eventually, she crawled backward and it looked as if they were ready to start bringing him up.

Fordham called to one of the medics to get the vehicle ready and to back it up closer to the action.

"I think we should talk to Allen right now," I said. "He's obviously freaking out a little. This might be a good time to get him to open up."

Fletcher nodded his agreement and we ambled over in Allen's direction. We came up behind and flanked him before he knew what we were doing.

"Well, you must be relieved that he's alive," Fletcher said.

Allen jumped a little, and his bloody fingernails came away from his mouth momentarily. His head whipped back and forth for a second, as he looked from Fletcher to me and back again. He took a deep breath and started to put his hands in his pockets, then thought better about that. He crossed them over his chest and cocked his hip out, trying too hard to look relaxed. He nodded his head.

"Ye…ahem. Yes. That's great."

"I wonder why he would do that," I said.

He shrugged. "You never know what someone is thinking, I guess."

When I kept looking at him, Allen filled the silence. "You never know what people will do."

"Must have been upset about his brother," Fletcher said.

"Yeah, that's probably it," Allen said.

"I bet Reggie knows who killed his brother. What do you think? You think he knows?" I asked.

"What? How should I know?"

"He might know, don't you think?" I prodded.

"I have no idea. I barely know the guy."

"You don't?" Fletcher asked. "Did you know Bobby better?"

"No. Most of the time I couldn't tell them apart."

"Maybe the killer couldn't either," I said.

"What do you mean?"

Fletcher picked up the logic. "Yeah, maybe the killer thought he was killing Reggie and he killed Bobby by mistake."

Allen shrugged as if it was too much to contemplate. His hand was half way to his mouth for more nail chewing when he caught himself and clasped his arms tighter around his chest.

"Of course, you couldn't tell them apart," Fletcher said. "You're so new to the unit. Some of these guys knew them for years though."

"I don't know," I said. "The way Bobby was killed, had to be someone who really hated the guy, right? I mean, jeeze. How sick was that? To bury a guy in cement. And he was alive at the time." I gave an exaggerated shudder to emphasize my point. Allen stared at me, his lips parted slightly, his eyes wide and unblinking. He looked like a kid listening to a horror story told around a camp fire. After a brief pause, one in which I wondered if he was breathing, he blinked a couple of times and he seemed to gather himself.

"Yeah," Fletcher said, watching Allen closely. "You're probably right. It had to be someone who knew him a long time. Someone who really hated the guy."

"But everybody liked the Larsons," Allen piped in, seemingly against his will. Fletcher and I focused on him, focused on the utterance we hadn't expected. He looked back and forth between us for a second or two, then gathered himself, shrugged, and this time his hands did go into his pockets. "They were both always nice to me."

Since most of the other men rarely spoke to the lieutenant, better treatment from the Larsons would have been an anomaly. It was always easier to have fond thoughts of the dead than to have evil ones. But Allen looked sincere, almost wistful of the friendship he claimed to have with the brothers.

"There was that fight though," Allen offered. He almost whispered it and looked around to see if anyone was watching.

"Go on," Fletcher said.

"Well, I guess Bobby was hitting on Paulson and Dr. Reece got mad."

"Staff Sergeant Paulson, from the medical unit?" I asked. The young woman I met earlier who had been crying so hard. "And Dr. Reece? Do you mean the veterinarian?"

Allen nodded.

"Why would Captain Reece get mad about Bobby flirting with Paulson?" I asked.

"Reece told me they were getting married. Him and Paulson. So when Bobby started hitting on her, he got pissed. It was at one of the poker games last week. Angela showed up with a couple of the nurses."

"Angela Paulson," Fletcher interrupted.

"Yeah, she's a dental hygienist. So anyway, she shows up and Bobby is hitting on her, and Reece got pissed and they ended up going to blows and money was flying all over the place…." Allen kept on like that describing the scene. Fletcher and I exchanged looks. Once he got started, it seemed Allen wouldn't shut up.

I glanced over at the rescue operation. The Honduran soldiers on the hilltop pulling hand over hand as they raised the injured man from below, veins in their necks and faces strained with the effort. They wore gloves, but the slickness of the rope, the light but steady rain and the mud everywhere had to be making their job difficult. Harry counted for them so that they were pulling in rhythm, a steady pull, pause, pull, their cheeks puffing out as their breath became ragged.

The crowd that had been waiting patiently along the tree line now started to creep forward as if they couldn't wait any longer to see the injured man. They murmured and shuffled closer as if they wanted to help make that final pull to bring the stretcher up to safety.

"Keep that crowd back now, lads," Harry yelled, still lying on his belly. "Easy now. Another 10 meters should do it."

"If I were you, I'd be talking to Reece," Allen said, bringing my attention back to him.

I glanced around and didn't see Reece in the crowd.

"So you think Reece did it?" I asked.

"I didn't say that."

"But he could have."

"I don't know," Allen said, a whiney note in his voice. "I don't know the man. I'm only saying they had a fight. A pretty big one."

"At the poker game," I said. "The poker games the Larsons organized."

"The Larsons?" Allen asked. "Who told you that?"

"Well who did organize them then?"

Allen kept his mouth shut but his gaze went directly to Dodd, Porter and Judd who were all staring at us. They were probably dying to know what we were talking about.

"So Dodd organized them?" I asked.

"I didn't say that," Allen said defensively.

"A poker game that is against General Order number one," Fletcher said.

"I don't play," Allen said. "I just kind of watch."

"You watch," I said. "You watch while a bunch of your soldiers break an Army regulation."

He narrowed his eyes at me but kept his mouth shut. We let the silence linger for a long pause.

"Well, if Reggie does know who killed his brother," I said, "we might find out shortly."

"It's possible the killer is part of this crowd, waiting for him to be brought up," Fletcher said.

Allen looked at Fletcher, then at me as if he had lost his patience with us.

"If you think he's going to point the finger at me, you would be wrong," he said angrily. "Yes, I was here last night, but I didn't kill him. Now leave me alone." He stomped off in the direction of the camp and shouldered his way through the crowd. He didn't stop, but kept going as if he had lost interest in the drama.

Fletcher and I looked at each other over the gap that had contained Allen.

"Who knew he would start flapping his lips like that," Fletcher said, eyebrows raised.

I chuckled. "Yes, but he also left. So if Reggie was about to point out his brother's killer…"

"Allen won't be here to choose from."

Harry and Gutierrez reached down now and pulled the stretcher up and over the lip of the cliff. They moved backwards, dragging the stretcher and the wounded man with them. After several yards, they stood up and medics raced forward to help them with the stretcher.

The crowd closed in and it was difficult for Fletcher and I to get a look at Reggie. He was securely strapped to a backboard on the stretcher, his neck wrapped in a thick brace. His face was bruised and bloodied but his eyes seemed to be open. It was difficult to tell if he was aware of what was going on around him.

Dodd and his group crowded in, Dodd being more aggressive about getting close to the man. He pushed several of the villagers out of his way and strode into the crowd. "Don't you worry now, Reggie. We're going to take care of you," he said. "We'll take good care of you."

Dodd's words didn't sound as if they were meant to comfort the man.

Reggie was lifted into the back of the Humvee ambulance, Fordham and her medics climbed in and drove away at an almost sedate pace, probably in an attempt to prevent jostling the patient in the back of the truck.

The trio of men stood silently and watched the vehicle. They didn't look angry, or anxious, just sort of blank, tired maybe. They glanced at each other and ambled slowly away from the scene along the path the vehicle had just traveled.

Fletcher and I watched as the crowd streamed around us. People murmured quietly and seemed a bit deflated at the end of the dramatic rescue.

I glanced behind me and met Harry's stare and felt a tiny jolt to my heart as he looked at me. He coiled rope around his arm, but his gaze was locked on mine. He was covered in mud and the camouflage paint on his face though smudged, had not washed off in the rain. He made perfect loops of the rope and stared, and kept staring. My heart fluttered along like playing cards pinned to a bicycle wheel.

When he finished, he handed the neat package of rope off to one of the soldiers near him, never taking his eyes from me. He glanced away to speak to Gutierrez and they came to some understanding. They shook hands and then his gaze snapped to me again. Fletcher may have been talking to me. If he was, I wasn't paying attention.

Harry came toward me, walking slowly. He removed his hat and ran a hand over his close cropped hair. Then he stood in front of me and looked down.

"Now then," he said, a slow smile spread across his face, his eyes crinkled to slits.

Chapter 18

Harry's gaze made me smile and blush and feel a little woozy. I dug into one of my cargo pockets, pulled out a packet of wet wipes and handed one to him. A straight line of color slashed across his forehead where his hat met the camouflage paint. He put the small, damp cloth to work on his face, scrubbed away the line and attempted to remove the rest of the black and green streaks. When the first wet wipe was used up, I handed him another. We stared at each other. I watched his familiar face emerge.

I wondered if everyone could see the electric current crackling between us. A current that seemed to dance across my skin. We must have made some kind of impression on Fletcher, because he backed away from us, clearing his throat as he went.

"Don't be too long, Sergeant Harper. We've got a lot of work to do," he said.

"I won't."

"Take an hour."

I froze, mouth open. I had expected him to say minutes. An hour seemed a luxury.

"Thanks," I said, surprised.

Fletcher shifted his gaze from me to Harry. They nodded at each other.

"I won't keep her too long, sir," Harry said as he put his boonie cap back on. "We've got a bit of catching up to do."

"One hour," Fletcher said.

"No worries, Sir. I'll bring her back on time."

The scene felt as if Fletcher was my father, lecturing Harry on our first date. I didn't understand why Fletcher was being so generous, but I wasn't going to question him. Harry and I watched him walk away, then he turned to me. "Come on then, luv. We've got sixty minutes. Let's use them wisely."

We turned toward the canopy of the jungle and walked, kicking our knees high to clear the tall weeds and grasses as we headed into the trees in a direction away from the village and the campsite and everyone. As soon as we entered the jungle, I let him lead me, my hand slipping into his. We stepped over fallen logs and splashed through shallow puddles and ignored the mud that splattered. We hadn't gone far, when we reached a small clearing. He turned back to me and stopped. He brought the back of my hand to his mouth and kissed it, leaving his lips there for several heartbeats, his eyes closed.

It was hard to tell if it was still raining, or if it was simply the abundance of water that still dripped from the thick foliage. It was dark under the canopy of the jungle. I would have been frightened there alone, with all the darting animal sounds, the strange bird calls and the constant furtive noises happening all around us. Harry's presence took all the scary parts away.

"What the hell are you doing here?" I asked him.

"I volunteered," he shrugged. "When you canceled our plans, I didn't want to take leave on my own. I volunteered for the first mission I could find. It just happened to be Honduras."

"And you ended up here." I said.

"And I ended up here. I hoped I'd see you, but I couldn't know that I would of course. We've been given a lucky break it seems. "

He started to touch my face, then seeing his own hand, stopped. "Christ, I'm filthy," he said. He dropped my hand and backed away from me. He looked down at himself. The front of his uniform was a black, sodden mess from low-crawling across the hillside. His hands were black with dirt, his fingernails thick with mud. I didn't want to say anything, but there were still green and black steaks of camouflage paint on his face, deep in the creases of his eyes and around his nose.

"Bloody hell," he mumbled under his breath, as he uselessly brushed at his uniform.

I grabbed his hands to stop him.

"Look at me, Harry. I'm just as dirty."

It was true. From the soaking wet boonie cap on my head to the fat, lime green rubber boots on my feet, I was covered in mud.

"Well, yeah. But you're still beautiful. I just look like a bloody, filthy, mess."

"You look like a soldier who just finished a difficult mission," I said, then smiled. "You think I look beautiful?"

His gaze roamed over me as he tried to hide his smile. "Well, now that I get a better look at you, you could use a bath and a change of uniform. And what the bloody hell are those things on your feet?"

We shared a brief chuckle, then he got serious again and stepped closer to me. He pulled the boonie cap off my head.

We had only known each other a few short, turbulent days while in Bosnia. Harry had seen me at my absolute worst, and it seemed that even though we hadn't spent much time together, we knew each other better than most two people did. We had shared a brief and chaste kiss. A kiss I remembered often. One I took out and examined when I was alone and thinking of him. I knew he was about to kiss me, and I was a little frightened by it.

"This is not how I pictured our reunion," he said, quietly as he closed the distance between us. "But if there's anything I've learned in my long military career, it's that one should take opportunities as they present themselves, don't you agree?"

I nodded and knew my voice would have come out in a squeak. He leaned down slowly, not touching me, as if afraid more grime would rub off. His eyes were open when his lips brushed mine. He was hesitant, careful, then his tongue licked out, testing my willingness. I stepped in closer, touched his face, then put my hand behind his neck and made it clear that I wanted that kiss, wanted to feel what his lips had promised. With a quiet moan deep in his throat, his arms went around me and he leaned over me, kissed me, pulled me into him, drew my soul up from my toes. I was lost. He cupped my head in his hand and the mud and filth were forgotten. His arms were strong and he squeezed the breath out of me as I had fantasized he would. I couldn't believe that he was here, that we were touching, kissing.

He pulled away, cradled my head as he looked at what his kiss had done to me, and his gaze roamed my face. I smiled, still breathless. "Well, then," he said. "I could do that for close to forever, I believe."

"I wouldn't stop you."

True to his word, he kissed me and kept on kissing me. We lay down on the jungle floor, adding more mud and dirt to our filthy uniforms. We kept our eyes open most of the time and watched each other, gasping at the wonder of how good it felt. He said things, murmured words, about missing me, about thinking of me, how good it felt and how unbelievable it was that we were here, living these moments. I marveled at his bulk and felt breathless with the size of him above me. My arms barely reached around his broad back. I wanted to feel my naked skin against his, and told him so, but it was impossible, so we moaned with frustration and after a time, he rolled over onto his back and pulled me into the crook of his arm, my head on his chest, and we lay there, as we caught our breath and held each other.

"So, how did he get down there then?" he asked. "That soldier over the cliff."

I groaned. I didn't want to think about it. "Long story," I said.

"That's what the man in the flight suit said. That it was a long story. You'd better just skip to the essential bits."

I told him about Cordovan and my mission, how we found the body in the cement. That it was the brother of the murdered man who had driven himself off the cliff. I explained about the weather and the roads. That I knew something rotten was going on in the unit and that I wanted to find who did it. And that Fletcher and I were working together to figure it out.

Then I wanted to change the subject.

"Where is your camp?"

"We don't have one, luv. We've been on patrol for over a week. Living out of our packs, eating snakes and wild chickens and fish from the streams."

"You're kidding."

"Cross my heart," he said. "These blokes are Honduran Special Forces. They don't mess about. I haven't had this much fun since I went to that survival course in Australia. A canteen of water and a knife is what they let us have there and we were on our own. But this lot aren't in training. They do this stuff every day. Hunting out drug crops and the like. We've been hearing about this little village the last couple of days. They've got quite a crop from what we've heard."

"The pot plants here? Most of the farmers I've seen look like they're barely scraping by. How could these few marijuana plants be so important.

"It's not just marijuana, luv. Although this group I'm working with will probably come back to burn that to the ground. No, it's the coca plants these blokes are after, and this village supposedly has its share of them."

Coca plants. The leaves of the coca plant are the basis of cocaine and crack and the myriad of crimes that stemmed from such activity.

"What will they do if they find coca here?"

"Slash, burn and take people to jail, most like. If they find it here, as our intelligence has directed us we will, then this will be our second major strike since I've been with the team. And I do mean major. There are millions of pounds worth of drugs here."

I'm as against drugs and the crime associated with it as the next guy, and if there were coca plants around, I hoped they'd be destroyed, but their existence was hard for me to imagine. This village was too poor. If someone was profiting from the drug trade, their affluence was hidden from plain view. Everything I'd seen so far reinforced the fact that these folks needed the help we were giving them.

Harry ran his finger across my forehead. "What's putting wrinkles in that brow?" he asked.

"I'm wondering if the entire village is in on this or if it's just a few. They seem like a bunch of dirt poor farmers to me. Where is all the money going?"

"There's probably one guy, one group who runs the whole thing. The marijuana crop is close to the village to be sure, but the coca plants will be further away. They do that on purpose to make it look like it could belong to anyone."

"I've only been here a day but the only guy I've seen so far that could possibly fit that bill is Senor Bonilla," I said. Harry sat up on an elbow and looked down at me obviously interested in the information.

"Why him?"

I shrugged, "It's just a feeling really. The man definitely has influence around here and the men who hang out with him seem afraid of him."

It had to be Bonilla. He didn't seem richer than anyone else, but he had influence and money could buy influence. Harry looked down at me, his gaze lazily wandering over my face. I liked having him above me and I especially liked the possessive look in his eye.

"Do you have a plan?"

"For what?" he asked, as he planted a slow kiss between my eyebrows, followed by another on my eyelids and another on the corner of my cheekbone, leaving a trail of warmth and my thoughts fuzzy.

"A plan to figure out who is behind it all," I said.

"Destroy the crops first," he said, kissing me again on his path down my face. "That's what the group I'm with will do. After that, the state police will do their thing."

"And then you'll move on to the next one?"

"Yes, the next job," he said. "But what's with the bloke in the flight suit, luv?"

"What?" The quick change of subject threw me off. I had a feeling that had been deliberate on Harry's part. If we were going to talk about Fletcher, I didn't want to be distracted.

"The tall, handsome fella who didn't seem too happy that we

knew each other. Why did I get the feeling he is a bit jealous of you?"

"We dated. But that was a long time ago," I said. "Can we leave it at that? I don't want to waste time talking about Fletcher."

"As you wish. But I feel I should warn you. For years, I've kept bits of me locked behind walls of ice. I couldn't afford to feel anything, not with my chosen profession." He leaned down and repeated his trail of kisses down my face, pressed his lips to my forehead, my eyelids, my lips, then leveled his frank gaze at me again.

"I don't know how you did it, but you've managed to melt my frozen bits. It's like I can suddenly feel my heart beating where it lay dead before. Now, I want to know all of your secrets. I want to know what nasty habits you have. I want to see the dreadful pictures of you growing up. I want to know everything about you, Lauren."

"I'm not gonna lie, Harry. That scares me a little."

He chuckled. "It scares me too, darlin'. I'm practically trembling with it."

"Then why are you saying it?"

He ran a finger along my eyebrow, brushed my cheek with his thumb. The look in his eyes thrummed through my chest. It felt hard to breath.

"Because it scares me even more not to say it. Trust me. We will find the time to see where this will take us. We don't have much time left now, but we will. I promise we will."

I drank in every detail of his face, his shining green eyes, his wide mouth and full lips, the dark stubble on his chin. He slanted his lips onto mine again, his tongue going deeper, his grip tighter. We both knew these would be our last moments. There was no way to know when another opportunity like this would come around. Not days or weeks certainly, more likely months. I fumbled with the buttons but managed to open the front of my uniform jacket and yanked my t-shirt out of my pants. I pulled it up to expose my breasts, feeling smug that I had chosen a black, lacy bra that morning.

Harry's gaze slid from my face down to my breasts. He hooked his finger into the lace of my bra and pulled down. I held my breath while he lowered his head and gasped in pleasure when he ran his tongue gently across my hardened nipple. He wrapped his lips around the nub and bit down playfully. We moaned together, breathless, desperate, wanting to stop the progress of time.

He took my hand and guided it to his hardness. When I ran my palm along his length, he threw his head back with a strangled curse. I drank in the sight of the cords on his neck, the way he strained into the pleasure of my touch. When he looked at me again, the fire in his gaze nearly burned me. Our kisses became more frantic. He trembled beneath my hands and our moans began to sound more like cries of pain, rather than pleasure.

He rolled onto his back, bringing me with him, slipping his leg between mine, presenting the hard press of his thigh as a perfect place for me to ride out my frustration. I bucked against him, so taut with need, my cries muffled by his mouth and his seeking, darting tongue. He pushed against my shoulder, sitting me higher, rising with me, his shoulders off the ground, changing the angle and increasing the friction. He watched me, his mouth open, his knowing eyes burning with encouragement. "Yes, Lauren, yes," he said, but I couldn't. It wasn't fair and it wasn't the way I wanted our first time together to be.

I wanted to cling to him, to stay there, to get naked and give myself to him. It was impossible, and overwhelming to be denied what we wanted so badly.

Finally, I slowed then stilled and gazed down at him, and we stared at each other and panted as our heart rates slowed. I closed my eyes and swallowed a sob, acceptance finally, that we had to stop.

He drew me down to him, his arms coming around me like a vice. "Oh darlin'. Don't fret, now."

I lay there trying to catch my breath, so frustrated with our circumstances, at the last minute orders, the lack of time, the inability to even have a meal together.

I love the Army, but there are so many times when I'm sure the

Army doesn't love me. But then, without the Army, I never would have met Harry and we'd never be half-way around the world, laying in each other's arms on a jungle floor.

"This will definitely be on my list of most unusual make-out locations," I murmured.

I enjoyed the rumble of laughter deep in his chest, my ear pressed against him.

He ran his hand over my head, and rolled me onto my back, tilted my chin up and gave me closed-mouth kisses while he slowly righted my bra, pulled my t-shirt down, closed my uniform jacket. It grew very late. I could barely see him in the graying light, but there was just enough illumination to swim in the depth of his eyes for one last moment.

There was a lot about Harry I didn't know, a lot he didn't know about me but I wanted more than anything to correct that lack of knowledge. What I did know about him assured me that it would be worth the wait.

Then he tucked away the lust in his gaze. He put on his senior NCO, all-business face, kissed me quickly but fully on the lips and pushed himself up in one smooth movement. He held his hand out for me to grab. We spent an awkward couple of seconds straightening our uniforms, picking leaves and brush off our clothing. He scooped my boonie cap off the ground and handed it to me. I thanked him and it sounded foreign.

"I've worn this uniform for 15 years," he said quietly. "I've never kissed anyone like that whilst wearing it."

I knew what he meant and I smiled. It accounted for the sudden distance, as if he had only just realized how inappropriate it all was. Giving someone a hug was frowned upon while in uniform, let alone what we had just done.

"Well, Sergeant Major Fogg. Let's hope it doesn't happen again."

"No," he said. "Next time we have a snog, it will be out of uniform. No worries on that score." The corner of his mouth and an eyebrow went up while he said it. The double meaning wasn't lost on me. I wondered just when that might be, and couldn't hide the sudden gloominess I felt at the long wait.

"It'll be sooner than you think, luv," he said, as if reading my mind. "Just you wait and see. Sooner than you think."

He then offered me his arm in a formal way, as if we had been called into dinner. I linked my arm through his and leaned on him cozily as we strolled out of the jungle.

Chapter 19

Harry was of the school that believed it better to rip the band aid off in one go.

"Goodbyes. I can't stand them," he said.

"Me either."

"The worst part about this job."

"I agree."

He had returned me to the site of the rescue, then consulted his map and checked his compass.

"Right then," he said as he tucked the map away in a cargo pocket and turned in the direction of his compass barring. "Ciao, luv," he said simply, and disappeared into the jungle.

I felt the ghostly warmth of his arms around me and the rawness of my face where his stubble had left its mark. I hung onto the slim hope that we might find more time together before this mission was over. Knowing he was near wouldn't help my concentration.

The cloud-shrouded sky meant there weren't any stars or romantic moonlight to guide my way back to the village. I was grateful for the small flashlight I always wore in a sheath on my uniform belt. The light provided some help, but it was sound that led me back to the camp.

The clamber of hammers at work reached my ears long before I got near the construction site. Judging from the noise, two or three teams were at work removing the body from the cement. The clatter of cement chunks and the metallic ding of chisels on rock was an assault to what should have been a quiet night in the jungle village. Light from behind the tarp cast a blue glow across the construction area and dark shadows played eerily on the plastic. I was glad not to be involved in that morbid business.

I continued past the school site and headed to the headquarters tent where I knew Fletcher expected me. My progress down the center road was slow and slippery. My rubber boots didn't have much traction in the mud that had grown deeper as the rain continued to fall through most of the day. I struggled to keep my balance and my dignity.

Harsh florescent light spilled into the road through the mesh walls of the headquarters tent. The constant drone of generator engines covered the sounds of nighttime jungle noises. Fletcher hadn't dropped the canvas walls of the tent, so he was clearly visible as he paced around inside. Porter sat in the chair facing the desk.

The generators made it impossible to hear what was going on from my position. Fletcher seemed tense, his arms crossed over his chest. He watched his feet as he paced, and occasionally glanced at Porter who seemed to do all the talking.

I pushed open the tent flap and stepped through the door and Porter turned to look at me. There was a brief flash of irritation on his face before he replaced it with a fake smile, his lips stretched to reveal his teeth, but his eyes were watchful and serious.

"I hope I'm not interrupting anything," I said.

Fletcher looked from me to Porter and I felt the tension in the room.

"Sergeant Porter was just telling me a little about the unit. The kinds of relationships the men have with each other, on and off duty," Fletcher said.

"Oh?" I said, glancing at Porter.

"Yeah. I was just telling the Chief here, that ah, we're all pretty close, you know. We ah, we do our soldier thing every month but we, most of us anyway, are friends when we're civilians too." His eyes bobbed back and forth between Fletcher and me, that fake smile making his already skeletal face look stretched and unnatural. He licked his lips nervously. "We hang out sometimes, you know. That's only natural, right?"

He went on like that for a while, talking about barbeques and get-togethers. I didn't understand why he was trying so hard to convince us of their friendships. It was the same thing Dodd had told us, that they were one big happy family. Even their children played together. They didn't go to the same schools, but the wives were very sociable and fixed play dates often. Everyone was friendly with everyone according to Porter.

"Hell, my wife looks forward to me going on these things so she can get together with all the gal pals from the unit. They go shopping and so forth."

"And the Larson brothers are part of this tight knit group?" Fletcher asked.

"Well yeah, sure." Porter said. He scooted to the front of the chair his hands going into action now. "Why wouldn't they be? They work on everybody's lawns, you know. A lot of their business is tied up in doing lawns."

There wasn't anything wrong with doing business with people you served with, but the rank structure, even in a National Guard unit, could get tricky. If people who out ranked you owed you money from some business transaction, that could complicate things.

"So the Larsons worked on your lawn?" Fletcher asked.

"Yeah, like I said."

"On First Sergeant Dodd's lawn?" Fletcher asked.

"Yeah, and on Judd's and a few others." His eyes darted back and forth between us. "Ain't nothing wrong with that. Ain't no regulation against it anyway," he added defensively.

"Was everyone happy with their work?" I asked.

"Sure, at least I was," he said, scooting back in his chair. He crossed his legs and tried to appear relaxed. "My wife has these huge flower beds. She never had much of a green thumb but them

Larson boys have brought a lot of color to our yard. Talked her into letting some of it grow natural, without any chemicals or pesticides. Now we got this little pond with a fountain surrounded by tall wild flowers. It took a couple years, but it looks real nice. We got more than an acre and a half and ah, well I don't much like riding a lawn mower."

"Isn't it expensive?" I asked.

His brow wrinkled as if I had asked an inappropriate question. Then he looked down, suddenly interested in mud splatters on his pant leg.

"Naw," he said. "The Larsons use a lot of illegal Mexicans. Pick 'em up off of them corners where they hang out looking for work. Besides, they only come couple times a month. It's worth it." He continued to find interest in his clothing, his foot bobbing nervously now. I figured he was hiding something and decided to push some buttons just to see what would happen.

"Does anyone in the unit owe them money for the work they did?" I asked.

"I don't know. How would I know that?"

"Did you owe them money, maybe a lot of money for that pond and the wildflowers?"

"No! I'm all paid up. Ask Reggie. He'll tell you." His face grew blotchy with red spots. I pushed a little further.

"What about from the poker game?"

"What about it?" he said. He glanced at Fletcher who raised an eyebrow at me.

"We've heard about the poker games, the ones you guys have been playing most nights,."

"Yeah, so. A lot of us played. What's wrong with that?"

"It's against regulations for one thing."

He wrinkled his brow at me. "Don't nobody pay attention to that. Hell, we've been playing poker for years."

"That doesn't make it right," Fletcher interjected.

"How much did you lose?" I asked.

"We played for quarters, for Pete's sake," he said with a sneer. He stood up and jingled the change in his pocket. "I might have lost five dollars. You want to arrest me over that?" He sat back down and crossed his legs again, then uncrossed them, slumping down in the chair and splaying his legs wide to show his disdain. He was getting on my nerves.

"Were you playing poker last night?" I asked.

He hesitated a moment, flicked his eyes at Fletcher again. "Like I told the Chief here. I wasn't feeling well last night. I turned in kind of early."

"How early is early?"

"I don't know. It was after dark."

I pointedly looked at the watch on his wrist and waited.

"I didn't look to see what time," he said defensively. "It was early, that's all,"

"Anyone else turn in early?"

"I don't know. Maybe Judd," he said. Of course they would supply each other with an alibi.

"And I suppose the Larsons have done a great landscaping job at Judd's house too."

Porter glared at me.

I decided to push him a little just to see what would happen if he lost his temper.. "Who didn't they get along with?" I asked.

"Nobody."

"No one fought with them?"

"No."

"Nobody was jealous of their business?"

"No."

"Jealous of their good looks?"

"Awe, come on!"

"There had to be someone who didn't like them."

"No. Everybody liked the Larsons."

"Everybody?"

"Yeah," Porter was getting louder, more defensive with each question. He was almost as quick to lose his temper as I was. Now he wasn't just angry, he was defensive too. "They were good guys," he said loudly, with a red face to match. "Good men."

"Then why is one of them dead?"

He was about to make a quick retort, then stopped himself. He sat up in his chair, put his hands on his knees, his lips pressed together. He locked eyes with me for a long moment, then shot up out of the chair.

"To hell with this," he said and made for the door.

Fletcher stepped casually in his way and Porter stutter-stepped to avoid a collision then backed up a pace or two. "Do you have any idea who did this?" Fletcher asked. "Or why someone might want to do such a thing?"

Porter looked him in the eye. They were almost nose to nose. "No, sir. I do not. But I'd sure like to find the son of a bitch who did. Bobby and Reggie are both my friends."

It was exactly what I expected him to say. This unit was one big happy family.

"Okay, Sergeant Porter," Fletcher said. "I guess that will be all for now."

Porter didn't hesitate. He bent to duck through the tent flap, but I stopped him.

"Porter, one more thing," I said. He froze, then put that plastered fake smile back on his face before he turned to look at me expectantly.

"What did Judd mean before, when we were at the cliff. He said, he deserved it after what he did. What did he mean—after what he did? What exactly did Reggie do?"

Porter flicked a glance to Fletcher, then back to me. He licked his lips nervously.

"It's like I said out there. Reggie tried to kill himself and he couldn't even get that right. And he, he put everyone in danger out there. It was just a stupid thing to do, that's all. That's what he meant."

"You're a liar, Sergeant Porter," I said. I expected him to get angry or to deny it. He did neither. His mouth dropped open as if he were going to say something to defend himself, then he just smiled at me. A big toothy grin.

"Prove it," he said, and he ducked out of the tent.

Fletcher and I shared a look, eyebrows up. "Well, I'm not sure who surprised me more," he said. "You or him."

"Well, he is a liar. They're all liars and I'm sick of it." I suddenly felt filled with frustration. I mentally ran over a bunch of things I should have asked, should have said to the asshole Porter, before he walked out. We were wasting our time. We had nothing to go on and no one would cooperate, not with Fletcher and I who had no power to really do anything if anyone refused.

I pulled the boonie cap off my head, brushed a strand of hair from my face and realized my hand shook, then realized my whole body shook. I took a couple of steps to the nearest chair and collapsed into it. Fletcher immediately knelt in front of me looking worried.

"I'm okay," I said. "I just…" I didn't know what to say. My whole body trembled and it pissed me off that I felt out of control. I had such a strong feeling that the man who had just walked out the door had murdered Bobby Larson and then smiled at me about it. I had been close to evil like that before. I had felt impotent, powerless to do anything about it. I was feeling the same way again and it made me angry.

"Lauren, what is it?" Fletcher asked.

"Just give me a minute," I said. I took a few deep breaths and tried to get control of myself. Porter had something to do with the murder, I was almost certain of it. The thought that he had buried a man alive under cement and then walked around as if he had a right to was maddening. I wanted nothing more than to see the men who did it punished. My belief in Porter's guilt was instinctual, a gut feeling I couldn't substantiate. If the boot prints at the crime scene matched Porter's perfectly, I had a good start. If Porter and Judd were the killers, Santos would find them out somehow. Until then, Fletcher and I just needed to collect what information we could. I didn't know how we would do it, but I wanted to catch them. I wanted to find a way to prove they had killed Bobby Larson.

I found it hard to look at Fletcher.

"You okay?" he asked.

"I'm sorry," I said. "I just… He got to me, that's all."

"Understood." He stood up slowly, still watching me.

I folded my arms across my chest and probably looked pretty dark. When I glanced up at Fletcher he was trying not to laugh.

"What?" I said.

"You have leaves and stuff in your hair. And, well, your face. It looks like you've been making out with a man who hasn't shaved in a while."

Heat immediately rushed to my cheeks. I flushed further as images of Harry leapt to mind. I picked absently at my hair, knowing it was going to take a mirror, a wide toothed comb and a lot of patience to get my hair right again. The stubble burn would only go away with time. It was something I couldn't control. What I could control was the amount of time I spent thinking about Harry. I decided thinking more about Harry was better than thinking about brutal murderers. It wasn't a tough choice.

"Before I got here, was there anything I missed when you were talking to Porter?" I asked, hoping to change the subject.

"Pretty much said the same crap Judd gave me. They didn't see anything last night. They were just hanging out, playing poker with a bunch of people in their tent. They turned in early. They didn't hear anything, one big happy family, yada, yada, yada."

"See, a bunch of liars."

He shrugged, "Well, that seems obvious, but Porter is right. We can't prove that they're lying. I'm not cut out for this shit. If they were playing poker last night, there should be plenty of people in the medical unit who could vouch for their whereabouts. If they left early, they have each other as an alibi. I don't even know what to ask at this point."

He avoided looking at me. He was the kind of man that excelled at everything and couldn't stand the thought of being defeated. His shoulders were hunched in frustration. He walked to the desk and fiddled with the computer, not bothering to sit down. His nervous energy was contagious.

"Have you heard from Santos?" I asked him, as I stood and started my own nervous wanderings about the room.

"He says the forecast calls for some clearing late tomorrow

evening. Until then we're on our own. When I checked on her, Fordham said the removal was going well, but they'll be at it for hours. About the only thing going right is that she's here. We can be grateful for that."

"And Reggie?"

"Lots of broken bones. Colonel Scaporelli says he broke both legs, one minor, one pretty serious. Cracked a couple of ribs, broken collar bone, bruised vertebrae, but no serious internal injuries. Got a good bang on the head which is the most worrisome of his injuries, but overall, he should be okay. He may still be in surgery but we should go over there soon. See if we can talk to him."

"Okay," I said, and waited for him to move, but he just stood there looking at me. He didn't want to ask and I didn't want to volunteer the information, so I just waited. Eventually he asked.

"So, who is that guy?"

"Someone I met in Bosnia. We were supposed to go on leave together but I was ordered here."

He nodded, staring hard at me.

"What?" I finally asked.

He shook his head. "Nothing. It's just that..."

"It's just what?" I wasn't comfortable with him poking at my personal life. He hadn't any right to it, but I figured we might as well get it over and done with. Still, I wanted him to work for it and didn't volunteer anything.

"Have you known each other long?"

"No, not long."

"But you were going on a trip together?" He mumbled the question under his breath. I chuckled and shook my head.

"Fletcher, you and I went on a trip fairly early on in our relationship, didn't we?

"Yes, but that's different." He grinned at me, and the mood lightened.

"Because it was you?" I said, returning his smile.

"Of course."

"Are you ready to go question the guy who just tried to kill himself, or would you rather sit here and ask me questions about my love life?"

He thought about that for a minute.

"I could ask you questions about your love life on the way."

"No, you couldn't," I said and moved toward the tent door in an attempt to end the interrogation.

"Ah, come on," he teased, as he followed me, ducking through the tent flap. "It's the accent right? That's the big turn on."

"You have to admit, it is a great accent, but he's also very handsome," I countered.

"Okay, accent, and handsome. That's all it takes?"

"He's also SAS. That's pretty cool."

"Okay, accent, handsome and a trained killer. That's all it takes?"

"Shut up, Fletcher," I said.

Chapter 20

Night had fallen like a curtain on a stage, smoothly but rapidly in one swift go. The darkness wrapped the village in an unbroken blanket of black, no street lights or wash of the moon to lessen the disorientation caused by wide-open eyes that saw little variation filtering through. Each of us carried flashlights, mine thin but solid, Fletcher's wider but less effective. Our mud-soaked steps sounded funny in a splat and squish kind of way. I stifled a chuckle the noises evoked, knowing any explanation I offered for the laughter would only make me sound crazy.

With the night, voices grew quiet as if the lack of illumination muffled them. Absent the long lines of clients, the area outside the hospital complex at first appeared deserted, but a buzz of activity continued only much more quietly and evidenced in lowered voices, the bright glow of a burning cigarette, the occasional giggles of children as they played and splashed through mud.

Closer to the hospital, yellowish light spilled onto the dirt road. Inside, a general hush had settled over the place. The reception tables were empty, clipboards, pencils and medical armbands sat organized and waiting for the next day's group of patients. We went through the back of the reception area, through a short tunnel and into the main examination room, drawn on our path by the sound of voices. The curtains surrounding exam tables were pulled back and secured neatly except for one near the end. Silhouettes of several people danced behind the white sheet. Colonel Scaporelli stepped out and saw us. He must have performed Larson's surgery himself because he still wore blue hospital scrubs, his head covered by a surgical cap. He moved slowly, shuffling over, as if pulling a heavy burden.

"He's sedated now. You'll have to wait and talk to him in the morning," he mumbled, as if talking required too much energy.

I wasn't surprised, but it was still frustrating. "Has he said anything about why he might have done this?" Fletcher asked.

"Nothing coherent," Scaporelli said. "He moaned about his brother. He kept saying he was sorry. That's about it."

"And his injuries?" Fletcher asked.

"He'll live. He'll not only live, he'll walk and should fully recover. Considering what he did, going over a cliff in a vehicle, he's very lucky."

Fletcher wandered over to the examination area ducked behind the curtain. Scaporelli ignored him as he stifled a yawn, then flipped through his chart making notes, his eyes red-rimmed and a stark contrast to the pastiness of his skin. He was one of those men who needed to shave twice a day, his chin and neck covered with stubble flecked with grey. His pallor and evident exhaustion didn't reduce his attractiveness. Still, it was evident he had had a long day. We all had.

Scaporelli glanced up and looked past me to something that made him straighten and wrinkle his brow. He gave a tiny shake of his head. I wouldn't have noticed if I hadn't been looking right at him.

I turned to see what had captured his attention and caught Bonilla ducking out the door. He stilled, then turned back, as if he'd intended to enter.

"Excuse me, doctor," Bonilla said, confirming that he could speak English after all. And he spoke it well. "Many of the people are wondering how the young man is," he went on. "They are saying prayers for him."

My gaze bounced between Scaporelli and Bonilla and wondered what they really had to talk about. Scaporelli, who didn't seem the least bit surprised by Bonilla's fluent English, gave him the rundown of Larson's injuries; darting glances at me punctuated his report. The relaxed and exhausted man I had just observed had disappeared. The doctor's speech was now energized and his posture ramrod straight. The conversation between them seemed only for my benefit. Bonilla didn't care about Larson's medical condition and Scaporelli knew that.

"Oh, I forgot to tell you," Scaporelli said, turning to me. "Dr. Fordham would like to speak to you. She's down at the construction site."

"Dr. Fordham."

"Yes, she said she had some information about your ah, investigation."

The awkward attempt to be rid of me only increased my interest. Scaporelli was a terrible liar. In my work with the media, the press often implied that I lied to them. They never came right out and called me a liar but the implication was usually there, that I was somehow hiding information or twisting it to make the Army appear in the best light. I've never lied to the press and I never will. Get caught in one lie and your reputation never recovers. I had some strong feelings about lies, and now I was getting pretty damn tired of everyone lying to me.

I let my gaze flick between them. Bartonelli hadn't put much thought into the execution of his lie and I hadn't been fooled by their scene. Bonilla's benevolent look changed to a smirk but he didn't give up on the fiction.

"Ah, doctor, in light of all that has happened today, we are wondering if the clinic will be open again tomorrow."

"Of course," the Scaporelli said as he turned to walk away, Bonilla felling into step beside him. If the men wanted it to be a natural looking exit, they failed. "We'll have regular hours tomorrow, all of the same services we provided today." He kept up the monologue of banal information until they reached the door, taking one more glance at me before they left.

"Curiouser and curiouser," I said.

"Are you talking to yourself?" Fletcher asked me, poking his head outside the curtain.

"Yes. You would be too if you'd seen what I saw." I joined him at Reggie's bedside, the injured soldier looked in pain even while unconscious. We spoke in whispers to avoid disturbing him.

"Curiouser isn't a word by the way," Fletcher said.

"It's a perfectly good word to describe what just happened."

"What was curiouser about it?"

"No, see the way you just used it doesn't work."

Fletcher, smirked at me and folded his arms, waiting for an explanation. I glanced at the patient and winced at how banged up he looked.

Reggie's eyes and cheeks looked shiny and puffy, his face scrunched up because of the thick collar that surrounded his neck, his head tilted at an unnatural angle.

They had secured his hands and arms to the rails of the bed with thick padded restraints, which sort of made sense considering his attempt to kill himself, but it seemed obvious he wasn't going anywhere. A hard plastic cover wrapped his torso, and a plaster cast covered his entire leg all the way up to his groin, the leg raised in traction by a pulley.

Two soldiers, one young woman and an older male NCO stood next to Reggie's bed checking the quietly beeping monitors.

"Ouch," I said.

"Yeah, he really wracked himself up didn't he? So, what was it you saw that had you talking to yourself?"

"Scaporelli and Bonilla. It was weird."

"Weird how?"

"They appear to know each other. I mean, of course they know each other. But it's like there's something going on with them."

Fletcher raised his eyebrows at me. "Something going on? Like what?"

"First of all, Bonilla speaks English. He's been pretending to need a translator all day. Second, Bonilla came to see the doctor about something, but when he saw me, he pretended he came to see him about something else. I don't know. It sounds strange now that I try to explain it."

We turned our attention back to Reggie, taking in the mangled mess he'd made of himself.

"Scaporelli said he's lucky to be alive, but Reggie may not think that when he wakes up."

=============

When we left the hospital, a light rain fell again. The village street seemed empty, the weather or the late hour having driven everyone inside.

We trekked into the construction site and immediately noticed that the hammering and chiseling had stopped. The constant buzz of nighttime insects filled the silence created by the lack of the tools at work. People moved around inside the tarp area, the walls occasionally pushed from the inside as if the makeshift tent wasn't large enough to hold everyone inside.

"They must be ready to move the body," Fletcher said. He trotted forward, not wanting to miss the action. I followed him but stopped in my tracks when Harry stepped out of the enclosure. He exchanged a polite nod with Fletcher, holding the tarp aside for him to enter then, hands in his pockets, strolled my way.

He folded back the brim of my boonie cap and smiled down at me. "God, you're lovely," he whispered.

My knees turned to jelly. If I didn't get a handle on all this moony-eyed business, I'd be a goner.

"What are you doing here? Not that I mind it at all." Harry's slow perusal of my face made me purr under his scrutiny.

"Looking for you, luv." He brought his arm up to his nose and sniffed the fabric. "They've managed to free the body finally. It's smelling bloody ripe in there. Don't know how they can stand it." Harry hunched his shoulders and shuddered. "I'd help, but there's too many people in there already. I'm only getting under foot."

Fordham gave instructions. Someone had already backed a pickup truck onto the site, the tailgate lowered and waiting for the load. Fletcher threw back one side of the tarp while stepping out. Harry trotted over to grab the other side of the flap as six soldiers, three to each side, heaved under the strain of the body.

They had created a sling using the woven canvas straps normally used to tie down pallets for transport. The straps provided plenty of handles, the men shuffled sideways and took frequent stops as they carefully moved the awkward load. By the time they had it out of the shelter, they panted, red-faced. It was obvious they would never be able to lift it into the truck bed.

Their work on the cement had revealed much more of the corpse. They had not only cut around the body but huge chunks of cement had been lifted from the top and sides to reveal his torso, one arm and tops of both legs. His head remained encased, and his grotesque position was as we had found him, with his clawing hand, the legs that looked like they had been caught mid-kick. His uniform jacket had been opened, and the t-shirt cut to reveal pasty grey skin that looked bright in the darkness. Larson had worn the sleeves of his uniform rolled up in regulation fashion to about mid-bicep, a tattoo of the engineering symbol, a red castle, still partially hidden by the sleeve cuff.

The exposed parts of the body were covered in a thin dusting of cement making him look hard as stone, like an ancient Roman statue with a missing head and arm. I kept looking at his chest, expecting it to rise and fall with the breath of life. It stayed immobile and I had to look away to take a deep breath of my own as if to reassure myself that I could still breath.

The men conferred, Fletcher and Harry offering suggestions as they discussed how to get the body into the truck. They finally decided to put the slab on a wooden pallet and then use a forklift.

While soldiers went to get the necessary equipment, Harry returned to my side.

"I've got to head back, luv, " he said. "I wanted to tell you that it appears we have an operation at first light."

"You mean, you and your commando friends?"

"That's right." He slipped my cap off, then chuckled and picked a couple of bits of leaf out of my hair, with full knowledge of how the debris got there.

"Anything you can tell me about?"

"I can tell you we won't be far from here," he said, in a lowered voice. "Could be this village won't be so friendly after tomorrow morning."

"Will people be arrested?"

"Not by us. We'll hold them until the local authorities get here, but they'll do all the arresting. Our only job is to find the stuff, destroy it, hold the bad guys. We're priming up the flame throwers for the job."

"Drugs, guns, danger. Is that your world, Harold Fogg with two Gs?"

I tried to make light of the question but my stomach churned. Harry didn't miss my sentiment. He glanced around to see if anyone was looking, then took my hand and we walked a few feet away from the activity. Under the canopy of a tree he pulled me into a hug. He wrapped his arms around me and I felt the tension leak out of me, as if wrapped in a comforting blanket. He cradled my head in his hand.

"Promise me you'll still come to London to meet the family," he said, his breath a warm whisper against my ear.

"Of course. As soon as possible."

"And then we'll go someplace warm, like Majorca or Crete, someplace where people wear very little clothing."

I chuckled. "I'd like that. Very much."

He stepped back and looked at me. "It's my job, luv. And you know I'm good at it, so there's no use worrying." He ran a finger down my cheek and traced my lips.

"Of course not," I said, but I knew I would worry. How could I not?

"I'll try to come see you afterwards, before we move out."

I nodded, not sure if I could say anything, afraid of how it might come out. I couldn't ask him to call me. Neither of us had phones. I didn't know if I would even hear how the raid went, didn't know when I would see him again. If he were injured or worse, I would have no way of knowing. I touched his face, marveling at his square jaw, the cleft in his chin, the way his green eyes seemed luminous in the meager evening light.

"I know it goes against everything in your nature, but don't be a hero, Harry." I smiled, trying to appear okay with the whole thing. The last thing he needed was a whiney woman on his mind.

"A hero? Me?" He smiled, and backed away and was just about to turn to leave when he stopped. "Oh hell," he said. And in two strides he was kissing me. A deep open mouth kiss, full of soft exploration. One that took ownership, and my breath away. Someone could have seen us, but I didn't care. I wanted to disappear into that kiss. When he stopped, he dropped his arms and backed away immediately, knowing the proximity would only make another kiss possible, and he had to go.

"Caio, luv," he said. "I'll see you very soon."

I watched him leave. His thick neck and broad back gave me much to contemplate. I instantly felt lonely. I continued to watch him, wondering if he would turn around to get one last look at me. He didn't.

Chapter 21

The pickup truck sat low on its axles, the huge slab of cement with its gruesome tenant centered on the flatbed. Dr. Fordham, her face streaked with cement dust, wiped her brow with her arm. She drank greedily from a water bottle and glanced at me. "There you are," she said.

"You look exhausted."

"I am, and starving and I need to take a piss in a big way," she said, then smiled at me. "You look thoroughly kissed."

"Is it that obvious?"

"Your lips are all swollen and your cheeks are red. I'd say you've been sucking face with somebody."

"Well, I feel thoroughly kissed."

"That big handsome British guy?"

I simply smiled at her. She took that as a yes, but kissing wasn't all she wanted to talk about. She got right to the point.

"At least two people did this," she said, her voice lowered. "Bruises and scratches on one wrist plus a large bruise in the middle of his chest. The one on his chest," she paused and looked down, shook her head. When she glanced back up at me, her eyes were red rimmed. "I'm sorry. I just keep thinking about what he must have felt when this was happening to him." She raised a slightly trembling hand and pushed a wisp of blonde hair away from her face.

I was surprised to see the seasoned coroner acting like this.

"I've examined hundreds of dead bodies. This is the first time it's been a soldier, and it's, well it's different." She looked away, her eyes glistening, then took a deep breath and pushed on. "The bruise on his chest looks like a boot mark. Specifically a combat boot."

"Someone forced him down by standing on his chest," I said. My stomach took a flip at the thought.

"Yes, while someone else held his wrist down. "

"Could it have been one boot on the wrist and one on his chest?"

She shook her head. "No, the bruises on the wrist are from fingers. If I were back in my lab, I might be able to lift prints from them, but here I'm not so sure. One thing is certain. At least two people were involved."

I pictured two people holding him down while one of them poured cement over his head. I glanced at the slab in the back of the truck and shuddered.

"It gets worse," Fordham said. "I haven't been able to examine his other wrist yet. It's still buried in the cement. If someone held that wrist down and the bruise marks don't match…"

"You could be talking about three people." I said.

"Yep."

I guess I shouldn't have been surprised. The soldiers we had interviewed wanted us to think they were a big happy family. If they were so tight, it was only logical that the murderer wouldn't have acted alone. He would have had help, not only to physically hold Larson down. They were lying for each other and withholding information. The liars were just as complicit in the crime as the guy who put a boot in Larson's chest.

My money was still on Judd and Porter. I didn't have a shred of evidence to back up my gut feeling other than that they had been here at the time, the two of them were pals and they obviously knew something they weren't talking about.

"So we know that at least one of the killers was wearing combat boots," I said.

"Yep. Not absolute proof that it was a soldier but it's looking that way. And, unless they're brand new, the tread on them would be solid evidence against any suspect."

"What's next?" I asked.

"I tried to do some preliminary examination while they were still chipping away at the cement. Unfortunately, we don't have any refrigeration large enough to keep him cool. I'm going to have to work through the night to get the rest of this cement off of him before I can continue my exam."

"You need some rest," I said. "You can't go on at this pace."

She took a deep breath and glanced over her shoulder at the cement slab resting in the back of the truck.

"I'm doing okay. I'm tired, but I'm okay." She fixed me with her red-rimmed eyes that looked glassy and ready to spill. "We've got to get the men who did this."

"Believe me, that's the plan. Chief Mayes and I don't have any experience with investigations, but we're doing our best. On another subject, how well do you know Colonel Scaporelli?"

"Not as well as I'd like," she said with a sly smile. "I think he's kind of sexy. Don't you?"

He was a very good looking man, but the more shady he appeared the less attractive he seemed. "Do you know what kind of relationship he has with Senor Bonilla?"

She seemed surprised by the questions. "Bonilla? That guy from the village that's always surrounded by his little posse?"

I nodded that she had the right man.

"I don't know that they have any kind of relationship," she said. "Why?"

"Was the entire medical team up here all weekend?" I asked.

"We sent four soldiers down to base camp to renew some supplies and to send lab work out for testing we couldn't do here. The four of them came back up with you on the convoy. Other than those folks, we were all here. We've been running the clinic as usual on weekends and we had some patients overnight in the hospital."

"So Scaporelli was here," I said.

She narrowed her eyes at me. "What's the deal?"

"I don't know. Just seems like something, I don't know, something sneaky is going on between him and Bonilla." She continued to stare at me with a question on her face.

"Do you know if Scaporelli ever got involved in the nightly poker games?"

Her hands went to her hips and she seemed reluctant to answer. "You don't suspect him, do you?"

"Frankly, I suspect everyone at this point. Could you just answer the question, please?"

She consulted her boots a moment then looked up at me with a sigh. "I have no idea if he played poker, but I doubt it. I've seen him working late at the hospital most nights. I don't know when he would have had time to get involved in card games. And it doesn't seem like something he would do, hang out with a bunch of enlisted guys on his time off." Fordham had been open and friendly with me so far, but my questions made her reassess her opinion of me. Her attraction to Colonel Scaporelli appeared to be more then idle admiration.

"He's a good man, Harper," she said. "I can't believe you suspect him of involvement in this."

"I'm just eliminating possibilities. Everyone who was up here this weekend is potentially a suspect," I said.

"Including me?"

"Including everyone," I said.

"But somehow Scaporelli has risen to the top of your list," Fordham said, her eyes narrowed.

"I didn't say that," I said, but she didn't seem mollified. "Look, I'm sure it's nothing. I know you've got a lot on your plate. Let me know if there's anything I can do to help you."

My offer of help didn't repair her newly negative feeling toward me. "I'm going to go take a whiz and then head to the lab," she said. "If you come by in a couple of hours, I should have more information for you."

I glanced at my watch and saw that it was already way past dinner time. No wonder my stomach was making embarrassing noises.

"You're not going to make me stand there while you cut into him are you?" I asked. "Because I'm not into that whole autopsy witnessing thing."

My reluctance brought a smile to her face. "No, you don't have to see any gore unless you want to. Although if you've never seen one, an autopsy can be very interesting."

"I'll take your word for that," I said.

I told her I would stop by the lab later and walked away from her hoping she wouldn't think too badly of me. I liked her. Under other circumstances, we'd probably be friends.

My stomach told me it was time to grab another MRE for dinner, but first I wanted to find Sergeant Mora and the journalists to see what they had been up to. Unfortunately, Fletcher wasn't ready to wrap things up.

"Don't you think we should call Santos again?" he asked. As much as I didn't want to admit it, he was right. There was a lot of new information to pass on and putting it off until tomorrow wasn't going to help anyone. I told him I would meet him at the headquarters tent as soon as I had spoken with Mora.

I looked for the sergeant and the journalists in their tent but it was empty. When I searched in other tents, I found them all empty, darkened shells of canvas filled with rows of cots.

Where is everyone? I wondered.

A sudden burst of laughter drew my attention further down the road, just as Dodd stepped out from between two tents. He stood looking through the mesh at a room crowded with people, his hands on his hips and his cheek puffed out with a wad of tobacco chew. He didn't look happy.

"Have you seen the journalists?" I asked him.

He spit a long stream of tobacco on the ground. "In there," he said.

I looked through the mesh. "Looks like half the unit is in there."

"Yep, looks like." He crossed his arms over his wide chest and seemed willing to look anywhere but at me.

I wondered what pissed him off. I pushed the tent flap aside, stepped in, and understood what had put Dodd's underwear in a knot.

"All right, ante up," Porter said.

The room looked like a make-shift casino instead of a military tent. Large square cuts of plywood lay on top of empty cots to create tables. Around each table, men sat shoulder to shoulder, perched on the edges of cots. They palmed their cards, faces expressionless. Porter dealt a new hand; Judd sat next to him.

The three young soldiers I had met earlier in the clinic, Granger, Paterson and Burke sat around a second game. Captain Reece, the veterinarian, now sported sunglasses in the poorly lit tent and wedged into yet another group. Reece told me everyone played. He hadn't exaggerated.

I'd played Texas Hold'em a few times, but never with so many people. Despite the numbers, the tent was quiet, very little of the banter you would expect in a normal card game.

Each player is dealt two cards of their own. The rest of the hand is made up of five community cards everyone uses. As community cards are revealed, the pot grows larger until the stakes are substantial. The drama of the game happens when someone declares, "all in," an aggressive move in which the player bets everything they have, a dare to either win it all or lose everything. If these games had been going on over several weeks, I wondered how often the pots simply shifted from one man's pocket to the next then back again.

Everyone seemed to look at me as I ducked into the tent, but Mora was the only one to greet me.

"You gonna get in on one of those games?" I asked him.

"No way. I've never understood poker and these guys seem like they know what they're doing. Cordovan wants to play, though."

"Of course he does. Play some cards, get people to open up. Absolutely anything they say or do could be used in his story."

"I can't stop him, can I?"

"No. Let him play, but pay attention to what people say to him, would you?"

"Okay, no worries."

We discussed some of the interviews Mora saw the pair had recorded throughout the day, who they had interviewed, what angle they might be going after.

"So far, if you would ask me, I'd say they were working on a positive story. They didn't ask anything I wouldn't have asked," he said.

"Nothing unusual?"

He thought about it for a minute and shook his head. "No, nothing. They seemed to ask the same questions of everyone. They had some interesting conversations with a group of the older women in the village. They asked what they did for medical care when the military hospital wasn't here. Some of the old women described some of the traditional remedies they used."

"Traditional remedies?"

"Yeah, like roots, or local plants they might use as curatives. You know, like folk medicine."

"Local plants. Did Cordovan ask them about these local plants?"

"Yeah, now that you mention it. He was the one who brought it up, but the women talked about several different things that grow in the area. I didn't understand all of it…"

Mora kept talking, but I stopped listening. All I could think about were the two kinds of local plants I knew grew in the area. Both could be used for medicinal purposes. Both were illegal to cultivate. Marijuana and the leaves from the coca plant.

I glanced at Cordovan and caught him looking at me. They were here because of the drug crops. That had to be it. The tingle of discovery shortened my breath, a cold chill raced down my back.

"How could I have been so dense?" I said.

"What is it?" Mora asked, but kept quiet while I rolled things around in my head. Did Cordovan think Scaporelli was involved with the growth or worse, the distribution of drugs? Why would an oncologist be involved with the drug trade?

Then it clicked and I wanted to kick myself for how long it

had taken me to see it. Marijuana was sometimes prescribed to cancer patients to relieve pain. Scaporelli was an oncologist and Cordovan's wife was a cancer patient. There had to be some kind of connection between those three things. If Scaporelli used his trips here to smuggle drugs into the U.S., it would be a serious story about criminal activity.

It was difficult to picture the handsome doctor getting involved with drugs. His relationship with Bonilla felt suspicious, though. A smuggling partnership would explain why they didn't want to be seen talking to each other.

I was sick of the guessing game. Sick of listening to people lie to me. When Cordovan strolled over smiling I figured it would be more of the same.

Even after a full day of working in the hot jungle temperatures, his safari jacket looked crisp and wrinkle-free, his hair still perfectly in place. The only sign that he had been working all day was the mud on his brand new boots.

"I heard they managed to get the body out of the cement," he said.

"Yes. Dr. Fordham has him in the lab now."

"Will you allow us to shoot the hole where he was found? I haven't asked a single question about the murder, but I can't ignore it."

"I'm not asking you to. You can shoot video of the construction site tomorrow. The investigators should be here in the afternoon, and I'll have an official Army statement for you. I can probably get you some preliminaries on the investigation as well."

Cordovan's look of surprise was almost comical. "I didn't expect you to be so cooperative."

"Like I said before, I'm not here to stop you from doing your job. I just didn't want the gruesome video of the body all over the airwaves."

"Isn't that what murder is?" he said. "Gruesome. Tabloid. A sordid, ugly business?"

The first murder I had ever been involved with had been a sordid, ugly business. This one wasn't any different.

"You must see a lot of this sort of thing in your trade," I said.

"Me? No. Larceny, embezzlement, political corruption, yes. But murder? That was the first dead body I've ever seen and I hope it's the last," he said. "Hey, do you think you can get Dr. Scaporelli to give me an interview? As the head of the medical mission, it would be a shame not to get a chance to talk to him."

Cordovan's smile came off smarmy, like a car salesman.

I put my fake smile on and flashed it at him. "Sure, I can try to convince him. It would be helpful if you gave me the questions you want to ask. It might help reassure him that the interview will be harmless."

Cordovan kept the smile on his face, but the charm left his eyes. "I'd prefer to get responses that are unrehearsed."

"If you were going to ask him about medical care or about service in the National Guard, you wouldn't have a problem giving me the questions. But that's not what you want to talk to him about, is it?"

We stared each other down for a minute. I didn't have time for his games.

"When you're ready to tell me what this is really about, I'll be ready to help you. Until then...." I shrugged.

Cordovan narrowed his eyes at me then and walked away. He went straight to Dropic to tell him what I had said.

"He's not happy," Mora said.

"Neither am I. He's after something and I'm pretty sure I know what it is."

"Do you want to share?"

"Don't worry about it. I'll see you in the morning."

By the time I left the tent, the poker games were in full swing. I noticed that some of the quarters had been replaced by dollar bills. I strolled closer and saw there was actually quite a bit of money stacked up around the cots.

The games were inappropriate and I understood why Dodd had looked pissed. It was Dodd's responsibility to enforce good order and discipline. The games put him in an awkward position, one which forced him to tell his buddies they were out of line. I didn't think Dodd the kind of NCO that would let a friendship intimidate him from doing his job. It seemed out of character that a man who ran his construction sites so cleanly would allow such a blatant thwarting of the regulations. They were his men. If he wasn't going to stop it, neither was I.

Chapter 22

I found Fletcher in the headquarters tent hunched over his laptop.

"I'm putting together some notes for our conversation with Santos," he said, glancing up at me. His bald head glistened with rain, and his skin appeared golden brown under the odd lighting in the tent. He sat with shoulders hunched up around his ears. Even from several feet away, the tension was evident.

"Tired?" I asked.

He flicked his bloodshot, puffy gaze to me for a long moment and took a deep breath, relaxing back into his chair.

"Did Dr. Fordham tell you about the bruise? The one on his chest?"

I nodded.

"Who could do that?" he asked. "It was so clear. Like a tattoo on the middle of his chest. This big boot print. I just," he shook his head, unable to say any more.

"I've got a few things you need to add to your notes," I said and described the poker games going on down the road.

"They had just started playing when I got there and by the time I left, I would guess there might have been twenty bucks in a couple of the pots. That can start to add up if they're playing night after night."

"Reece told you the Larsons were the ones who put the games together, but Allen said it was Dodd, Porter or Judd?"

"Well, it's definitely not Dodd. But the other two, maybe. Still, who knows what, if anything, poker has to do with Larson's death. Reece is the one who failed to tell me that he and Bobby had gone to blows over a woman. I think he told me about the poker games to take focus away from himself."

"So not the most reliable witness," Fletcher said.

"It's pretty clear the Larsons aren't his favorite people,"

"Is Reece a killer?" Fletcher asked.

"Who knows? Maybe. Even if Reece killed Bobby out of jealousy over a woman, he would have had help."

Someone fired up a new generator, but it was far enough away that we could still hear the constant buzz of insects as they cycled through a pattern of nocturnal communication. The rain slowed down to an annoying drizzle, but the night felt drenched and heavy. I wondered where Harry was, whether he was cold, wet. I shook my head to clear it of thoughts of him.

Fletcher had his chair tilted back on the rear legs, gently rocking back and forth, looking out at the camp through the tent mesh.

"Did I tell you what my friend Harry was doing here?"

He looked at me and plopped his chair down on all four legs as if he didn't really want to hear about it. I told him about the drug raid scheduled for the morning.

"Is it a crop associated with this village?" he asked.

I shrugged. "I have no idea. Harry didn't say, but he did tell me it was nearby so I guess we can make that assumption."

Harry hadn't said if the target was marijuana or a coca field. Either way it was danger close, with a full squad of trained killers against men who might defend their crop by any means necessary. Dangerous for anyone in the vicinity.

"We're basically cut off from civilization, surrounded by narcotics, with a dead body," Fletcher said. You gotta figure the drugs and the murder are connected. Maybe Larson saw something and the villagers involved with the drugs killed him."

"Drugs and murder seem a likely combination, but you saw the bruise. Those were combat boots. At least one of the killers was a soldier. I haven't seen any villagers wearing anything other than sandals. Maybe some cowboy boots scattered here or there, but no combat boots. Have you?"

Fletcher shook his head in the negative then rocked back on the legs of his chair, thinking.

"I think it was Porter and Judd," I said.

"Based on what?"

"Based on the way they've been acting. The way Dodd seems to be covering up for them somehow. Dodd wasn't here, but it's obvious he knows something about what happened. And Porter and Judd are down the road running that poker game right now. Dodd isn't happy about it, but he's not doing anything to stop it."

"That doesn't prove anything," Fletcher said.

"I know. And if I talked to you all night, I couldn't give you anything other than innuendo to back it up, but my money is on those two. I just feel it."

"All we can do is rely on the hard evidence, and right now that evidence points to the killer being a soldier," Fletcher said. "What if we make the connection that the soldier is also involved in the drugs somehow?"

"If there's a soldier involved with the drugs, it's Scaporelli."

I told him about Cordovan's interest in local plants and traditional medicine. I explained Scaporelli's background in oncology and the connection with Cordovan's wife.

"Which points to Scaporelli somehow," Fletcher said. "The only way some kind of drug running plot could happen is if the soldiers involved had been here before. This exercise has been going on for years, but this is the first time this particular engineer unit has been here. The only ones who keep coming back…"

"Is the hospital unit," I finished for him. "Which means that little tête-à-tête we saw between Scaporelli and Bonilla…"

"Could be significant," he finished for me.

Fletcher and I exchanged a look, then laughed at the verbal dance we had just finished. Somehow, considering our rough start, it seemed as if we had found a way to make it work. Now we were finishing each other's sentences. Who knew?

I went to the container of MREs stashed in the corner and found a couple of meals. I guessed Fletcher would want the Chicken Fajitas and was right. I took the Cheese Tortellini. We added water to the heating elements and set the meals aside as they cooked, then went over our notes before we put in the call to Santos. Despite all the questions and information we had for him, there was really only one thing I wanted to know, so I asked him as soon as he answered the phone.

"When are you guys getting up here?"

"Maybe just before night fall tomorrow," he said.

Less than 24 hours. Still, it seemed like a long time to be mired in the investigation on our own. We gave him the run down on what we had learned so far. I told him about the drugs and the raid scheduled for the morning. I told him about the weird scene with Bonilla and Scaporelli.

"Scaporelli has a history with that place," Santos said.

"Yes," I said. "It was his idea to start bringing the whole hospital up here."

"It could simply be a friendship," Santos offered.

Fletcher and I exchanged a look and didn't respond. I wanted Scaporelli to maintain the image I'd first had of him, as the kind doctor who seemed intent on saving lives and not associated with any criminal activity. He seemed genuinely concerned for the people of the village, but his relationship with Bonilla seemed suspicious. Bonilla was a shady character.

We told Santos about the bruises on the body and Fordham's conclusion that it had to be more than one person and that at least one of them had been wearing combat boots. Talking it over with the investigator, speculating about what might have happened felt creepy. I looked out at the camp's pale yellow lights strung up in a wide pattern that barely illuminated the road. The construction area was well lit, but amongst the tents, deep shadows prevailed, leaving whole sections where the night felt thick and unbroken. I didn't like knowing there were people capable of murder out there. I wasn't usually scared of the dark, but the dark road seemed like a danger area now. I knew I wouldn't feel comfortable moving around alone on this night.

We told Santos about Lieutenant Allen's report of the fist fight between Reece and Larson over a woman.

"We haven't interviewed Reece yet," I said. "But when I did talk to him, he left that information out and instead gave me false information about the victim."

"What false information?" Santos asked.

"That Larson hosted the poker games. But it wasn't him." I paused, a sudden thought stopping me. "You know, when I look back on the first conversation I had with Reece, he was downright evasive and dishonest. He tried to come off friendly and informative but he was really just making sure we didn't look in his direction."

"That's good insight," Santos said. "Sounds like you've formed a gut opinion about the suspect. There's nothing wrong with that in an investigation."

It sounded like a compliment but it pissed me off. Fletcher noticed my change of mood and sat up, waiting to see what I would say next.

"That's what you and Ramsey did with me in Bosnia." I said. "You formed a gut opinion about me as a suspect based on nothing. And you were wrong."

There was a long silence on the other end of the speaker phone. Finally, Santos took in a deep breath.

"Point taken," he said. "Can we move on now?"

He and Ramsey had apologized, but it had not been heartfelt. I wanted him to explain why he and his partner had decided so conclusively, that I was a killer. I stood up and paced the room, hands on my hips, taking deep breaths. I wanted to blow up at the man, vent at him about how close he had come to ruining my life. Fletcher, with a wary eye in my direction, continued to report, but I tried to block out the sound of their voices and paced the room, remembering Bosnia and the stress I had been under, the way the investigators had treated me. Eventually I looked down and saw my stupid rubber rain boots flopping about as I paced. The boots looked ridiculous. They made me feel ridiculous.

I sat down and struggled to get the overshoes off. It took a bunch of pulling and tugging, and by the time I was able to toss the damn things in a corner I was out of breath. The exertion had worked off my frustration with Santos.

Fletcher had continued his conversation but now stared at me, probably wondering if I was going bonkers. I gave him a small smile and he relaxed. I tried to catch up on their conversation.

"One thing's for sure," Santos said. "This case is much more complicated than it first appeared."

Hearing that from Santos made me chuckle. I had been feeling like I was completely out of my league. There was too much going on to know who was telling the truth and who wasn't. There were too many threads, too many possibilities. I glanced at Fletcher and saw the look of concentration on his face. He was a smart man capable of a lot of things most men couldn't do, but I had little faith that he or I could sort out what had happened here. To say I was discouraged would be an understatement.

"Chief Mayes has sent me the audio files of your interviews and the crime scene photos. Considering your inexperience, you've both done a good job of starting the investigation. I think we've got enough to work with. My investigators and I can take over as soon as we get there," Santos said.

"Wait, what?" I asked. "Are you telling us to back off?"

"Yes. Until we can examine the forensic evidence and get some expert interrogations done, it doesn't seem as if we can go any further."

Santos kept talking, but I wasn't really paying attention. I glanced at Fletcher and we exchanged a smile. I'd wanted to help the investigation and we had, as much as two people could who didn't know what they were doing. While I was a bit disappointed we hadn't solved the thing, I knew it was only a matter of time. I leaned back in my chair and allowed myself to release the burden of it.

"Please keep an eye on what is going on around you. I'd be interested in hearing how that raid goes in the morning. And keep an eye on Bonilla and Scaporelli. You might see them reacting differently tomorrow after the Special Forces soldiers get in there. Also, I'm surprised that if Dodd, Porter and Judd are involved with that poker game, they aren't worried about the possibility of disciplinary action against them. They have a dead body on their construction site. If they thought they could get away with the games before, they couldn't possibly think they could fly under the radar now. Violation of General Order Number 1 is serious business."

"Don't worry Mr. Santos," Fletcher said. "We'll keep our eyes open and report anything unusual that happens."

We began sorting out the logistics of the investigators' arrival the next day. Fletcher let Santos know that his helicopter would probably be ready to fly the next day as soon as the weather cleared. It was possible he might leave in only a few hours. I figured Cordovan and Dropic would want to send some tape back with him, and I was just about to mention it to Santos when a commotion outside the tent drew our attention. One of the engineers was running down the road shouting for Dodd.

"He's dead! He's dead!" he yelled. "Top, you gotta come. He's dead."

"Oh no," Fletcher said.

Santos asked what was going on. "There's some commotion outside," I said. "Someone is screaming that someone is dead. He must be talking about Reggie," I said. "Who else could he mean?"

"You'd better go check it out," Santos said.

We signed off with Santos, promising to call back immediately once we figured out what the heck was going on. Scaporelli had said Reggie had only suffered a few broken bones. Something must have gone terribly wrong, and I was afraid to find out what it was.

Chapter 23

We ran toward Dodd and several others, who had come out of the tent where they had been playing cards. Dodd grabbed the young soldier by the shoulders and gave him a hard shake.

"Where?" Dodd asked.

The kid was panting, red faced and sweaty, his mouth open, eyes wide. He pointed toward the construction site. "Under the blocks. At first I didn't see him, but then … Oh hell Top, you gotta come. There's blood everywhere."

Fletcher and I followed the soldier as he led everyone toward the site. He veered to the left toward the parking lot. A tall light post at the corner of the lot bathed the area in a pale amber glow, giving off a high pitched florescent hum. In front of the lot was an open area filled with neatly stacked construction materials, wooden pallets, bags of cement and stacks of roofing tiles. At the edge of the supply area, a wall of cement blocks lay tumbled in a haphazard pile.

Boots crunched and shuffled on fine gravel. A general murmur of questions grew louder as more people drew closer and realized what they saw. They stood staring. Some cursed; others backed off. Fletcher moved to the front, ordering everyone to stand back, taking charge of the situation. I moved up next to him. When I finally saw the body, I had to turn away, but the vision had already seared itself into my memory.

Legs splayed out from under a large pile of cement blocks, looking crushed and lifeless. I had no idea how much one of those blocks weighed, but an entire stack of them? No one could survive that. A forearm, purple and bruised rested in the middle of a thick pool of blood. Small mounds of dirt had been pushed up near the heels of the boots, making it clear that the victim had been kicking into the gravel, struggling under the weight of the blocks. He had kicked down to the sand in his desperate attempt to get free.

Reece kneeled next to the body, lifting a wrist to check for a pulse. After a few seconds he lay the hand down gently, no urgency in his movements.

"Someone go get Major Fordham," Fletcher said. "Move it!"

One of the soldiers sprinted off in the direction of the medical unit.

"Let's get some help moving these blocks," he ordered. "Slowly now. We don't want any more of them tumbling down."

"Wait," I said. "We'd better get some pictures."

I looked at Sergeant Mora, and he took off to get his camera. The rest of us waited. I wondered who it was. I scanned the crowd trying to determine who was missing. A bird screeched a high piercing call. Insects swarmed around the yellow light, a warning zap sounding each time one got too close. The jungle soundtrack wasn't helping to ease the tension. Soldiers stood about, jaws clenched, popping their knuckles, shaking their heads. Two of their number were dead now, another badly injured, and there was little they could do about it.

I had run out of the tent without my hat, and wisps of my hair blew around in the night air. I pushed the curls away from my face and was surprised at how much my hands shook. Another body. More blood. I wished for Harry.

When Mora returned, he set about taking snapshots of the scene. The thump of the flash going off, followed by the high-pitched whine of the unit powering up made me even more jumpy.

After several minutes of this, Mora nodded at Fletcher.

"All right now," Fletcher said. "Someone give me a hand here."

Dodd, Hank and Reece bent to the task along with Fletcher. They started near the top of the body, where his head might be. After a few minutes, Dodd cussed.

"Shit! It's the lieutenant," he said backing up and moving away from the horror.

Lieutenant Allen. The awkward new officer no one seemed to like. He had reluctantly opened up to Fletcher and me, telling us about Dodd's involvement with the poker game and about the fight between Reece and one of the Larson brothers.

I looked at Reece to gauge his reaction. Could he have done this because Allen told us about the fight he had with Bobby? But Reece looked pale and shaky. He took several staggering steps away from the pile of rubble, turned with his back to the crowd and puked, bracing himself with hands on his knees, his back arching up as he heaved. The soldiers in the crowd kept their backs to him, letting him have his moment of weakness.

Dodd, his face red, cursed in frustration. "God damn it!" he said. "What the fuck is going on here?" He stood, staring at the pile of rubble panting, his forehead streaked in cement dust, his face pale. Then he scanned the crowd of soldiers, as if his stern look could draw the killer out. When his gaze landed on Porter and Judd, he stopped. The two men stared back at Dodd. The first sergeant spit a long stream of tobacco juice on the ground, shooting his angry look at the pair. Porter shrugged innocently, shook his head in the negative slowly, but kept his focus on Dodd. Something about Porter's stare read defiance. Judd's eyes flicked from Porter to Dodd as if he were worried about getting between the two. Dodd took a step in their direction, then stopped, clenching up, his whole body rigid as if he wanted to spring at Porter but fought down the urge.

Fletcher continued to remove the blocks of cement. I wanted him to see the exchange, but feared that if I said anything, it would distract them. I kept quiet.

By this time, Dr. Fordham approached. Soldiers with her carried a litter. She moved slowly, as if she didn't want to see another body.

"Christ, Sergeant Harper, another one? I haven't even finished processing the first body." Then she lowered her voice, leaning toward me. "This is really getting scary now, you know? I mean, it's like one of those slasher movies or something. Don't go in the basement. Don't get separated from the group." She shuddered, glancing around at the soldiers watching. "One of these guys is a killer," she said. "Who says they're done killing people?"

A slasher movie. As much as I hated to admit it, her dramatic summary of events felt spot on. Stuck in the middle of nowhere, cut off from civilization and no way for the law to come to the rescue.

"I take it you've written off the idea of one of the villagers as the murderer?" I asked her.

"Those boot marks on Larson's chest pretty much sealed the deal for me. No. My money is on one of these guys."

This group of soldiers who claimed they were like a family had set to killing each other off for some reason and I felt more and more clueless about what that reason could be.

With a final deep breath that sounded like dread, Fordham stepped forward and began an examination of the body. Fletcher backed away. He took out a flashlight and began to survey the scene around the pile of cement blocks.

The place where Allen's face should have been was just a bloody mess. The golden bar of his rank pinned on the collars of his uniform and the embroidered name tab on his chest were the only solid identifiers. I wondered how old he was. Wondered about his family, if he had a girlfriend, a career that kept him busy when he wasn't serving in uniform. All of that was over now.

Dodd stood away from the group, his arms crossed over his chest, lower lip line puffed out to accommodate a wad of tobacco. His forehead deeply creased as he glared in the direction of the body but didn't seem to be seeing anything. I wondered what he thought about. Nothing good, that was for sure. I didn't blame him for his anger. Any First Sergeant would be angry to learn that another one of his soldiers had died.

When someone touched my arm I almost jumped and felt embarrassed.

"Hey, it's only me," Fletcher said. "What are you staring at so hard, Lauren?"

It took a couple seconds to catch my breath and for my heart to slow down. Dr. Fordham had hit a nerve with the talk about a slasher movie. I glanced around at the people standing in the thin pool of light. Heavy clouds obscured any moonlight there might have been. Add the unfamiliar insect sounds, wails and screeches from jungle animals, along with a murderer, and it was no wonder I felt skittish.

"You okay?" Fletcher asked.

"A little freaked out. Aren't you?"

He nodded, then glanced around, his gaze stopping on Dodd. He watched him for several seconds, then shifted his attention to where Porter and Judd were eyeing the first sergeant from several yards away.

"This is getting way out of control," he said. "I'll be glad when Santos and his crew get here."

"I'll just be happy to have this night end. Things might be a bit easier to take if it wasn't so damn dark around here."

"I want to show you something." He indicated I should follow him as he walked around to the other side of the pile of bricks, slowed down, stepping carefully, then crouched down and directed his flashlight to the ground. He ran the light back and forth over fat Humvee tire tracks which led away from the point where the pile of cement blocks had been stacked neatly. A vehicle had been used to knock over the pile.

"Could someone have backed into the pile, not knowing Allen was on the other side?" I asked.

"That's what I was thinking. It's impossible to tell if these are tracks from a truck backing into the wall, or driving into it," he said, standing up. "A trained investigator might be able determine that, but I can't, especially not in this light." He glanced around at the soldiers. Lowering his voice, he leaned closer to me. "And no matter how the truck knocked them over, those tracks won't tell us if it was an accident or intentional."

When I had first seen the body, I immediately assumed it had been done on purpose. I felt slightly relieved at the possibility it could have been an accident.

Reece's reaction to the corpse popped into my head. If he had backed into that pile of bricks knowing Allen was on the other side, he might have been shocked to see what his actions had produced. Reece had spun away and been sick at the sight. For a veterinarian, it seemed out of character that the sight of blood would have that effect on him. Maybe seeing the results of what he had done caused the sickness.

"We'd better tell Santos about this," I said.

I glanced at my watch and was shocked to see that it was after 2200. I should have felt tired, exhausted even. We'd started the day at oh-dark-thirty and that seemed like ages ago. No matter how many hours it had been since I last slept, or how much stress and exertion I had endured during the day, the likelihood that I would be able to sleep felt remote at best.

I hoped that news of Lieutenant Allen's death might light a fire under Santos and his team. We were in serious need of some help. The sooner civilization came to us, the better.

"I'll get some help to preserve these tracks first," Fletcher said. He called Mora over to get some pictures of the tracks. Then he assigned a couple of soldiers the task of marking off the area so that no one would disturb the evidence. They hammered tall stakes into the ground then loosely strung white cotton engineer tape around the area, fencing in as much of the tracks as possible. When they were done, two long lines of the white tape led from the concrete block tumble, away into the jungle.

Dodd continued to brood and glare at everyone around him, keeping distance between himself and the others. Most first sergeants would have objected to someone else giving orders to his people, but Dodd seemed past the point of arguing with Fletcher over the leadership mantle.

An animal screamed loudly in the distance as if in pain, startling everyone. I glanced in the direction of the noise then exchanged embarrassed looks with the crowd at how jumpy we all felt. The wind wasn't strong, but every leaf and branch in the jungle surrounding us seemed to move, as if it were a living thing. Despite the warm and humid air, I still felt chilled.

"Let's go make that call," Fletcher said.

I didn't need convincing. I turned my back on the bloody scene and followed Fletcher.

"I'll meet you there," I said. "I've gotta make a pit stop." I'd been ignoring nature's call for a long time. Normally, the two block long trip to the latrine wouldn't have seemed an obstacle. The bodies, the talk of killers lurking about and with the complete darkness that accompanied the jungle nightfall, the desire to ignore the inevitable increased; but I couldn't ignore it any longer.

"I'm going with you," Fletcher said.

"I don't need an escort to go to the bathroom."

"Shut up, Lauren. I'm coming and that's it."

He put his hand in the middle of my back and pushed me toward the latrine. I was grateful. I should have thanked him.

We both shined light around the entrance area, poking the small flashlight beams into dark corners around the tent to reassure ourselves no one else was around. I helloed the tent and when no one answered, ducked behind the flap, directing my flash light in every corner inside. Thankfully, the tent had light so I didn't need my flashlight, but I used it anyway, the added light providing some comfort.

I had my flashlight clamped between my teeth to unfasten my pants when Fletcher cried out. "Hey, what?"

The loud thud that followed sounded disgustingly like the smashing of a melon, then a grunt and someone falling.

I froze. Afraid to take a breath, fearing that something terrible had happened to Fletcher, I stood paralyzed for several seconds, listening. Someone moved around outside the tent, maybe more than one person. Yes, definitely two sets of footsteps out there. Cupping my hand around my flashlight beam to minimize its spread, I tried to find some other way outside the tent. Going out the same way I had come in would only mean danger, but it quickly became apparent that the canvas around the tent met the ground in a taut and obstructive way in every corner. I cursed Dodd and his ever-efficient engineers.

I had a Swiss Army knife on my belt. I doubted it would cut through the canvas but I pulled it out anyway. The shuffling continued outside the tent. Why didn't they rush in? What were they waiting for? They hesitated, but I didn't.

I did what my mother taught me to do in frightening situations. I screamed.

Chapter 24

You don't know how hard it is," my mother had told my sister and me. "When you're frightened, you might shout or gasp because you're startled, but to scream, to really scream? The kind of scream that means you want someone to come save you, that's much harder to do."

"That's not true," I had argued. "Of course your first reaction is to scream."

"No it's not," she said. "Your first reaction is to freeze. You have to think about it, gather up your resources and be purposeful in that effort to scream. When you're frightened, I mean really terrified, it's hard to think."

She would sometimes jump out at us, like it was a game to see if she could scare us. And when she did manage to startle us, she didn't want a frightened yelp. She wanted us to scream, to pretend something horrible would happen if someone didn't hear that cry for help.

I often wondered how my mother had firsthand knowledge of that kind of fear. What had frightened her enough to make her freeze? Frightened her enough to regularly train her daughters in the practice of crying for help as if their lives depended on it.

I worried that the tent might muffle any noise I made, so I called that practiced scream from my past and screamed until my body shook.

Almost instantly a lot of stuff happened.

The lights inside the tent went out, only the small beam of my flashlight remained. Two village men I didn't recognize, burst into the tent. I backed away from them, but there was nowhere to go. I crouched waiting, my flashlight in one hand, my small knife in the other. I continued to scream as loudly as I could. I must have looked a bit scary to them. They approached with wide eyes, hesitating as if I was something wild and dangerous. That's exactly how I felt.

When one got close enough, I leaned sideways and kicked out like a mule, my combat boot connecting squarely with his chest. He fell back against his partner, but only for a second. Then, they both rushed me. I slashed with the knife arm and cut only air. I followed that by swinging the flashlight as a club and struck the side of one head. He staggered, but the other managed to knock the flashlight out of my hands with the sweep of his arm and spun me around. He grabbed me from behind, one arm wrapped around me like a vice. I stomped on his foot and jabbed my knife into his leg. He cursed and jerked his leg back, but I kept hold of the knife and jammed it in again. This time it stuck. He screamed in my ear and I assumed, yelled at his friend to help. His friend did help, by way of a slug to the side of my head, making me stumble sideways. I found it too hard to scream after that. It was time to concentrate on not passing out.

The guy behind me clamped a cloth over my nose and mouth. I continued to struggle, to try to shake his hand away from my face, but eventually I had to inhale.

I had never smelled ether before, but I instinctively knew that the cloth enveloping my face had been soaked in the sickly sweet drug.

The guy behind me held my arms tightly to my sides, the cloth to my face, while the one in front got ready to hit me again. I leaned into the guy behind, raised both legs and kicked out at the guy in front, hitting him hard in the chest. He went sprawling back, yelling at his friend, and was slow to stand up, a hand to his chest like I'd hurt him. Good.

The man holding me would not let go. We stumbled about, I squirmed and tried to get the knife out of his leg, but it was slick with blood and wouldn't budge. I felt a sick satisfaction in his whimpers of pain each time I grabbed the handle. I slammed my elbow into his side, once, twice, and felt satisfied with his grunt in return, the cloth loosening from my face. Spurred on by my success, I screamed again, then snapped my head back, connecting with his face. When that didn't help, I stomped my foot down, dragging my boot down the shin on the way. This time, I think he yelled at his friend, screaming for help. The second man hobbled around nearby, giving angry instructions, staying out of kicking range.

No matter what I did, how I twisted and fought, the man didn't loosen his grip. My elbow connected again and again, but the ether slowly did its work. I grew weaker and unable to separate my face from the cloth.

More people came into the tent. The added manpower meant I wasn't getting out of this trouble, but I refused to stop fighting. I didn't know what they wanted to do to me, but I'd been at the mercy of men like these before. No matter what they had planned, I knew it wouldn't be good.

One of the fresh guys, someone unharmed so far, stepped in front of me and slammed his fist into the side of my head, and then my gut.

In movies, people get hit in the stomach and double over and in the next moment they come up swinging. In reality, getting hit in the gut is nothing like that. There is only pain and an instant loss of breath that feels as if you will never breath again. I folded in half, the pain so sharp and focused I could barely feel the pressure applied to the cloth smashed to my face.

The men spoke back and forth with each other in Spanish. I thought I detected an English accent from one of them, but it was a vague notion that seem to float unfettered in my muddled brain.

I hit the ground in what felt like slow motion, thinking about what Anne Fordham had said. I wasn't that stupid woman in the slasher movie who went off by herself. I had not gone alone, but my precautions hadn't helped.

==========

A sharp pain in my head dragged me back to consciousness. Raging thirst. Couldn't lift my head. Nausea. Wrists. Shoulders. Everything hurt.

I tried opening my eyes, but a bright light jabbed a sharp needle of pain straight through to the back of my head. I kept them closed. The worst pain came from my hands, like they were on fire. Slowly, I realized I hung from my wrists. It took me several seconds to understand that if I straighten my legs, my toes would touch the ground. I had to stretch, but my efforts relieved some of the pain in my hands. I tilted my head back and squinted up at them. They looked purple. Swollen. Alien.

"Fletcher." It came out in a croak. "Fletcher," I tried again. He groaned in answer. I felt relief that I wasn't alone, but felt no joy that he was in the same trouble as I.

I tried to open my eyes. It took a while. I filtered the light with my lashes and the unpleasantness of our situation became more clear.

The piercing light came from a vehicle, its headlights directed at us. Judging from the height of the lights, I got the impression it was a truck. Maybe one of the pickup trucks so popular with the farmers in the area. If anyone sat inside the cab, I couldn't see them, could only see the painful glare from the headlights on full blast and had to turn my face away.

Fletcher hung in a similar fashion several yards away from me. He looked unconscious, his legs collapsed under him as I'm sure mine had been. A shiny purple stain of blood almost covered his bald head, ran down his face and dripped onto the ground. A pool of the shiny black liquid formed underneath him. He'd suffered a terrible whack to the head and I worried for him.

We hung suspended from a metal rod that extended for several feet like a clothes line pole. With us on the rod were large branches of marijuana hanging upside down.

I searched the ground around my feet and saw a large stone a few inches in front of me. I stretched one foot toward it, pulling painfully on my wrists in the process, until I tapped a corner of the stone, finally managing to get it moving toward me. Eventually, I maneuvered it directly under me to stand on it. My precarious perch wobbled, but the pressure on my wrists immediately began to decrease and circulation in my hands returned in needle sharp jabs. For a long time, the pain left me breathless. I flexed my fingers. They felt like sausages.

Slowly, the pain began to subside and I tried to get a better look around. I almost lost my balance, rocks skittering down what sounded like a long slope behind me. I froze. Looking over my shoulder, I realized the pole we hung from sat very close to a tremendous gap. So close, in fact, that one small step back and I would have been dangling over nothingness. The shock almost made me fall off the stone. I struggled to maintain my balance.

It was too dark to see how far across or how far down the chasm extended, but I got the impression it was a large void. I pictured the spot where Reggie had driven himself over the cliff and felt grateful I couldn't see all of the details.

Heights. I hated heights. Just knowing that gap of nothingness was behind me made me tremble. Snatched by bad guys, hanging from my wrists, afraid for how badly Fletcher might be hurt, all of those things seemed like surmountable problems.

That gaping void behind me was a different story. My thinking became muddled, my breathing rapid. If I didn't get a handle on my sudden panic, soon I'd need to put my face in a paper bag. I took deep shuddering breaths and mumbled reassurances to myself as I tried to maintain my balance on top of the stone.

It's okay, you're not going to fall. Just don't look down. We're just close to the edge, not hanging over it. We'll get out of this. I repeated the reassurances in my head.

"Fletcher. Fletcher, wake up."

His eyes flicked open for a second, then squeezed shut. Probably feeling the same needle sharp pain from the headlights as I had felt. Slowly, he found his feet, straightened his legs, but seconds later he collapsed again. He was badly hurt and the bleeding hadn't stopped. A steady drip of blood added to the dark pool at his feet.

"Hey," I yelled into the darkness. "If you don't do something for Fletcher he could die."

No one responded.

"It's me you want anyway. Fletcher is no use to you. Dr. Scaporelli, if you're out there, you've got to do something for him."

That got some tongues wagging. Angry whispers in Spanish.

"I heard you back there, Doctor." I yelled. "I know you're involved in this. I'll cooperate. Just get Fletcher out of here. You don't want a murder on your head."

There was some scrambling around in the cab of the truck. Someone started to open the passenger door, then slammed it closed again.

I looked up at the sky, trying to judge what time it might be. Harry said their raid was planned for first light, but that could still be hours away. It didn't matter. I had a feeling that Harry and his men would have established surveillance on the crop they were planning to attack. He could be out there somewhere. The thought gave me some comfort but not much.

"Come on, Doctor. Let him go," I pleaded.

One hostage would be easier to free than two, especially if the second one was badly injured. If our capture had been meant as a deterrent for destroying the crops, I wondered how long they thought it would work.

The conversation in the truck became more heated, a back and forth that got louder the longer it went on. Eventually the voices settled down. The passenger door of the truck opened and someone stepped out holding a small bag.

Some instructions were yelled out and three men stepped out of the darkness, automatic weapons strapped to their chests. One of them limped badly, dragging his left leg. Another one had a large bandage across his nose and two black eyes. I smiled at them. They glared back.

The doctor moved toward them, and once he stepped away from the glare of the headlights, I recognized Scaporelli.

"It wasn't supposed to happen like this," he said, looking at me guiltily. I kept quiet.

The men cut Fletcher down and he collapsed in a lifeless pile. They stretched him out and Scaporelli bent to him. He opened his medical bag. I wanted to ask him if there was a bottle of ether in there amongst his supplies.

One of the men walked into the darkness, then came back driving another pickup truck, backing it toward where Fletcher lay.

"Is he alive?" I asked.

"Yes. But he's in a bad way."

The men struggled to lift him into the truck bed.

"Careful, now," Scaporelli said, climbing into the back of the truck. His apparent concern for his patient didn't convince me. His show of compassion, like the show he had displayed over his village patients, seemed like a role he knew to play. If he had true compassion, he wouldn't have involved himself in this violent abduction. He was a phony.

"Where are you taking him?"

"We'll drop him near the hospital, someplace where someone will find him. He's been unconscious the whole time so he won't be able to tell them where we are," Scaporelli said.

That must have been his argument with the man in the truck. No need to let Fletcher die since he didn't know anything.

"What did you think abducting us would accomplish? How long do you think you can hold the police off like this?"

Someone walked toward me, a silhouette in the glare of the headlights. I had a pretty good idea who it was.

"Long enough to harvest this crop," Bonilla said. "One day. That is all that we need."

"And you think they'll just stand by and allow you to do that?"

"Yes," he shrugged, then turned and walked away. Over his shoulder he said, "If they do not, you will die."

Chapter 25

Bonilla was a fool.

As I hung from that pole, my hands throbbed and my head ached. I watched Bonilla walk away and thought, the Honduran commandos would never hold off their raid simply because of me. Bonilla didn't have a clue.

He must have seen Harry and me together and assumed our relationship would have some influence. Even if Harry would consider trying to stop them—and I had no illusions that he would—the Honduran soldiers had orders to complete a mission. A pre-mission threat assessment would take into consideration that Bonilla and his small army were equipped with automatic weapons and who knew what else. In any operation, they would make predictions about casualties on both sides. I didn't think the death of one American soldier would mean much in the big scheme of things.

While walking away, Bonilla gave curt instructions to his men. Someone climbed into the cab of the truck, while the other men walked away in different directions taking up positions on the perimeter. They faded into the dark shadows of the jungle.

It appeared I had nothing left to do but wait for something to happen.

Even if Harry and his group did allow the drug traffickers to harvest their crop, I knew Bonilla would never allow me to live.

My survival wouldn't win him any points with the Hondurans and, in fact, showing any mercy would probably be taken as a sign of weakness from the men he usually did business with. I was in Bonilla's custody and if I couldn't get out of this mess somehow, I would be dead. No use in pretending otherwise.

I wondered about Scaporelli. Had the kind doctor, who had shown such empathy for the poor child with kidney disease, known that he was in partnership with murderers? I felt relieved that Fletcher was on his way to the hospital. I hoped his injuries weren't as serious as they appeared.

It was also a relief to know that I didn't have to worry about trying to get Fletcher out of danger. Extricating myself from this mess already appeared impossible. Add a six foot, two inch, semiconscious man to the problem and I may as well start writing both of our obituaries.

As soon as Bonilla and his men slithered into the darkness, the silence of the jungle descended around me. That silence made it easier to hear the rhythmic sound somewhere in the near distance. It took me a while to discern the sound as machetes, several of them, whacking away at Bonilla's crop. They worked in the dark, furiously attempting to clear the crop before the commandos arrived. Maybe Senors Rioja and Egberto and other villagers were out there laboring to bring in the cash crop before it was too late. Were patients that had been seen in the clinic out there helping the village muscle man with his illegal trade? I wondered how much they had to clear and how much time they had. I only wondered all of this stuff because I didn't have anything else to do.

I tried to ignore the pain in my hands, my shoulders, my neck. I tried to ignore the fact that I was hanging right next to a cliff. A cliff that felt, from some sixth sense of mine, like an extremely long drop. Mostly I tried to ignore the fact that I had to go to the bathroom in a big way. That was the hardest thing to ignore.

I had been on my way to the latrine when they knocked me out and dragged me here. When Fletcher and I had made the long trip down the road to the tented bathroom, I had already been holding it for a while. Now I was practically bursting. I thought about just letting go. I could end up getting killed because I was too busy thinking about using the bathroom, my preoccupation with bodily functions making me miss an opportunity to escape when it presented itself. If I just released, I could concentrate on other things, like getting free.

The thought of pissing myself in front of so many witnesses was a humiliation I didn't want to face. I'd been through much worse. In Bosnia, I'd faced humiliations I could barely remember without wanting to scream and cry. Still, I didn't want to add soiled pants to my list.

The man in the truck lit up a cigarette, his mustache and his direct gaze revealed in the orange glow of the lighter flame. Two people, somewhere off in the darkness, talked to each other in Spanish, the low murmur of their voices floated through the darkness unimpeded. These had to be Bonilla's men. Soldiers would never make the mistake of open flames and a conversation in darkness.

I bit the inside of my cheek. Crossed my legs. Counted the strokes of the machetes. Tried to make up a rhyme that went along with the rhythm of the work but somehow kept coming up with words like bliss, kiss, dismiss and yes, piss.

On long road trips, when rest stops were few and far between, my mom used to say it was mind over matter. "Think about something else, Lauren" she'd say. "Big girls don't wet their pants."

I tried to take her advice and think about the pain in my wrists instead of the pain in my bladder. I tilted my head back and looked at the dark and alien things that were formally known as my hands. Even standing on my tiptoes, the pressure felt excruciating, my fingers swollen and ugly. To my untrained eyes, my hands looked as if the only solution was amputation. I'd have two stumps where my hands were. If they had to cut off my hands, there'd be no more typing, no more writing. For a journalist, not being able to type would really suck. No more playing the piano. Okay, so I couldn't play the piano, but I'd always wanted to learn.

No way to undo my damn belt and unbutton my fly and pull my own damn pants down so I could use the damn bathroom.

A tear escaped my eye, followed by another one and another. That made me angry. Crying was not an option. I either had to piss myself or I would end up a blubbering fool and what would Harry think of me if I were crying like an idiot when they did finally get around to rescuing me?

I wiped my face against my sleeve, sniffled the tears away and grit my teeth. There wasn't any option. I had to simply let go.

At that moment, I felt a tapping on the bottom of my boot. Tap, pause, tap, tap, tap. It wasn't my imagination.

I looked toward the cab of the truck and the glow of a cigarette. The man on guard still faced me, his headlights illuminating everything I did. I let my head droop and my knees sag as if I'd passed out. I eased my body to the left, looking under my up-stretched arms to see behind me, my full bladder momentarily forgotten.

Harry hung just below the lip of the cliff. His face dark with camouflage paint, only the whites of his eyes visible. As soon as our gaze connected, he grinned behind closed lips and winked. Another tear escaped but I was fairly sure he couldn't see it.

In that moment, I promised myself, that if I ever got out of this mess alive, I would spend a great deal of time showing this amazing man how much I appreciated his help. I was prepared to show my appreciation in a variety of ways.

I shook off those visions to concentrate on what Harry was doing.

He wore a harness made of black rope and must have climbed to my location. If he hadn't let me know he was there, I never would have seen him.

He pointed to the watch on his wrist. Then he flashed both hands up, fingers spread. Wait ten minutes.

He mouthed a word. Boom. He clenched both hands into fists then spread them, fingers wide. They would create a diversion with some sort of explosion.

He reached behind his back and brought up a wicked-looking knife. The six inch blade must have been made of some sort of combat friendly material because the dull metal appeared just as invisible in the dark as Harry. He pantomimed cutting something near his wrists.

His pantomime done, Harry slowly, and I mean really slowly—I watched him and I couldn't believe how gradual his movements were—slipped that knife into the side of my boot, shoving it in there to ensure it wouldn't fall out. Any observer, even if they had their eyes on me the whole time, would have written the movement off as a shadow, something moving in the breeze. It was a crazy thing to do with those headlights flooding the area, but he used my body and his own stealth to ensure he remained unseen.

Once Harry slipped the knife into my boot, he crept back until his head was below the cliff line again. He repeated the pantomime of cutting near his wrists, then pointed at me and used the first and second fingers of one hand in a walking away gesture, only faster.

Wait ten minutes for the big explosion. Use the knife to free myself, then run away.

He waited to see if I had understood, his eyes wide and searching. I stared back at him and wondered about a man who would scale a cliff, coolly give instructions while surrounded by men equipped with automatic weapons. A man who calmly passed me a knife not meant for cutting rope, but for a much more deadly purpose. This was Harry's life. This was Harry's profession.

He raised his eyebrows, waiting for my response.

I nodded. He winked again, then disappeared into the darkness. No pantomimes of good luck, or be careful, or hope you survive what is about to happen. He simply disappeared and I was left alone with a decision.

Do I piss myself now, or wait until all hell broke loose?

Chapter 26

I pictured myself sitting on a toilet in the stall of a public restroom, searching for paper in an industrial dispenser, hearing someone running water in a sink. The warm spread of urine made my uniform feel heavy. The relief of finally letting go was severely tempered by the anger I felt at having been put in the situation in the first place.

I was pissed, in more ways than one and wasn't sure if I could follow Harry's instructions completely. Wait for the explosion? Check. Cut the rope? Check. Run away? That's where we ran into problems. What came after the cutting rope thing was up for debate in my mind. If someone near me — like the guy sitting in the truck for example, who lit up yet another cigarette and stared straight at me — should drop his weapon for some reason, the opportunity to get a few licks in myself might be too hard to pass up. The bastard was probably laughing at the huge wet spot that had appeared on the front of my uniform.

I glanced at the handle of the knife stuck in my boot, an instrument made for killing. The grip of the knife had rings for the placement of fingers giving the weapon a dual purpose. Designed for hand-to-hand combat, if the blade couldn't be used, the jaw-busting knuckle rings could come in handy. No matter its design, I needed to see it as my means for escape.

I tilted my head back and stared at my hands. The only way to use the knife would be to swing my legs up over the bar to pull the knife from my boot. I pictured the movement in my head and felt sure I could get that far. The problem was that my fingers were foreign objects seemingly incapable of anything useful. I tried flexing them and felt needles of pain. I concentrated on trying to regain some use of them. My greatest fear, was that I would get the knife out of my boot but drop it. If that happened, I would be finished.

Harry's instructions were to wait ten minutes. While dangling from your wrists waiting for the diversion, time was impossible to judge. I figured I'd simply take my cue from the big boom. Hopefully, the pickup truck sentry would go running in the direction of the explosion. If he didn't...well, if he didn't, my prospects for escape were much reduced.

The thwack of machetes in the jungle continued. Then, from somewhere in the darkness, came a strangled cry, cut off too abruptly. I guessed someone had taken out one of Bonilla's men. The pickup truck guy didn't seem to hear the noise, but one of the other men did. He came out of the jungle and approached the truck.

The two men conferred. Pickup truck man shook his head. He hadn't heard anything. The other guy insisted that he had, pointing in the direction of the sound. He must have been convincing because Pickup truck stepped out of the vehicle and they both turned in the direction of the commotion, their backs turned toward me.

That's right, I thought. Go check it out.

I took another look at the knife, flexing my fingers. Once I got the knife out of my boot, what would be the best way to hold it to get at the rope? How long would it take me to cut through the thick hemp? I'd have to be quick about it. No telling how long I would have before one of the guards glanced back to see about me.

By this time, both of the men had taken a couple of steps in the direction of the noise. I hoped they would continue in that direction, take it upon themselves to investigate, when a tremendous flash of light illuminated the jungle and both men crouched, alert now. Moments later the sound, a screeching thump, followed and the ground leaped underneath our feet. The explosion must have happened a few hundred yards away for the light and sound to be so distant from each other. Several smaller explosions followed but were much closer. Grenades. The blasts creeping closer to the clearing where I hung.

Both men took off running in the direction of the action.

I took a deep breath, grabbed the bar with my fat hands and felt shards of pain lance down my arms. I ignored it and swung my legs up, not high enough on the first try. The second try, I was able to get them high enough to hook a finger into one of the rings of the knife, letting my legs drop immediately. It had taken seconds. If my luck held, no one would have noticed what I had just done.

Another explosion rocked the ground and automatic weapons fire tore through the jungle. Tracer rounds bounced everywhere, some from the commandos, some from Bonilla's men. I thought both sides were equally equipped until a vehicle parked about a hundred yards away blew up in a tremendous roar from what had to be a rocket-propelled grenade. The good guys seemed to have a bit of an upper hand.

My fingers were useless. The knife, which looked like a perfect escape device, proved ill-suited for my purposes. The handle was too long. I couldn't grip it and get the blade close enough to slice through the rope which had my wrists so tightly bound.

Nearby, someone put their finger on a trigger and strafed back and forth with their weapon on full auto. It had to be one of Bonilla's men. No trained soldier would waste ammunition that way. Rounds pinged off the pickup truck in front of me and the ground around me, kicking up dirt and debris that stung my eyes. Things were getting dicey, and if I didn't get free soon, someone might come around to get rid of the useless hostage.

Holding the knife by the handle didn't work. I went for the blade, sliding my swollen and ineffective fingers closer to the tip. I sawed back and forth as quickly as I could. My fingers, now not only swollen and painful, they were slippery with sweat and my own blood. I grit my teeth against the pain each slice into the rope caused. When a large drop of blood hit my face, and dripped into my eye, I muffled a sob as the deadly knife made a ruin of my hands.

Then I simply couldn't hold on any longer and the worst happened. I dropped the knife.

When someone hands you the keys to your freedom, the least you can do is rise to the task. Sure, it was dangerous, bullets flying, explosions, whatever. I was damned if I was going to die because I dropped the one thing that would get me out of the mess I was in.

The instant my fingers lost grip of the blade, I drew up my knees hoping to catch the knife in my lap. Instead the blade embedded itself into my right leg, just above the knee.

I barely felt it. I hung there for several long moments, my knees drawn up to my chest, looking at that killing tool sticking out of my leg. I never thought stabbing myself would make me so happy. Now I only had to repeat the performance, bring my knees up to my hands and get a grip of the blade again.

Men were screaming and dying around me. The air was filled with the smell of cordite and blood. I had a sudden flash of realization that none of this had anything to do with Bobby Larson's murder. As horrible as his death was, his passing was a sideshow, an unrelated disaster to this war in the jungle. Cordovan and Dropic were missing the real reason they had come on this mission. I wondered if they saw the explosions from where they were.

There seemed to be only one way to get free. It was a large knife. At least one and a half of the knife's six inches was now stuck deep in my leg. The good news was that it was stuck far enough in, that it wasn't likely to fall out on its own. All I had to do was bring my knees up level with my hands, get a good grip and I'd be more than halfway to freedom. It had been awhile since I'd needed such flexibility, but desperation can bring out the best in us.

My first aid training had taught me that stab wounds were best left alone. If you find someone with something sticking in them, a knife, an arrow, don't pull it out. Get them to medical care but keep the blade where it was. I didn't have that option.

I drew my legs up and wrapped them around the pole I was tied to, then I pulled the knife out. It was stuck deeper then I had at first assumed, and I had to give it a good yank to release it. That hurt. It hurt a lot. I shook it off. The last thing I wanted to do was pass out but seeing so much of that blade come out of my leg, followed by a good deal of blood, was worse than feeling it land there. I don't think I'll ever forget that image.

All of this happened in only moments, a minute at most. I knew I had even less time to get myself untied now. I hacked away at the rope, sawing back and forth, knowing any moment the bullets flying all around me would eventually find a target.

I glanced around to see what was going on and saw Bonilla. He walked toward me, taking long strides, a determined look on his face. He raised his arm, pointing his pistol at me and fired, the muzzle flash blinding me for a second.

He missed, and I kept hacking away at the rope knowing I might not be so lucky with his next shot. Suddenly, the rope split and I was free. I dropped from the pole and landed hard on my back. Bonilla still stalked toward me, firing, ranging in on his target, getting closer with each stride. The fall had winded me for a second, but Bonilla's shots were landing too close. I had to get out of there. One shot pierced the ground near my head, dirt flying into my eyes. Another grazed deeply across my arm, just beneath my shoulder. It felt like a hot poker searing my flesh. I covered my face and head with my arms and rolled to get out of the way of his assault, trying to get to my feet.

I must have become disoriented in the fall. I thought my escape route was to roll to my right, crouch, then run away. That was the plan I had in my head. Instead, once I rotated, I found there was nothing beneath me. I had done Bonilla's work for him. I had avoided being shot, but now I was falling over the edge of the cliff.

Chapter 27

At one point in my military career, a senior NCO I worked with recommended I become airborne trained. If I wanted it, he told me, he could help me with the paperwork and maybe pull a few strings to get me a spot in the elite course. Soldiers who wear jump wings call the rest of us 'legs.' It's their way of reminding us that they are in a special class, have passed the rigorous training required, training the rest of us legs couldn't handle.

Most career soldiers would literally jump for the chance to earn their wings.

I thought about the offer long and hard. Completing the challenging course would have been a boost to my promotion prospects, add jump wings to my uniform and offer inclusion in the club for the select few. And as a journalist, the experience represented excellent writing material.

I turned it down. No matter how many times I imagined it, the fantasy ended the same. Standing with a string of soldiers, my ripcord hooked to the static line. At the green light, the jump string would shuffle to the door, soldiers before me disappearing one by one as they stepped out into the void. When it was my turn, I would get to the door and freeze. The jump master would scream at me.

"Get out that door, Harper. Now, now, now!"

No matter how much he yelled, there was no way I'd ever

willingly take that step. I couldn't voluntarily pitch myself into space on a rapid descent to the ground. It was impossible. No amount of training would prepare me to do that.

Now, to escape Bonilla's bullets, I had pitched myself into a void without the benefit of a parachute.

When I first realized there was nothing under me, that where I thought the ground would be was instead empty space, was like a punch to the gut. My breath whooshed out of my lungs. And despite my mother's training, I couldn't even scream. In those first moments, I remember thinking that dying this way would be pointless. Stupid. A colossal mistake.

Then my shoulder blades slammed into solid ground, spinning me over. Instinctively, I tucked into a ball and struck the ground a second time, this time my arms and knees crashing into the dirt. I realized that what I thought had been a cliff was actually more like a slope. A steep slope that sent me into a roll. Rolling was almost worse than falling. Rolling increased momentum. If I continued to roll, I'd splatter against a rock, go spinning into space. I had to stop myself. But how?

Staying tucked up would only increase my speed, so I tried to relax. Tried to turn my body so that my legs were pointing in the direction I was traveling; down the slope. I spun and bounced. With each bounce, the amount of time I spent airborne kept increasing. The spins increased and I quickly lost all sense of direction. Each time I hit the ground again was like a sledgehammer blow to my entire body. My breath smashed out of me in huge grunts.

Scrambling. Clawing. Spinning again. Dirt, rocks and small shrubs flying around me. I grabbed for anything that went by, digging my fingers and heels in, trying to slow my progression. My efforts were working, but not well enough. I was still headed downhill and I didn't know if there would be another edge, a moment when this slope would stop and I would go spinning off into nothing.

I slammed into what must have been a ledge, an almost level spot. Level enough that I was sliding instead of rolling. I threw myself onto my stomach, spread my legs and arms, trying to make as much contact with the ground as my body would allow. Still I slid. I scrambled for purchase. Fingers dragging, searching for anything to hold onto. Digging with the toes of my boots. Clawing. Praying.

Finally, I stopped.

Rocks and dirt continued to tumble by me. I lay my forehead on one arm, panting. Each breath caused a sharp, stabbing pain. Broken ribs, I thought.

Then I slipped again and realized I wasn't out of danger. The lower part of my legs were still dangling over the edge. Drawing one knee up, I pushed myself further onto the ledge, once, twice, creeping forward until I was laying almost flat. For a time at least, it felt like I wouldn't slide anymore.

I lay there for several seconds, taking tiny, painful breaths, assessing my situation. A quivering mass of pain pretty much summed it up. Releasing myself from the rope had returned circulation to my hands. With the circulation came feeling. There was no distinction between fingers, palms, wrists. It was all just a tremendous wave of agony at the ends of my arms. The place where the blade had penetrated my thigh throbbed. A new pain, one in my upper arm, where one of Bonilla's bullets had grazed me, started to throb along with everything else. Every part of my body felt bruised and scraped.

My thoughts were filled with long strings of cuss words. When I had rolled, and didn't feel ground beneath me, I thought I was surely dead. Instead I was alive but, damn it all, I felt damaged from head to toe. A sob escaped and a couple of tears, but it hurt too much to cry.

Come on, Lauren. Stop blubbering, I thought.

Looking around, I realized dawn was breaking. A pale sliver of light cast a grayish glow on the hills around me. The clouds had finally broken. It looked like we would have a sunny day, if I survived this mess.

Turning my gaze to the top of the cliff, the edge was a couple hundred yards away. Scanning the sloping ground above me didn't offer much hope. If my hands were okay and my leg wasn't injured, I might have been able to scramble up, inch by inch. My hands weren't okay though. Using them to find purchase, to pull myself up, was impossible. They were entirely useless. Besides, the bleat of automatic weapons fire and small explosions were still going on up there. Even if I made it to the top, I'd be in the middle of a battle again.

I looked down. About a foot from where the toes of my boots were dug in was the cliff edge. My legs had been dangling off that ledge a few moments before. While I couldn't see what was below the cliff, I had a feeling that I had averted disaster by only inches.

What was I gonna do?

Then something struck the ground right next to me kicking debris into my face. The sound of a gunshot echoed around the canyon behind me seconds later. Someone was shooting at me. I looked up. Bonilla.

He stood at the edge of the cliff, a pistol gripped in both hands, aiming. Suddenly his body jerked several times and he froze, a blossom of red, spreading across his chest, the sound of automatic weapons fire followed. His body tilted forward and he came tumbling down the cliff directly toward me.

Turning my face into the dirt, I wrapped my arms around my head. If he hit me on the way down, he could very well take me over the cliff with him. He crashed and tumbled closer, the ground vibrating beneath me each time his body struck the ground. After one last crash that landed very close to my head, there was silence. He must have sailed over the cliff after that. More rocks and debris rained down on me.

I listened for that final sound. The final blow that would signal that he had hit the bottom, but only silence followed. I shuddered knowing that very easily could have been me.

And then it was quiet. The firing and explosions had stopped. Only the sound of my own wheezing met my ears.

I looked up toward the top of the cliff. Harry stood there looking down, his weapon pointed at the ground. When he saw me move, he jerked as if surprised.

"Holy Christ!" he said. "Don't you move, luv. We'll be right down to get you. Do you hear me? Don't move."

I lay my head down again, feeling more tired than I ever had. "And just where would I go?" I asked no one in particular.

Chapter 28

Harry wouldn't look at me.

I sat next to him in the open back of a Humvee. The wooden benches that lined the side of the vehicle were notoriously uncomfortable, but we had no other alternative for getting back to the village save hacking our way through the jungle. Humvees were made for any terrain but riding in the open back meant that ruts in the road literally bounce you out of your seat if you weren't careful.

The ride to the village, which was only a couple of slow, rough miles, seemed painfully endless. Every bump made me wince. My every wince made Harry clench his fists and grind his teeth even more. I tried talking to him, telling him I was fine, but he wasn't listening.

A couple of ambulances from the medical unit had arrived at the battle scene. There had been plenty of others hurt far worse than me. Triage at the site determined that I hadn't rated much attention. Harry had tended to my wounds to the best of his abilities, doing what he could for my hands, and other injuries until we got to a hospital. A medic had injected me with something which dulled the pain , but aside from that, I was left to grit my teeth and endure the throbbing constancy of an overall ache. And I knew I smelled like piss. It was humiliating.

Harry and several of his men had managed to bring me up

from the ledge I clung to by way of a series of ropes and pulleys. Once he had repelled down to get me, Harry looked down at me, stroked my head gently and set to work preparing me for the long haul up the cliff. He avoided my gaze after that.

"How do you get yourself into these bloody messes?" were his first words. He had mumbled them through clenched teeth.

I chuckled, but it hurt too much. My brief laugh ended in a painful wince.

"Hurts, doesn't it? You think this is a joke?"

"No, of course not. I'm sorry."

"You're sorry. I don't bloody believe it. I think you'd be out here doing the same thing tomorrow if you had the opportunity."

When his inspections revealed a large patch of blood on my arm, he pressed his lips into a thin line.

"You know you've been shot," he said.

"It's just a graze."

"A graze is it?" He grabbed my uniform with both hands at the top of my shoulder and pulled in opposite directions.

"Entry wound here," he said, pointing to the front of my arm. "Exit wound here," pointing to the opposite side. "Gunshot wound. Through and through."

"Well it's not my fault."

"The hell it isn't"

He slapped a pressure dressing on the top of my arm, none too gently, then wrapped the gauze strips around my bicep to hold it in place.

"Hold it down here," he said, wanting me to help him get the dressing tied off. That's when he finally got a look at my hands. He froze for a moment.

"Sweet Jesus," he whispered.

It was obvious I wouldn't be able to help him, obvious my hands wouldn't be good for much of anything for a while. His gaze traveled from my hands to my face, his eyes betraying how bad the damage was. "Well, those will need looking after, won't they?" he said, gritting his teeth and looking away quickly. He cleared his throat, then kept himself busy with my preparations.

"Harry…"

"Shut it," he commanded. "There's nothing you can say that will make this right."

I admit, my hands were a shocking sight. Bloated and purplish. Sliced open in several places and covered in blood. I was afraid to bend my fingers, fearing my skin would split further. The sight of them was enough to stop his continued scolding but only for a while.

"Getting yourself held hostage. Is this what you call a good time? Are you enjoying this little tumble you've taken?" He went on like that while he quickly and loosely wrapped my hands in gauze and strapped them to my chest so they wouldn't get bumped around on the trip up the cliff. Even through his anger, he was gentle with me. Battlefield first aid was no stranger to him, but his chastisement continued as he hooked me to a harness, strapped me to his back and hauled me out of danger.

Even when we got to the top, he wasn't done. He continued with his harangue even while retying the field dressing on my thigh, pulling it a little too tight.

"Ouch!"

"You don't know what's good for you, you don't. Messing about with drug cartels, like you're out on a bloody lark."

"Now hold on, Fogg. Don't act like I did this on purpose."

'No, you hold on," he snapped. He stopped and took a deep breath, shifting his gaze to the now quiet battle scene around us. He was looking everywhere but at me, his jaw muscles jumping in his cheek, his eyes squinted to slits against the swirl of dust kicked up by everyone around us.

"Harry, please," I said. I wanted to run my hand along that strong, square jaw line. Run my fingers through his hair. I wouldn't be doing that for a while and regretted it.

"You almost got yourself killed, Lauren, and almost cost us this entire operation. We had a job to do. You got yourself in the way."

My entire body hurt. Pain was the predominant focus of my feeling, but nothing hurt me more than the accusation he was making.

"You talk as if I wanted to get kidnapped."

"Damn it, woman. I told you to be careful. I told you these men were dangerous."

"And what did you expect me to do with that information? Lock myself in a room and wait like a good little girl for you to make everything safe for me?"

It was a ridiculous argument. The worst part was that he was right about one thing. I would have done it all again tomorrow if I had to. Of course, I would never tell him that. Not the way he was looking at me.

He kept his mouth sealed tight after that, even when Cordovan strolled over. Dropic and Mora worked the scene, shooting video and stills of the battle's aftermath, Mora stopping now and then to scribble in his notebook.

At least one vehicle continued to burn. Small fires crackled some distance into the jungle. Several bodies lay around, all of them the inexperienced villagers working for Bonilla and unprepared for a war. Harry had told me some of the Honduran soldiers in the unit he worked with had been wounded. None of them killed.

Medical teams moved among the dead and wounded, treating some, leaving the dead for their final return to the village later.

"How did you get here?" I asked Cordovan.

"Your sergeant," Cordovan said. "It was Mora who figured out you were missing. He managed to find your boyfriend here in the jungle. Dropic and I just came along for the ride."

I glanced at Harry. He nodded in confirmation. I was surprised Harry had allowed the reporter to come along, but it was too late to worry about it.

I turned back to Cordovan. "Did you know Scaporelli was in this deep?"

"To be fair to him, I don't think he had much choice," Cordovan said. "I think he started out shipping just enough marijuana back to the states to prescribe to his patients. He wasn't even charging them for it. At least, he never charged my wife. But once Bonilla had his hooks into him, he started forcing Scaporelli to import his more expensive crop."

"Cocaine," I said.

The reporter nodded. "I knew where and when my wife was getting her weed. Then I started noticing patterns of cocaine arrests in the city, timed around the same periods my wife was handed her annual supply of pot." He shrugged.

"You did what investigative reporters do," I said.

"Hidden within the hospital shipping containers, the drugs were unlikely to be found. Not to mention Bonilla didn't have to pay for the transport. Scaporelli just got in over his head."

"What about his patients? What will your wife do for relief now?"

Cordovan ran a hand through his hair. I noticed his once crisp-looking safari jacket was grass stained and wrinkled. His face was smudged with dirt and locks of his hair stuck out wildly. He turned bloodshot eyes to me.

"He's been running rough shod over this village for years," Cordovan said. "Bonilla. Do you know how many of the village men were killed in this fight? They're not drug dealers. They're simple men who wanted to care for their families. Bonilla made them follow his orders. Even when it came to their daughters."

I remembered the tiny, torn panties I found in the latrine. The reports of young girls being sexually assaulted and the parents that seemed unwilling to do anything about it. The child molesting drug dealer had tumbled to his death. I shuddered at the memory of seeing him spinning by me into the abyss, but thought it a fitting ending to him.

"I'd like my wife to get the treatment she needs legally," Cordovan said. "From people who have respect for the law. Not like this," he said, sweeping his arm across the battle area. "Not like this."

Now, riding along in the back of the Humvee, Harry continued to avoid my gaze. I wasn't sure what I was going to do about that anger. Wasn't sure there was anything I could do. Despite how I felt about him, he knew I wouldn't give up my uniform. He wouldn't expect that, no more than I could expect him to stop being SAS and working for his Queen.

While riding toward the village, two Blackhawk helicopters flew overhead and I knew the CID team had finally arrived. Santos and his crew would finally be able to take over the investigation.

As soon as my mind turned back to the investigation, I realized that I had known who the killer was all along. It felt like a door opened to reveal a prize. I knew who had killed Bobby Larson, knew who was behind the gruesome murder. Now all I had to do was prove it.

Chapter 29

It was my fault.

"By the time they brought him in, he was already gone," Dr. Fordham said. "It was a severe skull fracture. His brain swelled. There was nothing we could do. He never regained consciousness."

The news left me drenched in an ocean of guilt. I had almost forgotten about Fletcher. Since Scaporelli had taken him away, I had been so wrapped up in my own need to survive and my own injuries, I had forgotten about the semiconscious state Fletcher had been in, about the pool of blood that had gathered at his feet. I knew he had been hurt badly, but never imagined it was that serious.

"How long ago?"

"Five, six hours," Fordham said, glancing at her watch. "I'm sorry Lauren. I know you cared about him."

Fletcher was dead. He had insisted on coming with me, insisted on providing protection. I wanted to hit someone.

"That bastard, Bonilla," I said.

"Easy, luv. He's dead too, yeah. And not too pleasantly."

"But, Fletcher."

Harry squeezed my shoulder. There was nothing to be done about it, nothing to say. Fletcher had been so enthusiastic about getting involved, about working together. His exuberance had annoyed me. Now he was gone.

The least I could do was ensure we caught the murderer who had started all of this.

"I've got to see Santos," I said.

"We've sent him a message," Fordham said. "You need to relax. You're not doing yourself any favors."

"Tell him I have to speak to him. Now."

She raised an eyebrow at me, not accustomed to being ordered around by an NCO.

"He'll get here when he gets here. In the meantime, lay back and relax."

After that, she and Harry simply ignored my demands. I asked Harry several times to go find Santos for me, but he was being stubborn as well. I asked once before having the x-rays that revealed I had several cracked ribs but no other internal injuries. I asked him again before Fordham injected both of my hands with a general anesthetic.

"Not until you're properly seen to," Harry said. "Now settle down and take your bloody medicine."

Fordham judged Harry's pressure dressing on my thigh was good enough. Harry had also correctly diagnosed the gunshot wound to my arm as through and through. His field dressing had reduced the bleeding to nil. It was the damage to my hands which took priority. The grime embedded in the deep cuts and scrapes presented a threat of infection that had to be dealt with.

"This is gonna hurt," she said. "No way around it."

Fordham patiently tweezed out bits of rock and dirt, doused my hands in antibiotic solution and then stitched the cuts I'd inflicted while trying to sever the rope that had bound my wrists.

Harry paced back and forth, glaring at her while she worked. Sweat beaded on my forehead. The stinging pulses of pain seemed to go on for hours. My teeth and jaw ached from clenching. I wanted to scream but swallowed the noise, muffling growls from the back of my throat, sounds I didn't know I was capable of making.

Fordham turned to Harry. "You should really go wait—" she

started.

"Not bloody likely," he said.

"Harry, I'll be all right," I said. "Dr. Fordham does know what she's doing."

He didn't reply. Instead he planted his feet in a wide stance and crossed his arms over his chest, refusing to budge.

"What about Scaporelli?" I asked, trying to break the tension.

Anne shrugged, her brow wrinkling in concern. "Disappeared. Might be why your investigator friend has been too busy to come see you." She paused and sucked in a deep breath. "Look, I heard what Scaporelli's been doing and I know he's in big trouble. It's just…he's a friend. It's hard to believe he could do what he's been accused of."

"He knew how badly Fletcher was hurt," I said. "That's why he insisted they drop him off here. But Fletcher is dead."

"I know," she said. "I should hate him for that, but I don't."

I felt sad for her. Major Fordham had been harboring feelings for the handsome doctor and now, if they found him, he faced an accessory to murder charge. His desire to help his patients may have started nobly. Now, if caught, he would be tried and jailed as the criminal he became. I wanted to see him pay for what happened to Fletcher, but I kept that to myself.

"What about Reggie Larson. Has he woken up yet?"

"We've been keeping Larson sedated. He woke up for a few minutes last night but didn't say anything coherent. Scaporelli's instructions were to keep him sedated until we can get him to a real hospital. I plan to put him on one of those Blackhawks this morning."

"Have you told anyone else that you plan to evacuate him today?"

"I haven't started preparing him yet if that's what you mean. We didn't know the aircraft would get here so soon today."

"Try to keep it quiet, will you?"

She exchanged a glance with Harry.

"Just don't tell anyone your plans," I said. "I think we can get Larson's killer to reveal himself. I just need Santos to help me do it."

"What you need is to bloody relax and let the good doctor here do her job," Harry said.

I knew he was right, but telling Santos my suspicions was more important. Sleep had to wait.

More than an hour later, a kind nurse had helped me out of my piss-smelling uniform, helped get me cleaned up and into a hospital gown. Both of my hands were wrapped in thick gauze and throbbed in painful rhythm to my heart beat. I felt totally spent.

"There's no permanent damage, but you're going to be without the use of your hands for a couple of weeks at least," the doctor said. "Now enough of this nonsense. I can stitch up your leg with a general, but that gunshot wound is going to hurt far worse then you expect. Stop being as stubborn as your boyfriend here and let me knock you out."

"How long will it take?"

"As long as it needs to," she said. "No one is going anywhere. You'll have time to talk to that investigator when you wake up. Please, stop being foolish and let me take care of you."

"Just make sure Santos is here when I wake up," I said.

"Oh 'fer Pete's sake! Would you take a moment to think about yourself for a change? Jeeze!" Fordham said before she stomped out of the examination area, calling for assistance as she hustled about in preparation for the procedures.

Harry hesitated, then stepped up to my gurney, as if afraid to be alone with me. Taking up one of my bandaged hands, he gazed down.

"Are you still angry with me?" I asked.

He shook his head, opened his mouth a few times to speak but couldn't. He trembled with the effort. Taking a deep breath, he let the words out, his voice quivering.

"When I first saw you down that cliff, Lauren, you weren't moving. I thought you were dead. I don't know that I've ever been so frightened."

Bending down, he pressed his lips to my forehead, then stayed close, his jade eyes inches from mine. "I can't lose you now, Lauren. Not now. Not when I've just found you."

"Harry, I'm sorry I frightened you, but I knew I would be okay."

He kissed my forehead again, allowing his lips to linger there. "That's what we all think when we go into these things, Lauren. We think we're invincible. I've known plenty who thought that and didn't come home. That bloke, Fletcher. He wasn't invincible, was he?"

If there was anyone who should have been invincible, it was Fletcher. He'd been full of life, a bigger-than-life hero.

"It wasn't like I was being reckless. Harry, it may sound crazy, but I was only doing my job. I'm a …"

"Soldier," he finished for me. "Yes, I know darling. A soldier." He leaned down and kissed my forehead again, laying my bandaged hand across my chest, the argument over, for now. "I'll be right here, waiting for you, hear?"

Despite all of the pain, I felt the depth of his stare in the pit of my stomach. He was filthy, covered in mud, blood and camouflage paint. Exhaustion etched into the red rims around his worried eyes. I wanted to camp out in this man's arms and never let go.

Fordham came bustling back, three people in her wake.

"All right, Fogg. Out you go. Now."

"Yes, Mum," Harry said with a smirk. "As you wish."

Looking at me, he said, "I'll be right out here, luv. Waiting for you." He winked and backed away.

Then a nurse threw the curtain closed around my gurney, blocking my view of him. I shut my eyes. I was ready to let her do what she needed. Knowing Harry was there standing vigil, I smiled. Before she could even administer any anesthesia, I went peacefully to sleep.

===========

When I woke up, Harry was sleeping. He'd moved a chair

close to my bed and sat with his head resting near my hand. His face was clean of the camouflage paint, his uniform free of dirt. I wondered how long he had been sitting there. I wanted to run my fingers through his close-cropped hair, but my hands were bulky lumps of gauze. I contented myself with staring at him, thinking that waking up next to Harry was something I could get used to. People moved around outside my curtained space, but for the most part, things were quiet. Laying there, I let myself imagine a time when I could wake up next to him when I wasn't battered and aching all over.

He would have to leave soon, I was sure. His group had probably left him behind to move on to their next mission. There was a chance Harry could be in some trouble for shirking his duties to stay with me. Once he left, there was no telling when I would see him again.

It's common knowledge that a relationship between two people in uniform is nearly impossible. The odds that you could be stationed together are close to nil. Add deployments and work schedules and chances are you'd have little time together. If the two people were in different services, one in the Army and the other in the Air Force, for example, the difficulties were even worse.

With Harry in the service of another country altogether, we faced impossible odds. But it was too late to think rationally about what we were doing. I was crazy about him.

"Good, you're awake," Fordham said, flinging the curtain aside. Her abrupt entrance startled Harry awake. He sat up, smiled at me, then winced.

"Oye, me neck may never be the same," he said, standing and stretching. "How're you feeling, Lauren?"

"Has Santos been here yet?"

"Don't start with that again," Fordham said. "He told us to send him word as soon as you woke up. I'll do that, but let me check you out first."

She poked and prodded, listened and gave instructions. My hands throbbed, it hurt to breathe, my shoulder and thigh ached.

All of that pain gave me a headache.

Then I remembered Fletcher was dead. We had been arguing just hours before he died. He had been especially irritating and I had wished myself far away from him. Now he was gone. Suddenly, the aches and pains seemed less important. I tried to appreciate that they were an affirmation that I was alive.

"Wait." I said, when I saw her come at me with a needle. "What is that?"

"I know you're in pain. This will take the edge off."

"No. Not until I speak to Santos."

"Christ, woman," Harry said. "You're stubborn, you are."

"Just get him here," I said, showing my frustration. "Let me talk to him and then you can shoot me up with anything you want."

Anne spun on her heel and marched out, taking her needle with her.

"You don't know what's good for you," Harry said.

I smiled, thinking that if anything was good for me, it was the bulky British soldier standing over my bed.

"How long can you stay?"

"I shouldn't be here now, but I'm not leaving. Not until we get you sorted."

"And after that?" It was a question I knew he couldn't answer, but I wanted to know if he had considered the possibilities, or lack of them. He pulled his chair up closer and picked up my bandaged hand.

"I've been thinking about that," he said. Those words alone made me feel warm inside.

"You need time to recuperate and I've still got leave coming. I'm picturing the Aegean sea, Mediterranean cuisine, me nursing you back to health. What do you say?"

"I like that picture," I said, smiling. "But not until I get rid of these boxing gloves on my hands. If we're going to be someplace romantic, I've got to be able to touch you."

The smile on his face slowly faded and his shoulders sagged. "We made plans like this before. Do you remember?"

"In Bosnia. How could I forget?" I said. The scenes were eerily similar. I had been in a hospital bed and he'd stood at my bedside. We had talked of going on a vacation together. "To properly get to know one another," was the way Harry described it. Our plans hadn't worked out.

He brushed a strand of hair away from my face and I realized again that he had never seen me out of uniform, never seen my hair unbound, hadn't ever even seen me recently bathed. The thoughts made me feel gloomy, as if it were all an impossible dream. We might never have the time we hoped for.

"Maybe we shouldn't make any promises," I said.

I regretted the words as soon as they were out. Harry stood up, gazing down at me, his mouth open as if he had something to say but couldn't.

"Harry," I began, but he shook his head, taking a step back.

Then Chief Santos finally arrived. The investigator stepped through the curtain, smiling. I had never liked the little man. His timing didn't win him any points either.

"Master Sergeant Harper," he said, glancing from me to Harry. "I hope I'm not interrupting."

"No, not at all, sir," Harry said. "I was just leaving."

"Harry, please," I begged, but he was already backing away.

"It's alright, Lauren," he said, but I knew that it wasn't. "I said I wouldn't go until you were sorted. I meant that."

He turned and stepped behind the curtain and out of my sight. I felt as if I were tumbling down that hill again, end over end.

Chapter 30

I was interrupting something, evidently" Santos said.

I didn't respond. Didn't know what to say. He stood there awkwardly, staring down at me, an eyebrow raised. Then he took a deep breath and launched into a long summary of everything he had learned since arriving, his hands clasped behind his back, pacing back and forth near the foot of my bed.

Crime scene investigators were going over both the school foundation where we found Bobby Larson's body and the parking area where we found Lieutenant Allen. Both scenes had been badly compromised as far as evidence was concerned, but he hoped his forensic experts could turn up clues. He had already met Dodd, Porter, Judd, Reece and several others, but hadn't questioned any of them yet. He'd heard most of the details about my kidnapping from Harry. He knew Fletcher had died. That Bonilla was dead. Scaporelli disappeared.

"We have some leads in that area. The fewer people who know them, the better," he said, as if I cared where the doctor had fled.

I wasn't sure if Santos wanted to brief me, or if he just wanted to make mouth noises long enough for me to recover from the awkward scene he had interrupted. It didn't really matter why he was talking or what he was saying. There was a massive, tangled knot in the pit of my stomach that hurt more than the bullet wound, or the stab wound or the throbbing in my demolished hands.

This was exactly why I hadn't let myself get involved with a man for so many years. My career in uniform wasn't conducive to relationships and besides that, men tended to walk away when my duties and commitments made life difficult. That tangled knot was a bit familiar. Much more tangled this time, maybe impossible to ever straighten out, but familiar. I didn't want to make any assumptions about what was going on in Harry's mind when he left, but whatever it was, I hoped he wouldn't give up, wouldn't give up on the promise of us.

But there wasn't time to dwell on all of that. Bobby's killer was within reach. If I could help settle that score, I might feel as if Fletcher hadn't died for nothing. Maybe it could help me believe that everything I'd been through had been worth it. And maybe that would help reduce the size of the knot resting in my belly.

I watched Santos pacing at the foot of my bed, droning on. He looked exactly the same as the last time I'd seen him. A small man, I wondered how he had met the Army's minimum height restrictions. His thick wavy black hair, solid dark eyebrows and olive-colored skin made him look similar to many of the Los Flores village men, only with a more sophisticated bearing. I remembered his black eyes, the same eyes he regarded me with now. They had made me nervous before, when I was the suspect under scrutiny. Now, they looked kind, sympathetic. I didn't want his sympathy. Not to mention that his pacing was getting on my nerves. I felt like a spectator at a tennis match.

"I think I know who was behind Bobby's death," I said, interrupting his litany.

That stopped him. He took a few hesitant steps toward me, and I realized I was making him nervous. Maybe all that talking he did had been his way of working through his nervous tension.

Something about his fear of me made me smile. My smile seemed to bother him even more.

"I'm not holding any grudges, Chief," I said. That wasn't all together true. Santos and Chief Ramsey had put me through several of the worst days of my life. Days when I worried from minute to minute if I would lose my freedom. It wasn't their fault. They were only doing their jobs, but it was hard not to resent the sleepless, nerve-shattering time in my life. and Santos had been at the center of those days.

"That's good to know Sergeant Harper," he said. "I ah, regret the mistake we made," he said, unable to look me in the eye. "Oh, and I should tell you that Colonel McCallen is here."

"But that's impossible," I said.

As if to prove me wrong, McCallen poked his head around the curtain.

"Alright if I come in?" he asked.

I tried to push myself up to a sitting position, but it hurt too much. McCallen was my commanding officer, but I was in no position to render him the proper military courtesies.

He told me to relax and explained that he had jumped on the first plane available as soon as he heard about the murder.

"There's no way you could have gotten here from Frankfurt so fast."

"I was in the states actually," he said, glancing at Santos. "I took Michelle and the boys to New Mexico to help them get settled. Headquarters authorized a commercial flight from there. That TV crew you were babysitting was making someone high up very nervous."

So Michelle had left him. Neil told me his wife was thinking about a separation. The last time I saw him, the strain, both from the death of their baby and the state of his marriage, had left him pale and visibly exhausted. Standing over my bed, he looked healthier, more relaxed. He could still use a few more pounds on his six foot frame, but he appeared at ease for the first time in weeks. His rust-colored hair had been freshly cut and his skin was bronzed from the sun. The tan lessened the appearance of the scar that slashed diagonally across his face from eyebrow to chin.

"I'm sorry, sir," I said. "About Michelle."

"Don't worry about all that. It was a long time coming. How are you doing? And what the hell happened?"

I was glad Santos was there. He'd want to debrief me and this would save me from having to tell the story twice. I was ashamed by all of the trouble I had caused. Sure, I knew it wasn't my fault, knew that Harry's accusations about my putting myself in danger were more about his feelings than about anything I had done. Knocked out, tied up, falling down. I wanted them to know how Fletcher had died, that he had tried to protect me. I was ashamed of how vulnerable I had been and I was feeling pathetic with my bandaged hands and injured body, but I told them what I knew.

"But I'm fine, " I said. I'd skipped a lot of the more humiliating details, but telling the story hadn't done anything to restore my self-esteem.

Santos and Neil exchanged looks. They had remained silent throughout my story, never interrupting with questions. Now they simply stared at me and continued staring.

"Well, say something," I said, wondering why they were both speechless.

Neil cleared his throat. "I'm sorry, Sergeant Harper. I never should have allowed you to go on this mission. Not so soon after what happened in Bosnia."

So that was why they were acting strange. They were feeling guilty. What had happened to me here was bad enough. Combine it with the experience in Bosnia, an experience they had both played a part in, and it was starting to look like I was either cursed or just plain stupid.

"I'll heal, sir," I said.

"You already demonstrated an extraordinary ability to endure extreme hardship," Santos said. "I have no doubt you will survive your current circumstances."

There wasn't much else to say on the subject. They stood there awkwardly, like boys caught in the middle of some mischief.

"The current circumstances can be wrapped up fairly quickly, if my suspicions are correct," I said.

"You said you thought you knew who the killer was," said Santos.

"Well, I think I at least have a plan to get to the truth."

I told them my idea. McCallen didn't wait for me to finish

before he shook his head.

"No way. That's ridiculous."

"Of course, you and the Chief would be here, waiting to see if anyone took the bait."

"It's a little obvious, but worth consideration," Santos said.

I thought, if it were so obvious, why hadn't he come up with it? But at least he hadn't completely dismissed the idea. I kept quiet, waiting for the men to come to whatever decision they would.

"I will not be a party to Sergeant Harper putting herself in danger again."

"But, Sir," I started.

"Chief, could I have a minute with my NCO?"

McCallen phrased his words in the form of a question, but Santos knew an order when he heard one. McCallen watched Santos walk away then turned his gaze back to me. His eyes were such a pale blue, they appeared almost white in some light. Despite the scar on his face and the flash on his uniform that displayed all of the special forces training he had undergone, his was a kind face.

He sat on the edge of my bed and took up one of my bandaged hands.

"How do you get yourself into these messes?"

"That seems to be the common question," I said.

"How are you feeling? This looks painful." He cradled the balls of gauze that were my hands.

"Actually, breathing hurts more than my hands," I said, chuckling, then wincing, then chuckled more. McCallen laughed with me, shaking his head.

"I send you on a simple media escort mission and it turns into this," he said.

"The escort mission wasn't as simple as it appeared. And Cordovan hadn't been upfront about what he was after. No big surprise there, being a reporter and all. But he was playing a dangerous game. Things are rarely safe where drugs are involved."

Someone at headquarters had to have their own suspicions about what Scaporelli had been up to. It would explain why I was assigned the mission at the last minute. If someone thought it possible to minimize the effects of the story, they were sadly mistaken. Scaporelli's drug smuggling would be a news scandal the Army would not be able to avoid.

"I don't like this plan of yours," McCallen said. He was scrutinizing my bandaged hands. Major Fordham had used a total of twenty-five stitches to repair the deep cuts I'd inflicted on myself while trying to slice through the rope. I decided not to give him any of the details.

"Harry is here, Sir," I said, trying to change the subject.

"Your British friend?"

"Yes, sir."

"I see."

He stood up slowly, laying my hand down, probably realizing the image someone would see if they walked in on us.

"Well, that's good. At least you were able to see each other after all. Not in the way you had originally planned, of course." A red flush traveled up his neck. My boss would never do well at poker. His emotions were usually colorfully obvious.

The relationship between a commanding officer and his senior NCO is typically intimate and sometimes complicated. My relationship with McCallen had become impossibly twisted when we had kissed. I remember that it had felt like the release of a tsunami of feelings that had been building over all the years we had worked and traveled together. His marriage and military fraternization policies had always kept a tight lid on any thoughts we might have had toward acting on those feelings. When we'd finally given in, the one kiss, that one passionate embrace, had resulted in a long string of events that we were still trying to recover from.

McCallen cleared his throat as if ridding himself of thoughts of our former intimacy.

"I'm sure Sergeant Fogg would agree that your plan is a no go," he said.

"Colonel, no one will ever get a confession in this case. Any physical evidence they might find won't stand up in court. A trap is the only way to be sure."

"That may be true, but..."

"Neil, you didn't see that body in the cement. You didn't see that young lieutenant with his head crushed."

He began to pace. I recognized the set of his shoulders, the way he crossed his arms over his chest while he walked, then spun on his heel and turned in the opposite direction. He didn't want to give in, but he would. Knowing the colonel as I did, it was time to keep quiet and wait for him to recognize the truth.

"I'm not sure why I ever argue with you. In the end, you usually do what you want." He gazed down at me, as if he had something more to say. Instead, he turned and walked out of the exam area, taking a good deal of my tension with him. I relaxed into my pillow, feeling exhausted.

I must have dozed off then. When I opened my eyes, Harry was back, sitting in the chair next to my bed. He was staring off into space, a tense frown on his face. It took him a while to realize I was watching him. When he noticed my eyes were open, he didn't waste a moment.

"Santos told me your plan," he said. "Christ, you're bloody stubborn."

"It's a perfectly safe plan, Harry."

"Stubborn. Pigheaded. Willful." He clenched his teeth and punched my bed with his beefy fist.

"And those are my good qualities," I said with a smile, trying to lighten his mood. It almost worked. He took a deep breath and turned his green-eyed gaze to me.

"When it comes to us, to you and me, I want you to be just as bloody pigheaded, Lauren. It's what it will take. Do you understand?"

I felt that knot in my stomach begin to unravel and sighed. "Yeah," I said. "I can do that."

"We do have to make a promise but only the one. Just the one. That we will be so bloody stubborn we'll cross the world if we have to. By and by, we'll have that time we want."

The depth of his gaze warmed me in the few parts of my body that didn't hurt. He was right. Between the two of us, we had enough pigheadedness to get us some extended time together. Time out of uniform. Maybe on a Mediterranean vacation. Maybe somewhere else. It didn't matter where or even when. We simply had to decide that being together was something we were going to do, and our stubbornness would get us there.

He stood, then leaned down and kissed my forehead.

"I've got to go. My being here won't be the right bait for your little trap."

"You'll be here though, when it's over."

He grinned. "Haven't you heard? Stubborn is my new middle name. Let someone try to stop me," he said. "Let 'em try."

I watched his retreating back and smiled, feeling safe. My ease wasn't misguided. Harry would be on watch somewhere, out of sight, waiting for our prey to take the bait. Just knowing he was thinking of me felt comforting.

Almost dozing again, I listened to the sounds in the hospital tent around me. The sides of the tent flapped gently in the breeze. I listened to the jungle noises, the screech and call of birds off in the distance.

A nurse came in to check on me, noting things in my chart.

There wasn't anything complicated about the plan. It was simply a matter of putting the right words in the right ears.

Reggie Larson had already left on one of the Blackhawks that had been flying the wounded to Soto Cano airbase for treatment at the hospital there. The helicopters had made several trips back and forth. On one of the trips, they had transported Fletcher's body.

In the meantime, Santos was planting the seeds of a story around the engineer camp site. That before I had been kidnapped, Reggie Larson had told me something, something that had me convinced I knew who had killed Bobby. Santos was telling folks that my condition was critical and I couldn't be moved. That as soon as I regained consciousness, Santos would learn what I knew and they would have their killer. I told Santos to be sure to tell Hank the information first. We could trust Hank to tell everyone and word would spread.

We still didn't know if Lieutenant Allen had been murdered or not, but I felt his death was too much of a coincidence. If it was murder, it was made to look like an accident, a well-planned, thought-out accident. It took place while most of the engineers were involved in playing poker and not paying attention. The killer knew Allen sat behind that wall of cinderblocks, his face buried in a book each night, too estranged from the rest of the men to participate in the card games.

My money was on the idea that whoever was behind killing Larson, had also killed Allen. At first, Larson's murder had appeared to be a poorly planned job, one that could almost be viewed as a crime of passion, a spur of the moment event possibly executed by someone who wasn't an engineer, maybe even someone a little crazy. The half-buried body. The smooth cement around the corpse. The wheelbarrow filled with hardened cement. Five men left behind to guard a site and two of them end up dead.

Logic would point to the three left alive. Hank seemed unlikely. That left Porter and Judd. But then there was the medical team and the villagers and the culprit was harder to determine.

Bobby Larson could have died in any number of places in any number of ways, but Honduras and the construction site were chosen for a purpose. It was remote, far from the eyes of investigators. Heavy rain this time of year was easily predicted, a given that it would wash away much, if not all, of the physical evidence. The construction site would be left mostly empty during the middle weekend of the project, allowing an opportunity to execute the plan without threat of being seen by the rest of the engineers.

Shadows around my bed grew deeper as evening settled on the hospital. The daytime jungle noises gradually transitioned to those of the nocturnal variety. The constancy of sounds from thousands of insects. The call of birds guiding families back to nests.

As the evening wore on, the hospital grew quieter. No one moved around outside my curtained-off area. I surprised myself by dozing off now and then, snapping awake at the slightest sound. I was exhausted, but my anticipation was too high to completely relax. Soon I began to question if anyone would come. Without a watch, I had no idea what time it was and had little choice but to lay there doing nothing. Waiting. Worrying. I had plenty of time to imagine the worst. My instincts told me it was growing late, and doubt settled in with the progression of time.

No one would come. This was a stupid plan. I should have listened to McCallen. I would be killed. My mind wouldn't settle down. One can find a terrific number of things to question when lying around waiting for a murderer to appear.

Just as I had resigned myself to failure, footsteps sounded in the exam area. They were hesitant. Furtive. I pushed myself up in the bed, silently wincing, the stabs of pain so sharp I almost cried out. The man approaching shuffled about, unsure where to go. He checked the first exam area, then moved on to the next. My bed sat behind the final curtain. In moments, I would know if I had been right.

And I was.

Chapter 31

He pulled the curtain back, saw me sitting up in bed staring at him, and froze. His first instinct was to back away, but it was too late. I had seen him. He couldn't pretend he hadn't intended to come.

"First Sergeant Dodd," I said.

"You're awake."

"Yes."

"Well, that's good," he said, trying to recover from his surprise. He glanced around the curtained area nervously. He slowly approached the head of my bed, creeping closer.

"They said you were in serious condition," he said.

"No, I'm actually doing quite well. I knew you would come."

That stopped him. He glanced around again.

"It's okay. No one else is here," I said.

"How did you know I was coming to see you?"

"Someone had to kill me. I imagine you weren't given any choice."

He wrinkled his brow and tried his best to look confused, but he wasn't a good liar. His bad acting had been part of what gave him away. He hadn't been so much outraged at Larson's murder when we found him, but he had been surprised at how gruesome the actual crime looked. You can plan and talk about killing someone, but actually doing it must come as a shock, no matter how much you may have wanted the person dead.

"Kill you? That's ridiculous. I was just coming to see how you were doing," he said.

"You don't know me well enough for an evening hospital visit. No, you heard Reggie had been talking to me. That Reggie told me your secrets."

"I don't have any secrets. You don't know what you're talking about."

"I know you were the only one who could have pulled off this plan, the only one who could convince all of your officers to stay at the base camp. Porter and Judd weren't capable of arranging all of the details. You're definitely the brains of this operation."

His face reddened. The muscles in his arms jumped.

"You're talking nonsense. You must have hit your head or something."

"No, I'm perfectly okay. For example, I remember what Reggie was saying, when he was in the jeep, right before he drove off the cliff. It should have been me. That's what he said, right before he stomped his foot on the gas. What did you say to him, right before that?"

"I didn't say anything to him."

"Yes, you did. You whispered it. I bet I can guess what you said. I bet you said something like, that's what you get for messing around with another man's wife, or something like that."

Dodd narrowed his eyes and took a step closer.

"I said no such thing."

"Maybe not. I can't pretend to have heard what it was. Still, you and Porter and Judd. One big happy family. A happy family where all the wives are suddenly interested in gardening. Lots of gardening. And two handsome gardeners who look great with their shirts off. And your wife. How old is she? Fifteen years younger, I heard. Must be hard to keep a beautiful young wife happy."

Dodd's breath was hissing through his teeth. His hands clenched into fists.

"Stop that. You stop those lies."

"Neither one of those boys could keep their hands off other people's women. If you had waited, you probably could have convinced Dr. Reece to go in on it with you, the way Bobby flirted with Reece's fiancé."

"I wasn't even here when Bobby died. I was with you in the base camp."

"True, but you were here when Allen died. Porter and Judd had everyone busy with the poker game, but I saw you outside the tent looking agitated. I suspect you were working up your courage for the task when I spoke to you. Porter and Judd told you to kill Allen, not because they thought he knew anything. They just wanted you to be as implicated in the plot as they were. They thought you were about to turn on them, so they made you kill Allen."

He started to speak, then thought better of it. His chest began to deflate, as if his anger leaked away. His shoulders sagged. The color drained from his face.

"You don't know what you're talking about," he said. "You can't make accusations like that."

"Sure I can. The three of you were working together at first, but soon the two men got out of control. You were in over your head."

He shook his head, backing away.

"You were able to kill Allen only because you weren't looking at him at the time. You won't be able to kill me now. You're not a cold-blooded killer. Not like Porter. Not like Judd."

He ran a hand down his face, stumbled into the side of my bed as if he would collapse.

"When you saw what those cinderblocks had done to Allen, you were sickened," I said. "More sickened then when you saw what Porter and Judd had done to Bobby. They weren't supposed to kill him that way, were they?"

Dodd shook his head. A tiny movement. I almost felt sorry for him.

"No," he said. "He was just supposed to disappear. Just disappear. I shouldn't have trusted them to do it right."

"What were they supposed to do?"

"He never would have been found if they had just thrown him over the cliff. What was so goddamn hard about that?"

"And Reggie? What would have happened to him?"

"You saw him. He won't be good for anything for a long time."

"Including sleeping with anyone's wife."

He stared at me, his eyes glassy, as if pleading for me to understand. After several seconds he jerked, shocked with the realization of what he had just done. Anger flared in his eyes and he took a step toward me. He thought better of it and turned, preparing to flee, throwing the curtain aside. But Santos, McCallen and Harry were there, flanked by several of Santos's armed military police.

Santos stepped forward, craning his head back to look up at the first sergeant.

"First Sergeant Dodd, I am CW3 Santos of the Criminal Investigation Division. I am investigating the murders of Sergeant Robert Larson and First Lieutenant Jerome Allen. I want to advise you of your rights under Article 31 of the Uniform Code of Military Justice. You have the right to remain silent."

Santos continued with his statement as the MPs put flex ties over Dodd's wrists. Dodd didn't resist. There was little else he could do.

"Do you understand these rights as I have explained them to you?" Santos asked.

"Yes," Dodd mumbled. He swayed slightly, but righted himself, drawing in a deep breath. "What about Porter and Judd?"

"They're already in custody. Please go with the officers now."

==========

Despite everything that had happened, the drier weather meant construction resumed. The engineers were already back to work on their school project. Since Santos had cleared the crime scenes, the walls of the school house had slowly begun to rise from the ground. Several courses of brick had already been laid. I wondered if there would be ghost stories associated with the school and the body that had been buried there.

I leaned on Harry's hand as I hobbled out to the landing zone. The Blackhawk crew waited, the side doors of the helicopter wide open. The crew chief walked around the aircraft making his final checks. We didn't have much time.

Santos and his crew had left with Porter, Judd and Dodd on an earlier aircraft, shortly after Dodd's confession. The three engineers had left quietly, the rest of the unit standing around in shocked disbelief. Hank had tears in his eyes as he watched Dodd being led away.

Scaporelli still hadn't been found. Santos speculated that he could be lost in the jungle, trying to make his way to some other village. Harry and his commandos would try to track him, but there was no telling if or when he would show up. Scaporelli had a family and a medical practice to return to in Minneapolis.

"He'll show up eventually," Santos said. "Once he realizes running means he's already lost everything."

McCallen would stay at the engineer camp until the unit's leadership arrived by vehicle to take over. He would bring Cordovan and Dropic back to Soto Cano airbase by land in a few days, once the rain-drenched roads had cleared enough for safe travel. I promised Dropic that I would pass his tapes on to his station's delivery service. Once I was assured the tapes didn't contain any images of dead service members, I would release them. Cordovan made it clear that news producers in Minneapolis were anxious to get the story out as soon as they had it. I wasn't surprised. What had started as a typical investigative reporter piece, had turned into something far more surprising. I could just imagine how the Minneapolis producers were salivating over the idea of an explosive drug war in the middle of the jungle. A war with a local tie.

I had a memory stick with Staff Sergeant Mora's pictures and a couple of stories in the cargo pocket of my uniform. He'd done a great job capturing the images of the villagers and the humanitarian mission. The Army News Service would snap them up for worldwide distribution.

McCallen followed Harry and me out to the landing zone. Harry wasn't a fan of my boss, so he remained stoic while McCallen was around. In Bosnia, Harry had deduced McCallen's feelings for me and didn't approve. He revealed his distaste now in the finely-etched line of his mouth and the way his left eyebrow twitched.

McCallen said, "I should be on my way to Soto Cano in a few days. Hopefully, you'll be on your way back to Germany by that time; but if not, I'll stop by the hospital to see you. I've already called headquarters to tell them you need leave. Lots of it."

"Thank you, Sir. I could use some time off," I said, glancing at Harry.

McCallen and I exchanged salutes.

"Take care of yourself, Lauren," he said and left.

Harry watched him walk away.

"Lauren," Harry said. "As if he has a right to call you by your first name."

"I'd say working together for over ten years earns him that right."

He made an angry noise at the back of his throat.

"Enough about him," Harry said. "We won't be making any promises about when we'll see each other next. That doesn't mean we won't see each other shortly."

I nodded, not trusting myself to say anything. I'd said goodbye a million times to a million people in my military career. The separation from people you'd grown impossibly close to in a very short amount of time became easier with repetition. This was different. I turned my face away, not wanting him to see that I was tearing up.

"You be that stubborn woman we discussed, alright darlin'? No giving up. I'll be done here in another week. It could happen. We could make it happen."

Despite my best intentions, a few tears escaped. I stepped into Harry's arms trying to control the waterworks. Behind me, the engine of the Blackhawk whined into life and the rotors slowly began to turn.

Harry cupped my head in his hand, staring down at me. "Now, kiss me. Before I start leaking like a bloody tosser."

I chuckled then winced and then lost myself in the feel of his lips on mine. He cradled my head and gave me a passion-filled kiss, his tongue exploring my mouth, a small moan vibrating through his lips as my arms snaked tentatively around his neck. He pulled me close enough that I could feel him tremble, but I knew he held back, afraid to hurt me further.

In the back of my mind, I knew it was too soon to feel so deeply for someone I barely knew, someone who seemed too out of reach. But I ignored that practicality. The feelings I had for Harry Fogg were simple despite how complicated everything else was.

By the time we broke the kiss, the engine noise from the helicopter was too loud for words. He leaned down, his lips next to my ear.

"Soon, Lauren. Very soon."

He brushed my cheek with the back of his fingers, stepped away from me, and saluted, looking very serious. Every bit the professional British soldier. I smiled and saluted back, trying to swallow the terrible lump in my throat.

I turned, and the crew chief was there, offering me his hand. Moments later, as I watched out the open door of the Blackhawk, Harry turned and walked away from the landing field.

He said he wanted stubborn and that's exactly what he would get. There was no way I would allow the vision of him walking away be the last I ever had of Sergeant Major Harold Fogg. I would see him again. We would make that happen. I settled back into the uncomfortable seat, the dark green jungle canopy rushing by beneath us, and wondered when that would be.

Army Acronyms –

Military jargon is filled with acronyms. It is impossible to list all of them here but I've attempted to include those acronyms used in this story. If you find any I've missed, contact me through my website at www.mldoyleauthor.com.

201 File – Army personnel file containing a soldier's training, awards, promotions, transfers from the date of first entry and throughout the soldier's career.

BDU – Battle Dress Uniform; a woodland pattern camouflage uniform. No longer worn by U.S. Army forces. Replaced with the ACU – Army Combat Uniform.

CID – Criminal Investigation Division; Unit tasked with the investigating federal crimes and serious violations of military law by members of the Army.

EOC – Emergency Operations Center; a twenty-four-hour center of support for emergency situations, activated when a situation is serious enough to warrant the input of multiple staff offices.

 EOD – Explosive Ordnance Detachment; a detachment charged with identifying unexploded ordnance, deactivating explosives and clearing minefields and a bunch of other stuff you have to be a bit crazy to do.

General Order Number One (GO1) – A military order used to outline prohibited activities which are thought to threaten good order and discipline during major military deployments. Activities can include drinking alcohol, gambling, procuring the services of prostitutes and many others. The list of prohibited activities is adjusted at the discretion of the officer in charge to fit the deployment or mission.

Humvee or HMMWV – High Mobility Multipurpose Wheeled

Vehicle; a four-wheel drive vehicle produced by GM which serves as the main vehicle for the US Military. The wide-bodied, fat-tired vehicle can be produced with a turret, be up-armored and have a wide range of other modifications depending on usage.

LZ – Landing zone; a place where a helicopter can safely land. Sometimes a permanent location or one designated hastily to accommodate emergency landings.

M16 – U.S. armed forces military rifle which fires 5.56 NATO rounds at semi-automatic or fully automatic rate.
MP – Military police.

NATO – North Atlantic Treaty Organization; an alliance of countries from North America and Europe used to seek peaceful solutions to member country conflicts.
or
NATO- Normal Army Tea Order; British slang for tea served white with two sugars.

NCO – Non-commissioned officer; grades of soldiers from corporal through sergeant major, sometimes called the backbone of the Army for their leadership skills, a most responsible for carrying out the day-to-day mission of an operation.

OPORD – Operations Order; a document outlining a plan, the objective, the associated tasks, equipment and staffing necessary to complete a mission.

PAO – Public Affairs Officer; an officer charged with providing advice and guidance to the commander on media and communication matters.

PMCS – Preventive Maintenance Checks and Services; a series of checks and services performed on military equipment before, during and after a mission to ensure the equipment is and stays in working order.

PSD – Personal Security Detachment; like bodyguards, soldiers charged with the safety and security of one individual, usually a high-ranking officer.

QRF – Quick Reaction Force; a standby force used by commanders to respond to emergencies.

Sapper - U.S. Army engineer specialized in digging and building fortifications, constructs combat expedient bridges, roads and air fields and handles the disposal of bombs, mines etc.

SAW – Squad Automatic Weapon or section automatic weapon; a weapon used to provide heavier automatic firepower to squads or sections. The type of weapon varies but is usually fed with an ammunition belt and can be carried or mounted on a vehicle or tripod.

TDY – Temporary Duty Travel; orders authorizing movement of military service members and civilians from one travel location to another for a short tour of duty.

TOC – Tactical Operations Center; the headquarters and center used to provide tactical support to the commander.

UCMJ – Uniform Code of Military Justice; the foundation for military law.

Acknowledgements

My years at the keyboard have taught me that I simply cannot write in a vacuum. My first writing group was born from a class I took at The Loft in St. Paul, MN. I lost touch with most of the members but more than a decade later, I can still thank Kathy Haley for being the one who shepherded us together and for continuing to read the stories I've cobbled together. Her advice has always been spot on and well appreciated.

The most recent cast of characters, the Novel Experience, is born from members of the Maryland Writer's Association. At the core are Gale Deitch and Cindy Young-Turner, authors to watch. You should also keep an eye out for Jonathan Allen, Brian Connors, Mark Willen, Victor Brown, Alma Lopez and C. J. Cooper.

Thanks to all of my beta readers, especially Loreen Doyle-Littles, Larry Doyle, Eileen McIntire, Ali Bettencourt, Colleen Riley, Barry Guertin, Kristin L. Wilson and the wonderful and talented Zander Vyne.

I'd also like to thank Liz Trupin-Pulli, for being so patient, trying her best and helping me navigate through this world of publishing.

A very special thanks go to Laura Michelle Hurst for the hook up and most especially Jaymie Hurst. You couldn't possibly know how valuable your responses to my ever expanding list of questions served in the shaping of my British character. Not to mention, it was just a heck of a lot of fun to learn so much from you.

My biggest thanks go to my family for being there for me. Rebecca Doyle, Reuben, Ramsey, Kyle and my niece Lauren. I didn't have to go too far to find a good name for my main character!

Most of all, to my mother, Ruth. Thanks for always having your nose buried in a book. I wish you were here to see this.

About the Author

M. L. Doyle has served in the U.S. Army at home and abroad for more than three decades as both a soldier and civilian. She is the co-author of two memoirs which chronicle the lives of prominent women in uniform. Her award winning fiction also features women who wear combat boots.

A native Minnesotan, Mary currently resides in Baltimore where she is furiously penning more adventures.

You can also look for Mary's adult romance series, *The Limited Partnerships Series*, which is written under the pen name Louise Kokesh. The series is available as four novellas. The omnibus is also now available.

Mary would love to hear comments from readers. Please like her M.L. Doyle Author page on Facebook. You can also reach her on her website at www.mldoyleauthor.com.

www.ingramcontent.com/pod-product-compliance
Lightning Source LLC
Chambersburg PA
CBHW030035180626
46810CB00001B/383